Drunk on a Plane

CARRIE JACOBS

Welcome to Hickory Hollow!

Each novel in the Hickory Hollow series is a stand-alone, and can be read in any order. There are some character appearances across books, so there may be some very minor spoilers if you read the books out of order.

For details about all of my books, visit my website at carriejacobs.com

For exclusive sneak peeks, behind-the-scenes information, and much more, sign up for my newsletter at carriejacobs.com.

For Scott
Time for another cruise! ♥

Chapter One

Megan's leg jittered with anticipation as she waited for her boarding call. This was it. The adventure of a lifetime. In under an hour, she'd be sitting inside an airplane, taking off, leaving Pennsylvania – and this cold November – far behind. For ten blissful days, anyway. Her phone vibrated again. In the time it took to go through security and find a seat at the gate, six calls had gone to voicemail.

With a sigh, she answered the phone. "Hello again, Mom." She kept her voice low so the growing group of fellow passengers wasn't disturbed.

"You're not going. The wedding's been canceled." Alice sounded relieved.

Dread wound its way through her chest and up her neck, making her tongue feel too large for her mouth. "What?" Her cousin's cruise wedding had been the only topic of family discussion for months.

"Brittney called the whole thing off. We'll head back and pick you up."

To Megan, it sounded less like an offer and more like a threat. Her heart pounded as she clutched her camera bag to her chest. She had to get on the plane. "Mom, I already paid for everything. I'll still be able to build my travel portfolio."

There was a pause, then Alice spoke slowly, like she was addressing a child. "Since you won't be taking any wedding pictures, there's no point in going."

"I said I wanted to build my *travel* portfolio." *You just didn't want to hear that part.*

"What on earth would you need one of those for? We're turning around." The phone muffled. "Turn around up here. Grant, you missed it – here, pull into this gas station."

No, no, Dad, please don't turn around. "I can't leave. I'm already through security."

"Of course you can."

"My bag's already checked."

"We'll call the airline and have it back in a few days. Grant, why aren't you pulling in?"

She hoped her mother wouldn't hear the desperation constricting her voice. "I gotta go, we're starting to board." The little white lie gave her a tiny pang of guilt as a nearby passenger looked up from his phone and reached for his bag, then frowned and settled back into his seat.

"We're coming back to get you." The words took on a sharp edge.

"No, don't. When am I ever going to have another chance to go on a cruise?" This was it. Do or die. If she didn't get on the plane, she'd never go anywhere. She'd waste the rest of her life in Hickory Hollow, putting the final nail in the coffin that already held her dreams.

"Your father and I can take you on a cruise. Maybe in the spring. Although I'm not sure why you'd want to go some-place so hot. We'll go to Niagara Falls instead. It's just as nice."

"I already spent a non-refundable fortune on this trip. I'll call you when I get to Orlando."

"*If* you get to Orlando."

"Gee, thanks." She forced her breathing to slow. The last thing she needed was to have a full-blown panic attack in an airport.

Alice's voice took on a whine. "Megan, you don't want to go on a cruise all by yourself. You'll be all alone. For ten days. Ten whole days."

It sounded like heaven. "I would have been alone anyway. Brittney and Eric would have been off doing their own thing. It'll be fine. Maybe I'll have a hot vacation fling with some exotic foreigner who barely speaks English."

She heard her dad chuckle in the background.

Alice snapped, "Why would you even joke about having a casual affair? It's not funny. And what about pirates? You know they hijacked a cruise ship last month."

Pinching the bridge of her nose, Megan said, "In Somalia. Which is on the other side of Africa, nowhere near the Caribbean."

"Fine. Go ahead. But don't come bawling to me when someone plants drugs on you and you end up in prison somewhere in Mexico, or when the plane crashes."

On the upside, the ridiculousness of the conversation calmed her down. "Getting on the plane, so I have to turn my phone off now. I'll text you when I land in Florida. Love you, bye." She hung up before Alice could say anything else.

Megan left her seat and went to the window. Out on the tarmac, a plane coasted closer, its nose facing her window. The sun winked off its silver shell, promising her adventure. Freedom. She wondered how it could seem both larger and smaller than she'd expected.

The door to the boarding tunnel opened and a stream of travelers walked through, laughing, talking, smiling, or staring at their phones. They all seemed so relaxed. She checked the time, had no idea what her watch showed, then checked again. Plenty of time to pee before boarding. She grabbed her bag and went to use the restroom.

Holding her hands under the dryer, she let the hot air blow the nervous chill from her fingers. She glanced in the mirror, taking a second to smooth a few stray strands of hair back to her blonde ponytail. The loudspeaker announced boarding for her flight. She gave her reflection a thumbs up and winked. "Here we go."

The line inched forward, and she wondered how obvious it was she'd never flown. Everyone else seemed to have their boarding pass on their phone. She handed her crinkled paper boarding pass to the man at the counter and followed the line of passengers through the doorway.

The hallway leading to the plane shifted slightly, bouncing with the movement of the passengers. The gaudy hotel-esque carpeting only added to her feeling of instability as the line slowly moved along. The flight attendant flashed a huge smile and grasped her elbow as she stepped over the small gap between the floor and the plane. The small gap her mother would surely imagine she was going to fall through, wherein she'd plummet to the pavement below, crack her skull open, and bleed to death.

Megan smiled back at the flight attendant. What a fun job. Always going from one city to the next, never being trapped in one place for too long. She watched the other passengers and followed their lead, finding her seat and carefully stowing her camera bag in the overhead compartment.

Inching across the empty row to the cramped window seat, she found the ends of the seatbelt and fastened it. She took a deep breath, watching as people of all shapes and sizes filled the plane. A woman a few rows back loudly discussed her husband's health-related bedroom shortcomings, while periodically insisting she had to hang up. Somewhere else, an already-cranky baby was wailing. The two seats beside her were occupied.

She watched workers out on the tarmac, driving carts of suitcases, then tossing them onto a conveyor belt leading to the belly of the plane. Workers in neon safety vests waved glowing wands to direct another plane out of its parking space. She watched it roll away and wondered where they were going.

Megan half-expected a loudspeaker announcement, calling her off the plane. She imagined being escorted by an angry flight attendant on a walk of shame past the scowling passengers whose mothers weren't over-involved in their lives. In her dark fantasy, she was frog-marched by security to her waiting parents, her mother sobbing, her father waiting in the car, people pointing and laughing and taking cell phone videos that would go viral. Someone would dash her bag to the floor behind her, breaking her precious equipment, so she'd have no way to make a living, and she'd be evicted from her apartment and forced to move back in with her parents.

Megan shuddered.

Thankfully, the plane door slammed shut, cutting off her overactive imagination. She watched as the pavement slowly started moving. The plane inched further from the terminal, backing out of its parking spot. Her heart pounded. What if it *did* crash? Just her luck. She finally gets to travel, and ends up splattered on the side of a mountain somewhere.

Stop it.

The speaker above her head crackled. "Ladies and gentlemen, welcome aboard flight 479 to Charlotte. We request your full attention as we demonstrate the safety features of this aircraft."

Megan sat in rapt attention. Right. If they landed in the middle of the ocean, she'd be sure to grab her seat cushion.

Emergency exits. Restrooms. Drinks. Drinks? Yes, please. No one else was paying any attention to the lecture.

Rubbing her neck, Megan watched the flight attendants buckle themselves into their backward-facing seats. They seemed calm enough, easily conversing with the passengers they were facing. A magazine peeked out of the seat pocket in front of her, so she pulled it out but couldn't focus on the cover.

The intercom dinged, and a voice announced, "Cabin crew, we are next in line for takeoff."

A few minutes later, the plane lurched, then drove leisurely past the airport, around a big loop, then stopped. Megan rolled the magazine up tight, then twisted it around and around in her sweaty hands. Would it be better to stare out the window and see them crash, or have the boring beige seat in front of her be the last thing she ever saw?

Maybe her mother had been right, and she should have –

Whoa. What? The thought instantly calmed the churning in her stomach. *Chill out. This is exciting, not scary.*

Exciting.

The plane lurched again, then started rolling forward. Faster and faster and faster. The trees lining the fence at the edge of the property blurred and suddenly, with a jump, the pavement fell away. Her stomach protested, twisting in her belly. She clutched the magazine, unable to tear her eyes from the shrinking ground. The plane leaned too far to the left, hiding the ground from her view, then too far to the right, until she was sure something was horribly wrong and they were going to fall sideways from the sky.

After a few nerve-wracking moments, the plane leveled and everything on the ground was in miniature. She wished she'd have thought to pull her camera out of her bag, but she'd been so preoccupied it hadn't occurred to her.

"It never gets old, does it?"

"Excuse me?" Megan turned to the woman beside her, a grandmotherly type. They both had their arms scrunched onto their laps, not wanting to be impolite and hog the sliver of an armrest.

"The view from up here. It still takes my breath away." Her Southern drawl added charm to her words.

Megan smiled at her and nodded. "It's amazing. I... I've never flown before."

The woman's eyebrows rose. "Well, isn't this fun, then? My friends call me Edie, so you can, too." She smiled warmly.

"Nice to meet you. I'm Megan."

"What's got you on a plane for the first time, Megan?"

"My cousin's wedding. Sort of. Apparently she called it off at the last minute. The wedding is – was – supposed to be on a cruise ship." She felt weird saying it out loud, like it was some kind of juicy gossip. She'd been so focused on getting away from home she hadn't thought much about the actual canceled wedding.

"Cruises are wonderful. A shame about the wedding, though. Were you to be her maid of honor?"

"Photographer."

"You take pictures for a living?"

Megan nodded. "Yeah, weddings, babies, family portraits... those sorts of things."

"But?" Edie was studying her face like she could see straight into Megan's soul.

"I'd like to be a travel photographer. I'd love to take pictures of the Great Pyramid or an active volcano or a Samoan tribal dance."

"But you don't travel?"

"I know. It's stupid." Megan felt the heat rising on her

cheeks, embarrassed, feeling like a fraud. Or a naïve little girl saying she wanted to be a princess when she grew up.

Edie reached over and patted her hand. "Don't ever call your dreams stupid, Megan. Dreams are living, breathing things. You have to nurture them. Care for them. If you don't, they wither and die."

"Did you follow your dreams?" For a second, she thought the question might have been too personal, but Edie's warm brown eyes crinkled as she smiled.

"Sure did. I always wanted to be a nurse. But right after high school, I got married and had six wonderful children, one right after the other. I didn't have time to breathe, let alone think about schooling for myself. One day, my precious husband, God rest his soul, handed me a college catalog and told me it was time. It took a while, but I was the first person in my whole family to ever get a college degree." Edie laughed. "One year before my eldest daughter got hers."

"How wonderful. Your family must be so proud of you."

"They sure are."

Megan turned back to the window and gasped.

Beside her, Edie chuckled softly. "It's incredible, isn't it? Seeing the clouds from this side?"

"I've never seen anything so beautiful." Megan touched her fingertips to her window, as though she could reach outside and touch the cotton candy skies. The mountains of white puffs stretched out, beyond her vision, creating a floor under a perfectly brilliant blue sky.

She took some pictures with her phone, wanting to remember these first impressions. She'd definitely be pulling her camera out of her bag during her layover.

The intercom crackled. "Ladies and gentlemen, welcome to Charlotte. We'll be landing in about five minutes. Local time is eleven-oh-five. Temperature on the ground is seventy-four degrees. Thank you for flying with us, we hope you enjoy the rest of your day."

The flight attendants hustled down the aisle, collecting used cups and empty soda cans, and checking on seatbelts before buckling themselves.

Megan swallowed hard as the plane leaned and seemed to drop straight down. She clutched the armrests and watched the ground rush closer and closer. Her heart raced. There was no way they'd stop before diving straight into the earth. The wheels made contact with the asphalt, jolting the passengers in their seats. The scenery streamed by. She dug her toes into the squishy foam of her sneakers, as if she could drag the plane to a stop.

The plane finally rolled to a speed that wasn't panic-inducing, and Megan released the breath she'd been holding.

Edie patted her arm. "You did great."

When the plane finally stopped at the terminal, the passengers stood, pulling bags out of the overheads and crowding the aisle. The interior of the plane became uncomfortably warm, and the man behind her kept bumping her seat. The baby in the back resumed his crying. When the aisle cleared, she stood and helped Edie retrieve her bag from the overhead.

The older woman gave her a hug. "You take care of those dreams, now."

"I will. I promise." Megan pulled her camera bag out of the compartment. She slung it over her shoulder and made it a promise, too.

They were going to see the world.

Chapter Two

Once she left the hallway and entered the building, Megan stepped out of the line of traffic to check her boarding pass.

"Megan? Meeeeeeeegaaannnnnn, ohmygosh, hey, Meg. Megmegmeg."

Megan's eyes widened, and she looked around, cautious and curious. "Eric. What are you doing here? I thought the wedd— um, I... I thought you weren't going to be here."

"Pfffffft," he rolled his bloodshot eyes. "*She* isn't here. *I'm* here." He pointed to the ground. "Right. Here. Me. I'm here."

"I see." She took his arm and pulled him down the hallway. "Have you had a lot to drink?"

"Let's see." He wiggled his fingers in front of his face. "I think four. One... two... three... four... Huh. Nope, musta been more, cuz' they're teeny." He held his index finger and thumb about an inch apart. "Teeeeeeeny tiny. Maybe eight."

"Okay. Let's see where you need to be, okay?"

"Mmmmmmmmmeg. Meg. In. The photo graffer." He squeezed one eye shut and mimed taking a picture. "Photo-graffer Meg. In."

"Yep, that's me." She steered him toward a nearby coffee

shop and claimed an empty table. "Let's get you a cup of coffee."

Eric slumped down onto the chair and unceremoniously dropped his bag at his feet.

"Sit. Stay. I'll be right back." Megan ordered him the largest black coffee they had. When she returned to the table, she set it front of him, then pulled the lid off her tea and dumped creamer in.

"Hey thanks. Whaddo I owe you?" He reached for his pocket, his arm swinging wide.

She grabbed his hand and pulled it back toward the table before he flailed into someone. "Don't worry about it. What's your next flight?"

"Geez, I don't know."

"Where's your boarding pass?"

He pulled his phone out of his pocket and flopped it on the table. "Guess in there somewhere, huh?"

Megan shook her head. "Drink your coffee."

"It's hot."

"Then pull up your boarding pass."

He squinted at the phone and poked at it, eventually finding his pass and showing it to her. They were on the same flight to Orlando. "I gotta pee."

Megan raised an eyebrow. "Can you get to the bathroom?"

"Pfft, no problemo." Eric stood and wobbled a little.

Pointing toward the restrooms, Megan said, "You sure you're okay?"

"Yep." He walked to the restroom in a surprisingly straight line. A few minutes later, he came back and carefully sat at the table.

"All better?"

He gave her a thumbs up. "How drunk are you?"

He snorted. "Pretty drunk."

She motioned to his cup. "Your coffee's cooled off. Drink."

"How come you're here?"

"I already paid for my trip, I might as well take it."

He slurred, "I'll make sure you get paid for the pictures. I mean, there's not going to be any pictures. Well, there will be pictures. I bet you take a lot of pictures. But like, wedding pictures. Not your fault though."

"It's fine. I'm not worried about it."

"Ha. I doubt it."

With her cup halfway to her lips, Megan paused. "What do you mean?"

"It's money. Money makes the world go 'round, right?"

"I wouldn't know," she said. "I'm not exactly rolling in it."

He made a noncommittal grunt, but finished his coffee. After a few minutes of silence, he blurted out, "Do you wanna know why she called it off?"

Megan looked up, but said nothing.

"Better options. She was always looking for an upgrade."

"Then why were you going to marry her?"

He held his hands up then slapped his palms on the table. "I don't even know anymore. At first I wanted to prove I was good enough for her. Then I think I got stubborn and didn't want to admit defeat. De. Feat. Failure."

"Sometimes things don't work out."

"Are you single because things didn't work out with somebody?"

She gave a humorless laugh. "Something like that. Let me grab you another coffee."

When she returned with the cup, Eric was staring out into the crowd. "Do you wonder where they're all going?"

Glancing at the steady stream of people moving past the coffee shop, Megan shrugged. "Sure."

"Pick somebody."

"What?"

His melancholy mood vanished and Eric grinned. "Pick somebody out of the crowd."

She looked around. "Okay, how about the guy with the Hawaiian shirt?"

"Psssht. Too easy. Headed to Florida. Retired. Was up north visiting his ungrateful kids who want him and his wife to move back home so grandma can babysit their brats for free. Next."

Megan laughed. "Hmm, there." She nodded toward a woman with three small children in tow.

"Sad story. They live in the airport. In fact, both of the younger kids were born here. Over in Terminal D. They live off scraps from the food court and water fountains. Sometimes they steal clothes from unclaimed baggage." His eyes unfocused, then he squeezed them shut. "So sad."

"You really are drunk, aren't you?" He hadn't been slurring his words, so she almost forgot how much he'd had to drink. "We should head to our gate."

"Yeah, I guess."

Megan checked her pass again, but Eric shook his head. "Check the board. Gates change. Like all the time." He pointed to the ceiling over a large bank of screens with all the flights listed.

"I'm glad you told me. My pass has E4, but this says A11."

His eyebrows rose. "A11? Crap. We better start walking." He grunted as he got off his chair and leaned a little too far as he reached for his bag.

Megan grabbed it and handed it to him, then pointed. "This way."

They walked. And walked. And walked. "How big *is* this place?"

"Big."

Turning down the massive hallway to Terminal A, Megan felt more and more like a sheltered hillbilly, staring around in wonder at all the shops and restaurants while everyone else looked at their phones or the ground, completely unimpressed.

They took seats in the waiting area between gates 11 and 12, watching the planes roll in. Eric dozed off and on. Megan took her camera out of her carryon bag and took some pictures out the window, then snapped some pictures in the terminal. When it was time to board, Megan hung the camera around her neck and nudged Eric. As a first class passenger, he was one of the first to board. She was one of the last.

Edie had been right. It was much easier on this leg of the flight, now that she knew what to expect. This time, her stomach didn't roll quite as violently when the plane took off.

The clouds captivated her, so she took dozens of pictures. They would probably be indistinguishable from each other, but she didn't care. This plane was smaller than the last, with no wall separating the more comfortable first class from the regular passengers. Eric dozed a few rows in front of her, his snoring undoubtedly annoying the people around him. She felt bad for him, but wondered why he was ever with Brittney in the first place. They didn't match at all. He seemed down to earth and Brittney was, well, Brittney.

The flight passed without incident. Megan's seatmate for this leg of the trip wasn't talkative, which suited her fine. She watched the passing landscape, fascinated with the topography they passed. Hills and rivers and trees and roads. Everything was so tiny. Tiny little things, built by tiny little people, with tiny little lives like hers. She wondered how many people on the ground were like her – shoved in a box she didn't belong in, living up – or down – to expectations of others and ignoring her dreams.

Enough. Stay in the present. Soak up every second of this adventure. She wasn't going to waste one minute of this trip.

The plane landed a little more smoothly this time. Megan waited until most of the passengers had moved before she got up to retrieve her bag from the overhead. She moved down the aisle and saw Eric's still-sleeping form. She plopped down in the seat beside him and reached over to shake his shoulder.

"Hey. Hey, we're here. The plane landed."

"Huh?" He moved his head slightly.

"Eric. Wake up. It's time to get up."

"Five more minutes," he mumbled.

"Come on, we have to go."

"Yeah, I'm good."

"Eric," she said louder, shoving his shoulder. "Get. Up."

"It's in the fridge."

Megan looked around. There were fewer than a dozen people left on the plane. The flight attendant manning the door was watching them. "Eric. You have to get up. Now. We have to go. We're in Orlando."

His face scrunched up as he managed to pry his eyes open. "Ah, geez. My head."

She shook him again. "You need to get moving. Now."

His eyes opened wider and he looked around. "Oh. Yeah, I'm up. Sorry." He stood and smacked his head on the ceiling. He yowled and his hands flew up, cradling the spot. "Holy crap, ow."

Megan winced. "Here, come out here so you don't hit it again." She pulled him toward the aisle. They were the last two passengers in the plane. "Let's go."

Eric groaned as he reached over his head to grab his bag. "Come on, come on, come on. You're going to get us arrested or something."

He managed a smile. "I think we'll be okay." The smile

transformed into a grimace. He walked down the aisle and stepped off the plane into the hallway. "This was a terrible idea."

"What?"

"This trip. I should have bailed like she did."

"Why didn't you?"

He gave a half smile. "Maybe I'm running away? Maybe I don't want to deal with all the crap back home? I don't know."

Megan shifted her camera bag. "Where's the baggage claim?"

"Out to the left." He pointed.

"You've been here before?"

"A couple of times. You?"

Megan laughed. "This is the first time I was ever on a plane." His eyebrows shot up. "You're kidding."

"Nope. Scout's honor."

Chapter Three

Eric considered turning around and immediately booking another flight back home. He shook his head. This whole trip was pointless and stupid. He should have stayed home so he could wallow in his... what? Misery? No, not really. Anger? Meh. Embarrassment? Humiliation? The truth was probably lurking in there somewhere.

In the end, he decided against it. A wave of booze-inspired chivalry convinced him Megan needed his help to navigate the process of getting on the ship. Besides, the trip was already paid for. Maybe it wasn't such a bad idea to go.

He'd have a big suite to himself. He could easily avoid being around people. But mainly, there was a good possibility he could score some coffees and teas for his brother's new shop, so it wouldn't be a wasted trip.

If nothing else, Stewart would be glad to have some exotic new flavors, and Eric would have time to think about what he wanted from his life. Or from a wife. He knew he wanted one of those, although given his current situation, he should be a little more selective about the woman he chose. Kids? He could take them or leave them. But forty was getting closer and closer, and if his wife wanted kids, he didn't want to wait around to get started.

The crowded terminal didn't help his pounding head at all. He was still half drunk, and the nap did more harm than good. His neck was stiff and his mouth felt like it was full of cotton. His eyelids scraped his eyeballs every time he blinked.

"I'm going to grab a drink." Cutting across the crowd, he veered off toward a fountain and took long gulps of the tepid water. It didn't help much.

Megan stood on the other side of a river of people, frowning at her phone. He waited for a break in the travelers, then pulled his bag quickly across the flow.

"...I can't talk now... No... Mom, I have to... No... I have to go get my baggage. I just... No, I wanted to tell you I got here okay... Yeah, I gathered as much from your ten voicemails... I have to go, the shuttle's waiting on me. Love you, bye." She poked her phone and shoved it into her pocket.

"Everything okay?"

She rolled her eyes. "It's fine. Ridiculous, but fine. I'm a grown woman, but my mother thinks I'm incapable of making it from Point A to Point B without being abducted or murdered or at the very least, run over."

"Overprotective, huh?"

"You have no idea."

He pretended not to notice her blinking back tears when she turned her face away from him. "Baggage claim is over this way. We'll grab our bags and then find the shuttle."

"Sounds good."

And he thought he had issues with his parents. His mother still worried about him when he traveled, but she'd long since gotten over the need to bombard him with calls when he was away from home.

Eric pointed. "This way."

They'd taken long enough getting off the plane that the bags were already coming through on the conveyor. People crowded around the carousel, yanking suitcases off and rolling them toward the exit.

"Which one's yours?"

"It's red with an orange tag. There it is."

Her pristine suitcase rolled around in front of them. Megan grabbed it and checked the tag. "Now where's yours?"

"With my luck? Probably Antarctica." He laughed, glad he managed to pull a smile out of her.

The crowd thinned considerably. Finally his battered black suitcase emerged from behind the plastic curtain. "There it is." When it came around, he pulled it off the belt. "Ready?"

"Yup." She looked up at the directional signs. "I assume the shuttle will be out there."

"Lead the way."

They pulled their suitcases through sliding glass doors. The wall of humidity hit them, erasing the comfortable air conditioned atmosphere they'd been enjoying. A man holding a sign with the name of their cruise line stood along the sidewalk a few yards away.

"Names?" He checked them off on a clipboard as they answered, then shoved their suitcases in the back of an already-stuffed minivan. Megan climbed in and squished over as far as she could on the bench seat, against the other two people in the row. Eric sat beside her, half his butt hanging off the edge of the seat. The driver consulted the clipboard, counted the people in the van, and slid the door shut.

Eric grumbled, "I hope this is a short ride. My balance isn't the greatest today."

"Here. Try this." She scooted forward to the edge of the seat. "Now turn sideways so your feet are there." She pointed to the floor between the seat and the door.

He turned and found more real estate for his behind. "Thanks." He wasn't too keen on being sideways in the mini-van, especially since the driver had barely pulled away from the curb and was already weaving across lanes of traffic, inspiring blaring horns and middle fingers. "Doesn't Florida have seatbelt laws, or maximum occupancy guidelines?" He whispered.

Megan held onto the seat in front of her and shot him a look. "I expected more palm trees and less concrete," she said.

Eric watched out the window. "Too much television."

"Ha. No doubt."

"I bet you got all your ideas about Florida from Miami Vice."

Megan giggled. "What's wrong with Miami Vice? Crockett and Tubbs were awesome. Those blazers and shoes with no socks? The height of men's fashion."

"Thankfully, we've come down from those heights."

"Oh, please. I bet you have a lemon yellow blazer in your suitcase."

He laughed in spite of his thumping temples. "No. I brought the seafoam green one instead. It matches my eyes."

"For the formal dinner, right?"

"Exactly. So did you bring your Aqua Net?"

"Hazmat confiscated it at the airport."

Eric grinned. "Good call. That stuff is dangerous. It ruined the ozone, who knows what it could do to a plane."

"Oh, please. If it was so bad, every woman who lived in the eighties would be bald."

He had to laugh out loud. The man on the other side of Megan, though, sighed loudly, apparently annoyed at their conversation.

Twenty minutes later, they reached the dock and unloaded

the van. Megan was wide-eyed and jittery. He followed her line of vision.

"I... I didn't imagine it would be so big. I swear Hickory Hollow could fit in there and have room left over."

"Just wait until we get on board."

"You've cruised before?"

"Once. I was a teenager and my grandparents took the whole family on a cruise to celebrate their fiftieth anniversary."

"How sweet."

"How about you? Where does your family go on vacation? Obviously nowhere too far, right?"

A shadow passed over Megan's face. "We never went anywhere after – I mean, the last time we went anywhere, I was about fifteen. We went to Ocean City."

Something in her voice kept him from digging deeper. "New Jersey or Maryland?"

"Maryland. I'm excited to see the ocean again."

He followed her through the welcome center and found a spot at the counter. He showed his papers, handed over his credit card, signed a few forms, and took his packet from the woman behind the counter. Megan was waiting at the doorway, clutching the strap of her camera bag.

They left their luggage with the attendant and walked across the catwalk to the ship. Her steps faltered. "I think I'm starting to freak out."

"Too late now. If I can suck it up and go, so can you."

She glanced over her shoulder at him. "Sorry. I forgot."

Eric gave her a shrug. "It's okay." *I did, too.* He didn't want to explore that any further. "What deck are you on?"

"Six. I'm in 6240."

"I'm 12238. Up on twelve."

They stepped off the catwalk and into a giant, grand lobby.

A football field could easily fit into the posh space. He nearly bumped into Megan.

She was staring at the room, eyes wide with wonder. "Wow, look at the chandelier. And the piano. And the staircase. What deck are we on?"

"I think we're on Deck Four."

They walked toward the bank of elevators, where ship employees were standing with trays of piña coladas. Eric lightly touched Megan's elbow and leaned over. "FYI, those drinks they're handing out aren't free."

She raised an eyebrow. "Thanks. I would have gotten one, too." They stepped into the elevator with a group of other people. Megan stepped out on Deck Six. "See you around."

Eric gave her a small wave as the doors slid shut.

Chapter Four

Megan pushed the door to her cabin open. A towel folded into the shape of a frog sat on her bed, guarding a newsletter and a few pieces of chocolate. She peeked into the bathroom. Small, but more than adequate. She pulled back the floor length curtains and took in the view. More cruise ships were docked nearby. Passengers were standing on their upper decks, waving, presumably, to passengers on the upper decks of this ship.

Grabbing her camera and her key card, she decided to join them. Maybe she'd even get some nice shots of the dock. For a brief moment, she wished she'd put some of her personal items in her carry-on bag. She would have loved to brush her hair before heading out.

The stairwells were filling with people of all shapes, sizes, colors, and ages. She returned the smiles of each person who glanced her way. Cruisers certainly seemed to be a friendly bunch.

Stepping out onto an outer deck, she pulled in a deep breath. The delicious thick tang of salt and heat in the air coated her nose and the back of her throat. The view from this side of the ship was dockside. She looked out over the scenery, mildly disappointed at the city feel of the tangle of highways and the surprising lack of palm trees and sand. She leaned on the railing, looking down into the murky water slapping the side of the ship. A tinge of anxiety fluttered in her belly. It was a long way down.

Walking around the front of the deck, she ran into more and more people congregating along the rail. She found an open spot and snapped some pictures of their cruise ship neighbor.

Someone behind her bellowed, "One, two, three," and the whole crowd yelled, "Bon Voyage!" A moment later, a return call came from the other ship, sending a ripple of festive laughter through the passengers.

Megan stayed on the deck for a long while, watching the other ship's passengers come and go as they did on her ship, until it was time to return to her cabin and take her life jacket to the assigned deck for the safety briefing.

Chapter Five

Eric stood on the deck, feeling stupid in his life jacket, but no more so than everyone else, he guessed. The crew pointed out how to use the life jackets, how to get to the row boats, and various other safety information. Unfortunately, the speaker had a heavy Russian accent, so even if Eric had wanted to pay attention, he wouldn't have understood the words.

His head was still pounding, and he hadn't yet gotten his luggage. A trip to the concierge had netted him some aspirin, but it wasn't helping. He yawned, wishing for the demonstration to be over so he could get something to eat and crawl in bed. The people surrounding him were entirely too enthusiastic and excited, their energy counteracting any benefits the aspirin could be offering him.

Coffee. He was here to find some great new coffees and make this whole miserable experience worth it.

Finally, the torture ended and he slipped back to his room, kicked his life jacket under the bed and checked the map of the ship. He found a burger joint on the top deck. Perfect. On the first night, most of the cruisers would be eating in the dining room.

He stepped out of the elevator and groaned. Every single person who populated Earth appeared to be standing on the top deck, shoulder to shoulder. He inched his way through the crowd when the ship's horn blew, nearly deafening him. The hollers and cheers from the crowd finished the job.

The rumble in his stomach propelled him onward. Just when he thought the crowd had calmed, he heard a distant cheer from the ship across from them. In response, someone counted, and on three, their deck yelled, "Bon Voyage," echoing back to the other cruisers.

"You look miserable," a familiar voice called from behind him. Megan grabbed his arm to keep them from being separated by the crowd.

He poked his temple. "My head's killing me."

"Not the best idea to come up here then, huh, genius?" She grinned up at him, tapping her temple.

"I came up to get something to eat."

"Me, too. I was heading to the burger place. My sit down dinner isn't until eight. No way I can wait until then."

Eric motioned. "Shall we?"

Megan led him through the crush of bodies. When they pushed open the restaurant doors, he was glad to see the place was nearly empty. He picked the booth farthest from the doors. When they sat, he rubbed the sides of his head. "I'm never drinking that much again."

"Is this a promise you need to make regularly?"

"Ugh, no. Two beers is usually my limit. Those tiny bottles threw me off." He glanced at the menu when the waiter came to take their orders. Burger. Cheese sticks. Iced Tea. His empty stomach rumbled.

Megan said, "You'll feel better after you get some food in you. And water. Stay hydrated."

The waiter brought their iced tea and basket of mozzarella

sticks. Eric broke one open, letting the oozing cheese cool, then pushed the basket for Megan to take one.

"I'm excited to see Nassau tomorrow," she said.

"What excursion are you doing?"

She shook her head and swallowed her tea. "None. I'm going to hit the touristy areas and get some beach photos. And flowers. There are such amazing flowers in the tropics. And I have to get some sand to take home."

"Sand?"

A slight blush colored her cheeks. "I want to keep a little bit of sand from each place I visit. I saw the idea online and I liked it."

The waiter brought their burgers and refilled their glasses.

"It's up to you, but I have a bunch of excursions that are already paid for. You can go if you want. Might get you some better photo ops than wandering around on your own."

"Oh. You mean I can use Brittney's tickets?"

He bit into his burger. "Yeah. I'm not going to use mine, either. It's for the dolphin encounter."

Her eyes lit up. "I'd love to see the dolphins."

"It's yours if you want it."

Megan sat back in her seat and shook her head. "Thanks, but if you're not going, I wouldn't feel right. Besides, I'll end up being the sad single girl some poor old couple tries to fix up with their nephew who is seeing the sun for the first time in decades because his mom finally evicted him from her basement."

Eric laughed out loud, then grabbed his head. "Sad."

"*He's* sad. I'm not sad, because I'm not getting fixed up with him."

"It seems like a shame to waste it, though. I wonder if anyone else would want it?"

"You could ask around."

He thought for a minute. The dolphin encounter was the excursion he had most wanted to take. "Or I guess we could both go. If you want to. I'll be there to keep the basement guy from hitting on you, you'll be there to keep his crazy mom from hitting on me, and we get to play with a dolphin. Win-win."

Megan looked down into her glass. "I'd like to go." She paused, scrunching up her face. "I don't want people back home to get the wrong idea. People might think it's... inappropriate."

Eric coughed on his soda. "There's nothing inappropriate – or romantic – about it."

"Obviously not." She sounded indignant.

"How about this? We'll split the excursions and in exchange, you help me scout some local coffee shops and decide which coffees are worth taking home."

"Well, I really would like to see a dolphin up close."

"The tickets will just go to waste if we don't go. Excursions for coffee. Deal?"

"Deal." Megan stuck out her hand.

He shook it, and the matter appeared to be settled.

"I bet the photos will be even better off the beaten path. Extra bonus." She smiled at him.

Eric relaxed and finished his burger. "I wonder if the crowd thinned out any."

"Doubt it. Do you want to go watch the shore disappear?" Megan plopped her napkin on her empty plate and swallowed the last of her tea.

"Sure." *No.* He wanted to go to his room and sleep. "How's your head?"

"Still thumping."

"I have Tylenol if you need any."

They walked out onto the deck and found a spot at the railing. The shoreline was shrinking into the distance. Eric closed his eyes and listened to the ship slicing through the water, its protesting waves slapping at the sides of the boat, loud enough to be heard over the festive cruisers filling the deck behind them.

The temperature dropped with the sun, and the breeze from the water gave him a chill. "I think I'm going to head to my cabin. I'll meet up with you when we dock?"

"Sounds great. I hope your head feels better."

Chapter Six

Megan watched Eric get swallowed by the crowd, then stood at the railing until the last of the lights from the shore were no longer visible. People left the deck, taking some of the noise with them. The pool area was full of laughter and splashing, and small pockets of people crowded the bar and covered a dance floor. Music blared through speakers all over the deck. Taking it all in, she wove around the deck until she found a door to the inside and took a few flights of stairs down to her floor.

Back in her cabin, she secured the locks, closed the curtains against the darkness and checked her phone. It had been a bad idea to leave it in the room. She scrolled down through nineteen text messages from her mom, and listened to three voicemails. All since she talked to her in the airport only a few hours earlier.

Sometimes, it was easier to go along with it. She knew her mother's issues, and she wouldn't add to her stress.

"Hey, I got your messages."

"Where have you been? I've been worried *sick* about you."

"Stop it. I left the airport and came to the ship. There's a big celebration when we pull out and I just got back to my room."

"By yourself?" The words were laced with something unkind.

"Of course." She held the phone away from her ear as she sighed heavily.

"Have you been drinking?" Alice barked as though speaking to a wayward teenager.

"Does it matter? I'm well over twenty-one, and it's not like I'm driving." Megan usually tried not to snark at her mother, but she was a grown woman. Drinking was legal.

"You don't have to be sarcastic."

"And you don't have to be ridiculous. I'm not calling you every ten minutes. I already told you I'll check in with you in the morning, and at night – when I can. I'm not spending twenty dollars a minute on international roaming, and every text message you send costs me money."

"Fine." The word was clipped.

"I'm an adult. I'm perfectly safe."

"You're a woman all alone in a foreign country."

"Florida's still part of the United States, Mom."

"Ha, ha, laugh it up. Someday when you have kids, you'll understand what I'm going through."

Ah, yes, the ever-present guilt trip. "I'm going to bed now. We have a big day tomorrow." She tried to share a benign topic. "I'm going to see dolphins."

"You're not getting in the ocean, are you? You're not a very good swimmer. You'll drown. And you saw on the news a dolphin pulled a woman underwater."

"Cheery thoughts there, Ma. I'll talk to you tomorrow."

Megan hung up and tossed the phone onto the bed. It might have been due to the long day, but the rope constricting her throat and her chest simply refused to loosen. Dropping to the edge of the bed, she closed her eyes and did some breathing exercises she'd learned from a therapist years ago. She hadn't had to use them in quite a while. Eventually, the tightness released its hold on her and she was able to relax.

Barefoot, she took the little plastic ice bucket from her room out to the ice maker in the hallway and filled it. The *clunk clunk* of ice clattering into the bin was soothing. Back in her room, she poured a glass of water. She considered the television, but she could watch at home anytime.

Instead, she changed into her pajamas, opened the curtains, turned off all the lights, and sat in a chair beside her floor length window. Tucking her legs under her, she watched the festive twinkling lights of the ship sailing across from them, marveling at the fact that she was here. On a cruise ship, heading out to sea, a thousand miles from home.

It was almost midnight before she slipped into bed, anticipating what it would be like to wake up the next morning surrounded by nothing but ocean. With a giddy laugh, she pulled the blanket to her chin. If she'd known how comfortable the bed was, she would have gotten in much sooner. Excitement tempered her exhaustion, but she fell asleep immediately.

Morning poured into her room, waking her a little before six. She'd forgotten to close the curtains, so sunlight streamed directly into her face. Excited, she kicked the cover off stood at the window, hands pressed against the glass, marveling at how the ocean stretched out into forever. She pried herself away from the window and showered, then picked up the newsletter from under her door and read over the little bit of information about the dolphin encounter.

She put on her bathing suit and covered it with shorts and a t-shirt. Nothing fancy. Her biggest dilemma was deciding whether to wear sandals or sneakers. Sandals. She put her essential items into her bag, checked that she had her key card and ID at least five times, and grabbed her camera.

Megan took the elevator to Deck Fourteen and followed her nose to the breakfast buffet. Eric was reading a newspaper at a table against the windows. He looked up and motioned for her to come over. "Might as well set your stuff down."

"You sure you don't mind if I sit with you? You don't have to hang with me if you don't want to."

Eric grinned. "If I minded, I would have pretended I didn't see you come in."

"Touché. I'll be right back. You need anything?"

"I'm good, thanks."

Megan picked up a tray at the beginning of the buffet line. Her mouth watered from looking at the spread before her. Every breakfast food, pastry, muffin, fruit, and beverage imaginable waited for her to dive in.

A chef stood behind an omelet station, smoothly flipping diced peppers and tomatoes and onions in a pan, then cracking eggs into the mixture. He looked up and winked at her. "You wish for omelet, yes, miss?"

His accent, she guessed Spanish or Portuguese, combined with his chocolate brown eyes and flawless face, gave her knees a little tremble. This was exactly the kind of man she'd envisioned when she joked about having a torrid affair, right down to his broad shoulders. She cleared her throat and shook her head. "No, thanks." *Maybe tomorrow.*

He smiled, displaying perfect white teeth. Then he winked.

Megan barely managed to contain a nervous giggle before quickly moving to a mountain of pastries. She finished loading her tray and went back to the table, her encounter with the omelet chef pushed to the back of her mind. She had more important things to think about. Like dolphins. "What time do we head out?"

"About an hour."

Megan popped another bite of pineapple into her mouth and sighed. "I have never had pineapple so sweet. This is amazing."

Eric sipped his orange juice. "It's easy to get spoiled on cruise food. Enjoy it, because you aren't going to eat like this back home."

"I'm going to gain five hundred pounds this week. You'll have to roll me onto the plane." She popped a mini muffin into her mouth.

"Maybe they have a forklift so we can get you off the ship."

"Don't make me laugh with food in my mouth."

"Did you see the chocolate chip pancakes? They were delicious."

"I didn't see any pancakes at all. Where were they?" She turned to see where he was pointing. "Holy crap, I missed a whole row of food? This is insane."

They finished with breakfast and went to the excursion checkpoint on Deck Five. Eric looked like he'd rather be anywhere else.

"You okay? How's your head?"

"Not as bad as I expected." He gave her a weak smile.

Megan wondered if he was thinking about the wedding that was supposed to have happened last night at sunset. "Terrible fake smile. It's okay to not be okay, you know."

"Yeah. I am okay, though." He shrugged. "I wonder if all these people are going with us."

"If they are, I hope they have extra dolphins."

A tour leader led them out of the ship, waiting on the dock with a sign on a tall pole, until everyone had scanned their ship cards and re-congregated on the sidewalk. "This way, this way, please."

The line of cruisers followed him through a tightly packed

shopping area. The thick air and heat mingled with the body odor, perfumes and colognes of at least a hundred people. Loud voices merged into a rumble that was almost a physical presence of its own.

Megan was focused on not losing sight of the sign when she felt a hand grip her arm. "You got money, pretty lady?" She gasped and jerked to the side, bumping into Eric, who immediately put his arm around her and kept it there until they left the building, preventing any further incidents.

"They think everyone on a cruise must be rich. Try to be more aware of your surroundings, okay?"

Megan nodded. "I should have expected it."

"You haven't traveled much."

His comment sounded like her overprotective mother, immediately setting her on edge. "Correction. I haven't traveled *far*." Deciding to let go of the annoyance he hadn't really earned, she added, "I'll have you know I was pick-pocketed in New York City."

"Are you serious?"

"Bus trip. We went to see Cats and after the show we were on the sidewalk waiting for the bus. This guy bumped into me and started apologizing while another guy took my cash out of my back pocket. It was such a smooth operation I was more impressed than mad."

"Impressed?" He looked horrified.

She lifted a shoulder and let it drop. "They only got ten bucks. I could afford to be impressed."

They boarded a rickety shuttle bus, which took them to a small dock, where they piled into a ferry. As the ferry wheezed and chugged out across the water, Megan snapped photos. The sky matched the ocean, blue on blue. After a while, they came upon a cove rising up out of the water. The ferry squeezed in between two fingers of land and came to rest against a metal docking platform where they disembarked.

Crossing a walking bridge, Megan pointed into the water and squealed, "Look!"

A dolphin swam under the bridge, then back the way he came. He poked his nose out of the water and chattered and whistled at them while Megan took pictures. A second dolphin joined the first, then they chased each other under the bridge and out of sight.

Megan's heart beat faster with the excitement of seeing the animals up close. She couldn't wait to actually touch them.

They walked into a little cabana shop nestled among picturesque palm trees. It was filled with stuffed dolphins and shot glasses and t-shirts. Rows of lockers lined a long wall. After a safety demonstration and a list of Dos and Don'ts, they were split into groups of ten. Megan and Eric stood off to the side while the first group was led down a ramp to the water.

"Why so nervous?" Eric asked.

"I don't swim very well. I know they said we aren't swimming, but what if I fall in the water?"

"Eh, I'm sure someone will fish you out. I bet they even have a tourist net because it happens all the time."

She appreciated his lighthearted joke. "Thanks. You're so reassuring."

Their group changed into their swimsuits and stood along the railing while the first group exited the ramp. Everyone seemed to be happy, except one man, who looked like he'd be sour even if he won the lottery. The metal ramp was hot against Megan's bare feet as they walked to the water.

"Step here, go the whole way to the end." A dolphin trainer held her hand as she stepped down the stairs into the warm, clear water. They stood in a square platform, about fifteen feet long on each side. A two-foot wide metal grate served as a floor, with a gigantic square of emptiness in the middle. A large canopy overhead shielded them from the relentless sun.

Megan swallowed hard and wished there was a railing. She followed the family in front of her the whole way to the end of the grate, trailing her fingers across the surface of the waist-deep water.

Once the group was settled, Megan focused on a little girl beside her. Fearless, she was standing on the very edge of the platform, looking straight down into the water. *If a little kid can do this, so can I.*

Soon, the trainer blew a whistle and a dolphin shot across the water, dove under the cove-side of the platform and popped up in the center. It chirped and clicked. The trainer waved his hand and the dolphin spun in a slow circle, waving his flipper.

The tension and fear oozed out of Megan and sank through the grate, gone for good. The trainer gave a command, and the dolphin ignored him, diving back under the platform and swimming out into the cove.

"Okay, folks, it looks like Chico isn't in the mood today. Our dolphins never have to perform if they don't want to. Sit tight and we'll see who's ready." The trainer motioned to someone in the cabana. While they waited, he explained, "All of our dolphins are rescues who can no longer survive in their natural habitat. Some of them were injured in the wild, and some of them were used in movies or television shows. We never force them to perform." He shared horror stories from the abuses some of the dolphins had endured both in the wild, and as entertainment props.

"It's awesome they don't have to perform if they don't want to," Megan said quietly.

"Wish I could find a job like that," Eric joked.

A few minutes later, another dolphin popped up and

chirped to them. The trainer threw a fish to the dolphin, then walked behind each person and handed them a fish so they could feed it. "Everybody say hello to Andy. We're going to start with hugs and kisses. Adults, get on your knees if you can, please."

The grate was hard against her knees, but the bath-warm water erased any discomfort. He made a gesture and Andy twirled and waved his flipper, slapping the water over all of them. The gritty salt clung to her hair and skin.

The dolphin swam past them, allowing everyone to reach out and touch him. Megan couldn't stop smiling. She was in the Bahamas, kneeling in the ocean, petting a dolphin. She looked over at Eric, who seemed to be just as enthralled with the dolphin as she was.

The trainer made another gesture. Andy paused at each person, leaning his head on their shoulder while a staff photographer took souvenir photos.

"Oh, this is not what I expected." Andy put his nose on Megan's shoulder. She carefully touched his sides, hugging him. She'd expected him to feel like a fish, floppy and pliable. Instead, he was heavy and solid, like a smooth rubber tire against her skin.

After the hug, the trainer blew a whistle and Andy leaned over for a kiss. Megan kissed the tip of his snout. Eric hugged the dolphin, but when it was time for the kiss, the trainer made a small hand motion, and Andy shook his head "no," leaning back over for another kiss from Megan. She laughed and kissed his snout. Andy swam back in front of Eric and blew water from his blowhole all over him before allowing Eric to give him a kiss. The group laughed.

"Okay, you two get close together." Megan squished close to Eric. Andy swam in front of them while the photographer snapped a picture. The dolphin went down the row as the trainer put each family together.

"Uh-oh. I didn't realize they were doing photos."

"Me, either," Eric answered.

After the photos were done, Andy waved goodbye, dove under the platform, then stood high in the open water, dancing backwards, whistling and chirping.

Megan followed the group up the ramp. "I wish I could have taken my own pictures in the water."

Eric handed her a towel. "But then you wouldn't be in any of them."

"Good point." She filled out an order form and spent entirely too much for pictures and a DVD of the encounter. They walked along the beach, watching dolphins playing in the open water while Megan took pictures and put a little bit of sand in a plastic zipper bag. Eventually, all the groups were finished, all the photo orders and DVDs were printed and copied, and the group was loading back onto the ferry.

Megan leaned her head back, savoring the feel of the breeze against her skin. "This is exactly what I picture when I think about a tropical vacation. Palm trees and sand and dolphins and salty air. I'm glad we did this. It was fun."

"Me, too."

"I can't get over the feel of the dolphin. I thought they'd be fishier."

Eric laughed. "I did, too. He was much more solid than I expected."

The ferry chugged through the crystal clear water.

"Someday, I'll stay there." Megan pointed to the massive clay-colored Atlantis resort they were passing by.

"It looks awesome."

"It looks expensive. But I bet it's worth every penny." She sighed, watching until the resort island was out of sight.

The ferry deposited them back on the island.

Eric checked his watch. "We still have a few hours before we have to be back on the ship. Stewart told me about a little coffee house beyond the touristy area. I'm going to go check it out, if you want to come along."

"Definitely."

Chapter Seven

Eric checked his directions and walked down a side street, turning from a paved road to a dirt path, leaving the color and chaos of the tourist area behind them. They glanced at each other before stepping through a tangled arch of foliage and entering a little run down shack with a sign insisting the place was a coffee shop. The screen door creaked in protest.

A weathered man sat behind a counter, watching them. As soon as they were seated on the rickety stools, he came over, a wide smile splitting his dark face. "You new around here, yeah?" He laughed heartily. "What can I get you?"

"Coffee, please." Eric replied.

"And for the pretty lady?"

"I'll have a tea, please."

"Comin' right up."

Eric looked around the room. It was dingy, dark, and in desperate need of repairs. But the place was reasonably clean, and the aroma of coffee was intoxicating. He could see Stewart buying a place like this, and if he ever did, Eric would volunteer to run it. He could handle an island life.

The man brought him a huge mug and set a tall glass in front of Megan.

He set them on the counter. "I make it special for you, friends. Try."

Eric sniffed at the coffee. "It smells amazing. What's in it?"

"Taste first. Then I tell you."

Eric took a small sip and savored it. Then he pulled a long swig into his mouth. The flavors harmonized perfectly. "Incredible." It was some of the best coffee he'd ever had.

The man laughed. "What did I tell you? This one have vanilla, raisin, and nut."

"Before or after it's brewed?"

He winked and leaned closer. "That is the secret. Put it all together with the coffee bean and brew. Then a splash of rum."

Eric glanced at Megan's untouched glass. "What's the tea?"

The man leaned over toward Megan. "Beautiful flavor for beautiful lady." He touched his fingertips to the bottom of her glass and slid it closer to her. "Try. You like it, I promise."

Megan shot Eric a look, then picked up the tea and took a sip. "Oh, this is delicious."

The man grinned. "Just like pretty lady. Delicious." He drew the word out.

Megan sat back in her seat, putting distance between herself and the leering barkeep. Eric casually reached over and put his hand on her knee. Immediately, the man took a step back. "Hey, no problem, friend."

Eric gave him a smile. "No problem at all, my friend. What's in the tea?"

Megan slid the glass toward him. "Try it. There's lime and lemon, and some other things I'm not quite sure of."

Eric tasted it. "This is delicious. I taste fruit, but what kind?"

"Ah, yes. Passion fruit." The man winked. "Hibiscus petals. And pineapple. True tea from the tropics."

"Do you sell your recipes?"

The man was taken aback. "Sell, no, no, my friend. But you wait here." He disappeared through a swinging door. It sounded like he was ransacking the place until he came back through with two small paper bags. "Here you go. Gift for my new friends. How long are you in Nassau?"

"Only a few more hours."

"Ah, you are on cruise ship?"

"Yes, I wish we had more time."

"Wait one minute." He vanished again and reappeared with several more small paper bags. "A few samples. You like these. You both leave me good Yelp reviews." He held up a hand with his fingers splayed. "Five star, please. Mention my name, Pedro. Yes?"

Megan answered. "I promise. Five stars."

He grinned and reached over to grasp her hands. He brought them to his mouth and kissed her fingers. "You are welcome any time, pretty lady. Enjoy my country."

After a long, awkward moment, he let go and firmly shook Eric's hand. "Safe travels, my new friend. Enjoy my country."

"We are. Thank you. And thank you for the gifts, Pedro." He led Megan out of the building, into the blinding sunlight. They stopped on the rickety porch to put their sunglasses on and stick the coffee and tea into Megan's bag. She took her camera out and snapped pictures of the ramshackle coffee house. Why, Eric couldn't fathom. The place was one strong breeze away from being a pile of rubble.

While she took pictures, Eric pulled out his phone and made notes in an app so he wouldn't forget what was in the coffee and tea they'd sampled. Stewart would be happy with their find.

He glanced over to Megan, hunkered down, taking pictures of some tiny lizard who was posing for her. "We should start heading back."

"Sure." She took one more shot, then stood. The lizard skittered off.

Their shoes crunched along the gravel path, but only a few short moments later, they found themselves back in the crowd. The entrance to the dock was conveniently located at the mouth of the shops they had walked through when getting off the boat.

Megan paused. "I'm going to shop and buy some horribly tacky, overpriced touristy stuff."

Eric chuckled. "Sounds great. Lead the way."

Chapter Eight

They wound their way up and down the row of colorful booths, all jammed together in the cramped building. Hawaiian shirts and sunburned tourists filled the aisles. Megan stopped at a booth and bought two spoon rests painted with a beach scene and "Bahamas" stamped on the handle, one for her mother, and one for herself.

In a different booth, she spied a drawstring tote bag she decided she must have.

"How about this?" Eric held up a monkey made out of seashells. Wearing a straw hat.

"Yes! I need one of those." She reached for it, but he pulled it back.

"My treat. For going along coffee hunting."

"Aw, thanks."

They left the shop with too many souvenirs.

"I left space in my suitcase, but I might need to buy another one if I shop like this at every stop."

Eric laughed.

"Now this is what I think of when I think of tropical scenery." Megan paused at the edge of the dock, looking out over the ocean with her arms wide open. Palm trees lined the shore, with an abundance of hibiscus and allamanda and bougainvillea blooming everywhere. "I need to take some pictures of this."

Eric offered to hold her bag while she took a lens off her camera and put it on backwards. "What are you doing?"

She grinned. "Photography trick. I could either lug around an extra lens worth about eight hundred dollars, or use a four dollar adapter and turn this one around. Basically it turns the lens into a magnifier for photos, but the tradeoff is you have severely limited depth of field."

"I don't understand anything you just said."

She bit her lower lip, trying to think of a way to explain it to him. "It's like layers. You're one layer, the ship behind you is another layer, the horizon is another layer. Are you with me?"

"I think so."

"When you take a regular photo, you can capture a whole bunch of layers in focus. Almost limitless layers."

"Okay."

"With macro – close up – photos, you can only capture one layer. A very thin layer. Depth of field describes how many layers you can get in a picture. Make sense?"

"Yes, it does."

Megan wasn't sure if he was just humoring her. She turned her attention to the flowers and took some macro shots of the petals, pistils and filaments, then flipped the lens back around and took photos of whole blooms. "Is it my imagination, or are the colors brighter and more vivid here than they are at home?"

Eric shrugged. "I have no idea. Maybe there are just more colors here?"

"Or maybe you're a regular guy and wouldn't notice such things."

"There's a definite possibility."

"Okay, I'm ready. Sorry to hold you up."

He frowned. "You're not. Why do you keep acting like you're inconveniencing me?"

Startled, Megan looked down and fiddled with her camera to hide her embarrassment. "I didn't realize I was. Sorry."

"Stop apologizing, okay?"

"Okay. Sor- Okay." She held up her hand. He sounded like her best friend Beth, who also told her to stop apologizing for everything.

They made their way to the dock and passed through a security checkpoint, then climbed the ramp onto the ship and had their passcards scanned in tired silence.

Eric yawned as they waited for the elevator to open. "I had fun today."

She agreed. "I can't even remember the last time I enjoyed myself so much. The dolphin was amazing. I'll have to journal about it right away so I don't forget the details. And I really enjoyed the coffee shop."

"That's a pretty generous name for it."

Megan laughed as she stepped onto the elevator. "I think I got some great shots there. It had a lot of *rustic charm*." She made air quotes around those words. "And the lizard was awesome. I can't wait to go through all my pictures from today."

"How many did you take?"

Megan felt the blush of embarrassment warm her cheeks. "Um, somewhere around sixteen hundred?"

"And it's only our first stop. Good thing you don't use film – you'd need a third suitcase to get your pictures home."

"Ugh. Speaking of home, I probably have a thousand messages waiting on me." She sighed and leaned back against the wall of the elevator.

"Are you an only child?"

She fidgeted with the buckle on her camera bag, never sure how to answer that question. "No."

"Do you all get the prison warden approach, or just you?"

Megan blinked rapidly. "Just me."

"Did I say something wrong?"

She looked up at him. "No. Of course not."

The elevator stopped and the doors slid open. Eric held the door open for a long moment, then simply said, "I'll see you later."

Hiking her bag higher on her shoulder, she nodded. "Sure. See you later." She got settled into her room, spreading her souvenirs across the top of the dresser so she could organize them. Eventually, she picked up her phone, unplugged it from the charger and turned it on. In spite of the warnings posted everywhere to keep cell phones in airplane mode to avoid exorbitant fees, Megan felt like she had to connect at least briefly, to keep the peace. She huffed out a humorless laugh. Peace. Hardly.

The phone went through its startup, then vibrated like crazy. Sure enough, between texts and voicemails, she had almost fifty messages. One text was from her dad. One voice-mail was from a potential client. The rest were from her mom.

"'Buying the wifi package is a waste of money,' huh? 'What do you need that for,' huh?" She grumbled as she connected to the internet and opened her Facebook app. She sent a message to both her parents, telling them she was having a wonderful time, and to *please* stop sending her texts and voicemails. They were going to cost her a fortune. Almost immediately, Alice messaged her back, scolding her for not messaging sooner.

Megan blew out a hard breath. For crying out loud, was her mother going to spend ten days doing nothing except glaring at her phone, waiting to pounce whenever Megan messaged her? Tears stung the backs of her eyes. She loved her mother. She understood her. But she couldn't keep living like this, feeling like she was tied to a short leash. It was choking her.

She sent another cheerful message, she had to go, it was time for dinner, and she'd send a quick message in the morning, and to *please* remember not to text or leave voicemails, knowing it fell on deaf ears... or blind eyes, whichever.

Sitting on the chair beside her window, Megan stuffed her frustration down. Again. After so many years, it was second nature. It was nearly a quarter to six when there was a knock at the door.

Eric stood in the hallway. "I'm headed up to dinner. Thought I'd see if you wanted to go along since my seating is so much earlier than yours."

"Yes, please, I'm starving. Give me five minutes to change?"

"I'll be over by the elevators."

Megan shut the door and picked a green sundress and black sweater from the clothes she'd hung in the closet. She ran a brush through her hair and swiped some mascara and lip gloss on, slipped her feet into her sandals and walked out the door.

"Wow, you're quick."

She shrugged. "I don't usually take very long to get ready."

"You look great, by the way." He followed her into the elevator.

"Thanks. You look nice, too." He did. The blue blazer he wore was a nice contrast to his crisp white shirt. "I have to admit, I'm a little disappointed, though. This look isn't very Miami Vice at all."

He laughed and tapped the elevator button. "I'm saving it for a special occasion."

The elegant dining room was crowded and filled with the dull roar of relaxed chatter, punctuated with bursts of laughter and the clinks of silverware against porcelain plates. They found Eric's assigned table – a round table for six – and sat down.

The woman to Megan's right immediately leaned over and grabbed her hand, pumping it enthusiastically. "I'm Sheila. This is my husband, Morty. We didn't see you last night."

Megan tried to extract her hand. "It's nice to meet you. I'm Megan, and this is Eric. We ate early yesterday."

"Megan. Eric. Okay, let me get your names in my brain. Megan, Eric, Megan, Eric. Okay, I got it. Where are you from? We're from New York. Brooklyn." Sheila's unmistakable accent made the clarification unnecessary.

"We're from Pennsylvania. Pretty much the middle of the state."

"Did you hear her, Morty? They're from Pennsylvania. We're practically neighbors."

Morty raised a hand in greeting, giving Eric a look that said, "Whatever she says."

"So you guys been married long?"

Megan balked. "No, no, we're not married. Just friends. Long story."

Sheila gave her a sly smile. "Friends, huh?"

"No, really. Friends."

"Too bad. You make a cute couple."

Megan was grateful when the waiter appeared, giving them a brief reprieve. Too brief.

"Morty and I have been married fifty years. Can you imagine?"

She couldn't. "Wow, congratulations." Megan guessed the last words Morty had spoken with Sheila around were "I do."

"Our kids got us this cruise for our anniversary. They're such great kids. Two boys and a girl. Light of my life, they are. Vincent, Christopher and Leah. Two boys and we thought we were done. Then six years later, surprise, Leah came along. We were sure I couldn't get pregnant again, then what do you know? I finally got my little girl. Now, I'm not complaining about my boys. They're the best sons a mother could ever hope for. But it was so nice to buy all those frilly dresses and hair bows. You know what I'm saying." She paused long enough to focus on buttering a roll.

Megan glanced sideways at Eric, who was suppressing a smirk. She gently kicked him. The other two seats at the table remained unoccupied. She wondered who they might belong to, and whether they'd experienced Sheila the evening prior.

Dinner progressed in much the same way. Sheila kept the silence at bay, and Megan periodically nodded and made an affirmative noise or comment, although her encouragement was wholly unnecessary.

"Oh, look. Cheesecake. Morty, did you see the cheesecake?" She held the dessert menu near his face. He made a noncommittal grunt. "Morty loves cheesecake. Of course, who doesn't? Are you getting the cheesecake?"

Megan answered, "I'm not sure."

Eric cleared his throat. "Yeah, sounds good."

While Sheila was distracted by making sure Morty was ordering his dessert correctly, Eric leaned over. "I see a lot of dinnertime burgers in our immediate future."

Megan took a long sip of water. "You could be right."

"Of course. I always am."

Megan rolled her eyes. "You keep telling yourself that."

"Ouch."

"Did you get the blueberry? I love blueberries on my cheesecake."

"Strawberry," Megan said.

Sheila's talking didn't slow down, even through bites of

dessert. By the time Sheila and Morty stood up to leave, Megan was exhausted.

When they were gone, she said, "I don't think I've ever spent so much energy listening to someone."

Eric chuckled. "You're not kidding. No awkward silence with her around, huh?"

Megan finished her cheesecake. "I'm glad I could savor the last few bites of this in peace."

Eric agreed.

They left the dining room. "Thanks for the dinner seat. The salmon was great."

"Chicken was good, too. I'm going to head back to my room.

See you tomorrow at breakfast?"

"Absolutely. Maybe I'll try an omelet."

Chapter Nine

Eric grabbed a beer from the mini bar in his room. One would be his limit. He twisted the cap off and slid the balcony door open. The rolling *whoosh whoosh* sound of the ocean filled his cabin. He sat on the deck chair, staring out into the darkness. The gentle hum of the ship's engines underscored the occasional peal of distant laughter from the upper decks.

He unbuttoned the top buttons of his shirt and leaned back, propping his bare feet on the balcony railing. On the one hand, he was sorry Brittney had bailed on him. On the other hand, it was becoming increasingly clear he didn't miss her, not the way he should.

If he were completely honest with himself, he didn't miss her at all, and he knew if the wedding had happened, they would have ended up divorced. And since he was being so honest, he admitted he was glad Megan was on board. As much as he would have enjoyed sitting in his stateroom alone for ten days, it was nice to have someone to talk to.

Even if it was his ex-fiancée's cousin. That part was awkward. Or at least it should have been. He guessed they'd never been very close, since Megan's name had never come up until Brittney's dad suggested they use her as their wedding photographer. With a snort-laugh, he realized he missed Brittney's parents more than he missed her. How messed up was that?

He finished his beer, then went back inside to throw the bottle away and sort through his coffee beans. Pedro had been more than generous with him. Several of the coffees would be making it onto the regular menu of Stewart's coffee shop if they could duplicate the flavors. The blend with shredded coconut would be Stewart's personal favorite, for sure.

The teas were less interesting to him, but he knew they would sell well. The hibiscus lime combination would be a big hit.

The buzz alerting him to an incoming message on his cell phone pulled him away from the teas. It was from Brittney.

I need to talk to you.

He bit off a curse. She'd said everything she needed to say – or at least everything he'd needed to hear – in the cowardly note she'd slipped under his windshield wiper.

He texted back.

Not interested.

Immediately the reply came.

I'm pregnant.

Eric smirked.

Congratulations, who's the father?

He knew for sure who it wasn't, so there was no point in continuing a conversation. When they'd reconciled, they decided to wait until after the wedding to have sex. Apparently for Brittney, it only meant she wouldn't be having sex with *him*. Irritated, he tossed the phone onto the bed and went to take a shower to scrub the disgust away.

Shampoo streamed into his eye. He cursed and wiped at his burning eye, but only succeeded in spreading the suds and making it worse, so he stilled, letting the stream of water rinse away the hateful bubbles. Getting angrier by the minute, he toweled off, wondering how much more she was going to try to humiliate him. If embarrassing him was her goal, she was succeeding brilliantly. He was embarrassed. Not only by her behavior, but by his complicity and laziness. He'd dodged a bullet, to be sure, but letting it go on for so long was all on him. What pissed him off most of all was his inability to justify his actions – or inaction – even to himself.

Everyone knew about her affair and tried to talk him out of forgiving her, but he did. Then she canceled the wedding. Part of the reason he'd decided to take the trip anyway was so he wouldn't have to face all the sadly shaking head and the inevitable "I told you so"s he'd hear the second he stepped foot off the plane back into Hickory Hollow.

He realized now he'd handed her the perfect opportunity to smear his name all over town, and he wasn't there to defend himself. Or Megan. His hand froze halfway to his mouth. A glob of toothpaste fell off the brush and into the sink.

She'd better not spread any rumors about Megan.

Yanking his clothes on, he stormed out of the cabin. He poked the elevator button, and when it took too long to open, he took long strides up the stairs to one of the open decks, found a deserted section, and leaned on the railing. The salty breeze ruffled his hair, but did little to blow away his tension.

"Hey." Megan came alongside him.

He turned and she immediately took a step back. "Sorry, I don't want to disturb you."

Forcing what must have been a murderous expression from his face, he said, "No, it's okay." He turned back to glare into the dark ocean.

"Looks like you have a lot on your mind. Did something happen?" She held up a hand. "Sorry. I'm being nosy."

"It's fine. Brittney texted me. Supposedly she's pregnant."

Megan's eyes widened. "What are you going to do?"

With a humorless laugh, he said, "Do? Nothing. It isn't mine."

She bit her lip.

"I'm sure you don't believe me. But it's not." He wasn't sure why it mattered so much to have her believe him.

"She cheated on you?" Megan asked, then immediately said, "Stupid question. Sorry."

He rolled his eyes. "You don't have to pretend you don't know what's gone on with me and Brittney."

"I don't. It's not like we're close, Eric."

"Yeah, well, families talk." And friends, acquaintances, and strangers. Everybody loves drama, especially when it's some-body else's.

She lifted an eyebrow. "Not mine. I'm only here because my dad wanted to help me get out and see the world. He and Uncle Doug thought this would be a win-win. I get to travel, Brittney gets a wedding photographer."

"So you expect me to believe you don't know anything about her cheating on me before?"

"I don't."

He was so used to being lied to that it took him a few minutes to recognize the sincerity in her eyes. He blew out a deep breath and rested his forearms on the railing.

"My business partner. One night he offered to work late and Brittney had 'something to do.' I forgot something in my office, so I went back and her car was in the parking lot. I went inside. I was going to storm into the office and confront them. But... I heard the noises and I didn't want to see it. I knew I'd never be able to erase it from my mind if I saw it."

"You're... are you sure they were...?"

"There's no mistaking what I heard." He mocked, "'Oh, Brittney, you're gonna make me...' Oh, and he finished the sentence. So yeah, I'm sure."

"Gosh, I'm sorry."

"Me, too. Sorry I let myself forgive them both, but sorrier I was fool enough to think life could go back to the way it had been."

Megan leaned on the railing beside him.

He continued, "Hindsight's 20/20, you know. Almost a year earlier, I had to fly to London. I'd asked Brittney to come with me. She'd always wanted to go to England, but she decided not to go along. I realized they'd been sleeping together the whole time. They played me for a fool for at least a year. A *year*."

"What did you do?" she asked.

"Confronted them. She swore it was over. He swore it was over. They both begged for my forgiveness. Quinn and I still had a business to run, so I went to work every day and pretended everything was fine."

Megan held his gaze but said nothing.

"She said everything I needed to hear, and I was willing to be gullible enough to believe she was telling the truth. *Again*. We stayed together and everything was going along okay."

"But you knew something wasn't right."

"Yeah. But by then we were engaged and the wedding and the cruise were planned. I thought maybe I was being paranoid. Living in the past, like she always accused me of. I let Quinn buy me out of the business."

"Why?"

"I wanted out. I was tired of the rat race. Flying all over the world to sit in meetings and shake hands with people who were slimy and fake. I hated it. Then my brother decided to open the coffee shop. I offered to invest in it and handle the books. Everything was finalized last week. I told Brittney we'd have a tighter budget for a while. That's part of why she bailed on the wedding. 'Budget' is a four letter word to her."

They stood in silence for a while.

"Sorry, I didn't mean to unload all my crap on you. I do appreciate you listening, though." Eric ran a hand through his hair. "If this could stay between us..."

Megan lightly touched his shoulder and shook her head. "Eric, I'm not going to tell anybody anything. What kind of lousy friend would I be?"

He felt better than he had all evening. "Thanks."

Chapter Ten

Megan changed for bed and climbed between the cool sheets. She reminded herself that every story has at least two sides, but if even half of what he said was true, Brittney was a jerk. It was a shame. Eric seemed like a nice guy. Maybe too nice. He must have some major issues, too, if those were the things he was willing to put up with. Then again, she didn't know what her cousin's issues were that would allow her to treat a man so horribly. Any man.

Sleep came easy on the swaying boat, and morning slid gently into the room. Megan picked up the daily newsletter from under her door. An entire day at sea. Megan was excited to explore the ship. She wanted to try some things she'd never done, like the rock climbing wall and maybe get a massage.

Or a pedicure. Spending money on something she could do herself felt like a frivolous indulgence. *But,* she reasoned, *this is a vacation, and if you don't indulge while on vacation, then when?*

She got dressed and straightened the blankets. A pedicure sounded perfect.

With her camera slung around her neck, she slipped her key card in the pocket of her shorts. Humming, she rode the elevator up to the shopping deck. The entire deck felt like a shopping mall, with little shops and stores everywhere. Few people were on the deck this early, and surprisingly, there were no customers in the nail salon yet.

Debating whether she should spend the money, she tried talking herself out of the extravagance, then she decided it was high time to treat herself. Denying herself simple, innocent pleasures was ridiculous, and it was time to stop. She worked hard, earned a nice living, and a spa treatment would hardly bankrupt her.

In spite of her hesitation, she thoroughly enjoyed the foot massage and pampering, so much so that she also got a manicure. She left a generous tip, then went out to take pictures all over the deck, pausing every so often to admire her French-tipped fingers and toes.

Her stomach reminded her she hadn't had breakfast. She went to the buffet and found Eric, sitting with an empty tray and a cup of coffee.

"Sunrise?" He gestured to her camera.

"Ha, actually not. I was on the shopping deck, taking some pictures there."

"Of what?"

"People. Designs. Neat stuff. Here, look." She leaned beside him, holding her camera screen so he could see, and clicked through the photos. "Elevator buttons. This is wrought iron on one of the trash cans. Wall sconce. Store display. Carpet."

Eric nodded appreciatively. "Interesting. I'd never notice those sorts of details."

"Exactly. It's one of the first things we learned in photography school. Look at the things nobody else sees."

"You're very talented."

Megan blushed at the compliment. "Thank you. I'm going to get food before they start putting it away."

Focused on filling her tray with food, Megan didn't notice the man behind the counter until he spoke.

The omelet chef winked at her. "You are enjoying your cruise, yes?" His voice was silk.

"Yes, it's been wonderful."

"What is your plan today? Since no trip to shore?"

"Um, I think there's some stuff. Like things to do and... stuff." Megan's heart was pounding. This was ridiculous. Just because a pair of chocolate eyes set in what was quite possibly the world's most perfect face were looking at her did not mean she could let her brain turn to mush.

"I'm Marco."

"Of course you are," she mumbled. He raised an eyebrow, waiting. "Megan. I'm, uh, Megan."

"Megan." Her name coming out of his lips sent a chill up her spine. "I'll be sure to see you around today, Megan."

She emitted some sort of nervous giggle before fleeing to the fruit station. Her hands were shaky as she tried to pick up pineapple wedges with the tongs. *This is ridiculous. He says that to everyone. EVERYONE. Even the ladies who are old enough to be his grandmother. Great-grandmother, even. Get yourself together.*

Eric looked up as she set her tray down. "You okay?"

"Yes, I'm okay. Of course I'm okay, why wouldn't I be okay?"

He held up a hand. "Sorry. You looked pale or something. Never mind."

"The omelet guy was hitting on me, and it made me nervous." She clamped a hand over her mouth. She couldn't believe she'd said it out loud.

Eric laughed.

"Knock it off. I know he uses the same lines on everyone, I'm not stupid." She stabbed at her food.

"You're eating grapes with a fork?"

"Yeah. So?" She glanced down in time to see a grape spin away from her fork and shoot onto the floor.

"Wait. Did he make you uncomfortable? If he upset you –"

"No, for Pete's sake, no, he didn't upset me. He didn't do anything. I'm just being a dork. Can we please let it go?" Megan groaned, shoving a bite of muffin into her mouth.

"Okay." Eric finished his coffee. "What's on your agenda for today?"

Grateful for the change in subject, Megan answered, "Deck photos for sure. Towel folding class, then I thought I might try the rock climbing wall."

"You don't strike me as the rock climbing wall type."

"Which is exactly why I'm going to do it." She hoped she sounded more convincing than she felt.

"Gotcha. Be adventurous. Try new things. Take advantage of this whole trip."

"Exactly. What's your agenda?"

"I was going to either wander around aimlessly or nap until it was time to eat again. But if you don't mind the company, maybe I'll go along to the towel folding class."

Megan wasn't sure whether she should laugh. "Are you kidding?"

He shook his head. "I read the newsletter. The other options aren't any manlier." He glanced at his watch. "When is it?"

"11:00 in the mini-theater on Deck Five. Give me a second to finish this and we'll head down." She swallowed the last of her orange juice and took her tray to the trash area. "What towel animals have you gotten in your room so far?"

He rolled his eyes. "Remember I've got the honeymoon package. Yesterday was two swans. Today was a pair of kissing bears surrounded by freaking rose petals."

"Aww, I bet the bears are cute."

"I suppose so."

"You suppose so. How can you be so cold?"

Flexing his biceps, then tapping a fist to his chest, he said, "Heart of ice, baby."

They laughed and made their way to the stage where the class was being held.

"Holy cow, how many people are coming to this thing?" Eric grumbled as they navigated the sea of chairs.

"Up there." Megan steered him to two vacant seats near the front, quickly counting at least thirty people in attendance. Four of which were guys.

A much-too-chipper ship employee bounded onto the stage and greeted everyone as he whipped and flipped a towel around and magically ended up with a swan. He told jokes and whipped a few more towels around and created a bunny, a dog, a monkey and a frog, which he set along the edge of the table. "Okay, everyone, decide which animal you're going to make with your towel."

"I want to do a bunny." She couldn't believe Eric had actually come along to the class.

Eric rubbed his chin. "I think I'm going with the dog."

They sat through the demonstrations for each animal, folding and rolling their towels when their turn came. It was harder than it looked. The instructor wound his way through the group, helping refold towel blobs into mostly-recognizable animals.

Megan held up her bunny with lopsided ears. "Poor little guy. I feel bad for him."

Eric made a face. "My dog didn't fare any better."

Before dismissing them, the demonstrator pointed out folders on the floor under each chair. Each folder had step-by-step instructions for creating all the towel animals he'd demonstrated.

"Sweet. We can practice."

Megan held her bunny close to her. "Surely you aren't suggesting I take my bunny apart to try again."

"Sorry, doggie, that's exactly what's happening to you." Eric pointed in the towel's face. "I'm going to turn him into a snake."

"Nooo, poor doggie. You can't." She reached over and scratched his ill-shapen head.

"Fine. I'll try it with another towel."

"Good." She leaned close to the towel dog. "You owe me."

"I think you're scaring him." He held the dog close to his chest and jiggled it like it was shivering.

Indignant, Megan pointed to herself, then at Eric. "Me? You're the one who was going to rip him apart."

"For his own good."

"Hmpfh."

"Do you want to do the rock climbing wall now?"

Megan swallowed hard. "Okay?"

"You don't have to do it at all, you know. You don't have to prove anything to anyone."

Looking at her bunny instead of him, she said, "Except myself."

"Why?"

"Why what?"

"Why do you need to prove anything to yourself ? You know who you are."

Megan frowned and looked up into his eyes. "I'm not sure I do."

Eric held her gaze for a moment, then gave her a nod. "Then let's go climb the wall."

They made their way to the wall and waited in line. "I'm freaking out."

"You'll be fine." Eric took her towel bunny and camera.

"This thing is huge." She squeezed her hands together as she took in the wall.

"You're only going one grip at a time. Look how close together they are. It'll be a piece of cake."

His calm voice helped her nerves, until it was her turn. She put on the special shoes and the safety guide adjusted the harness. With a relaxed smile, he had her touch the wall and showed her how to properly grip the multi-colored nubs.

"Have you done this before?" he asked.

Megan shook her head. "No."

Again, he smiled. "The grips are color coded. You see the lines dividing the lanes up the wall?"

"Yes." As soon as he pointed it out, she could see the pattern in the different colored pieces.

"This is your lane. Your grips are purple and green. All you need to remember is to grab purple or green. Okay?"

"Okay."

He explained how the harness worked, and how to get down. "Your goal is to ring the bell." He pointed to the top of the wall, to a large purple bell. "You get up there and ring the heck out of it."

"Okay."

Tapping the top of her helmet, he said, "Here we go."

She stood at the bottom and looked up at the wall towering over her. It seemed to stretch even higher while she stared. What had she been thinking? This was insane. It was unsafe.

She reached out and grabbed a purple grip. Unsafe? She had a harness and a guide. Worse than being unsafe was never reaching out, never taking a chance.

Shaking, she grabbed another grip and stepped her right foot, then lifted herself off the ground and put her left foot on a higher grip.

"Now reach up for the next purple one." The guide instructed her.

"Good job, Megan, you're doing great." Eric called to her.

With each step, she felt more confident. To either side, other climbers passed her, reaching the summit, ringing their bell, and falling off backwards, secure in their guides. One more grip. And one more. And one more.

Megan inched upward, listening for the voice of her guide, telling her which grip to grab onto. She trusted his experience, and his hold on the rope tethering her to the pulley above.

Finally, she reached the top.

"Ring the bell!"

She reached up and grabbed the rope, yanked it back and forth, ringing the bell, pride surging through her. She did it!

Eric's voice reached her from far below. "Yay, Megan! You did it!"

Her guide yelled up to her. "Lean back and let go."

She hugged the wall, sudden anxiety paralyzing her. "I can't," she yelled down.

"Trust me, Megan. I'll get you down safely. I won't let go of you, I promise." Her guide's voice was calm and reassuring.

"Are you sure?"

"I'm sure. I've got you. Just lean back and let go."

"What if I fall?" Tears filled her eyes.

"You won't fall. I promise."

"I can't." She was shaking. Her hands were sweating, so she gripped even harder to keep from slipping. She squeezed her eyes shut. *I'm going to die here, stuck to this freaking wall. What was I thinking?* The sound of her own rapid breathing only added to her fear.

The bell in the lane next to her clanged and she felt the person drop away. Why couldn't she just let go?

"Megan, you're doing great." Eric's voice rose up from the floor, followed by her instructor's.

"I've got you, Megan, just lean back and let go."

Taking a deep breath, she used every ounce of courage she had to push herself away from the wall and lean backwards an inch, then two.

Shaking like never before, she forced her clammy, freezing fingers to let go of the grips. She fell backwards with a short scream, then a whimper, dangling away from the wall, clutching the rope with a death grip. Her guide slowly let the rope out, bringing her down a few feet at a time.

Her feet hit the thick rubber mat on the floor. Her knees were shaking so hard she almost couldn't stand. The guide gave her a huge smile while he unbuckled her harness. "Great job, Megan. You did great."

"I got stuck."

Chuckling, he pulled her helmet off and said, "Happens all the time."

Slipping off the shoes and putting them in the marked bin, she stepped off the mat and burst into tears. Eric pulled her into a hug and she threw her arms around his neck and sobbed.

"I'm so proud of you," he said into her hair.

"Me, too," she mumbled. "But I look like an idiot."

"Nobody's even looking. You were amazing, and we're all proud of you." He handed her bunny to her and picked up his mushed dog.

Her hands still shaking, she wiped her face. "I'm not even sure why I'm crying. It was just a stupid rock climbing wall."

He slung an arm around her shoulders as they walked away from the wall. "Nope. Don't minimize it. It was a big deal, you were a freaking rock star, and you should be very proud of yourself."

She sniffled again. "Thanks."

"I took some pictures with your camera."

"You did?" She took her camera from him and stopped walking to click through the pictures he took. Of her. Conquering the wall. She might have gotten stuck for a minute, but she climbed it all the way to the top and rang the bell. *She* did.

"I hope you don't mind. I didn't mess with your settings or anything."

"I don't mind at all. Thank you. I didn't think you'd know how to operate it."

"Pfft, it's not rocket science." He grinned, then explained, "My mom has a similar camera. Older model, but basically the same."

"She's a photographer?"

"Scrapbooker. Dad got her the 'fancy' camera for Christmas one year so she could take better pictures. Mostly of Stewart and Jody's kids."

"That's so great. My friend Beth does scrapbooks for her five kids."

He dropped his arm from her shoulders as they went through a doorway. "Lunch?"

"Yes, please. After all the excitement, I'm starving." They went back to the burger place on the top deck and were seated at a table outside under a large canvas umbrella. The breeze ruffled the edges of it.

Megan fiddled with the corner of her napkin. "Thanks for encouraging me to do the wall."

"Hey, I just babysat the towels. You did all the work."

"Yeah, but I could hear you talking to me the whole time. I appreciate it more than I can tell you."

"You'd have done the same for me, right?"

"Right." She nodded. "So what are *you* going to do that

scares you?"

"Well, there's salsa lessons. Those sound rather terrifying, I'd say."

"Perfect."

The waiter brought their food. When he left, Eric changed the subject. "So I had an awkward visit before breakfast this morning."

"What kind of awkward visit?"

"From the wedding planner. She somehow didn't get the message the wedding was canceled."

Megan's jaw dropped. What an awful reminder for him. "Oh, no."

"Oh, yes. She had a bottle of champagne and some choco-late covered strawberries to congratulate the happy couple."

"Yikes."

"You should have seen her face when I broke the news. I think she took it harder than I did." He chuckled. "Then she turned beet red and apologized a thousand times and I thought she was going to cry. I felt bad for her."

Megan felt bad for her, too. "I'm sure she was embarrassed she didn't know."

"On the upside, I had paid for a non-refundable lobster dinner I didn't know about, to be served on a private balcony off the formal dining hall. So if you like lobster, here's your opportunity to indulge."

"I've never had it, actually. I love seafood, but I tend to stay with fish and shrimp."

"Great. Then you get to try lobster, and we get to avoid Sheila and Morty. Win-win." He picked up his glass and set it back down. "Assuming you want to, of course."

"Sure. Take advantage of every experience, right?"

"Right."

"What time's dinner tonight?"

"Six."

"Sounds good. This is our formal night, right?"

"Yep."

They finished eating, then went their separate ways.

Megan took her camera and explored the decks. She kneeled down, taking pictures of the horizon through the railing.

"Megan?" The rich baritone voice gave her a shiver. She took another photo to give herself a moment to wipe the shock from her face, then stood and turned.

"Marco."

"Ah, you remembered."

As if anyone could forget. "Of course. You're the only omelet chef I've ever met."

He laughed, low and sultry. "Would you take a walk with me?"

"Sure. Where to?" He was too smooth, too practiced. She half expected him to ask her back to his cabin.

He reached out and took her hand, sliding it into the crook of his arm. "Anywhere you like, *mi corazón.*"

"Oh." Her knees went a little weak. This was definitely the fantasy man she'd joked about.

"Here. Let me show you something."

Uh oh.

He led her to the stairs and walked up to the next deck, keeping her hand tucked firmly in his arm. They went down a hallway. He pushed open a door leading to a large room with wooden floor and a mirrored wall. Yoga mats and towels were rolled and displayed in baskets along the far side of the room. "I will teach you to dance, yes?"

"Oh. Okay." Megan set her camera and towel bunny on a bench while Marco turned on some music. Sultry, sexy, Latin music. Of course.

He held his arms open. "Come."

She hesitated before stepping into them, putting her right hand in his, and her left on his shoulder.

His voice was low and husky. "Is all in the hips." He held her waist and pulled her closer. "You watch me, follow my lead."

He held her captive with his eyes. The song ended, replaced with another. On a beat, he moved her backward, then pulled her forward, pulling her tight against him. He moved her expertly around the room. It was effortless, moving opposite his sensual lead, like they'd been dancing together for years.

"You've danced before."

Not trusting herself to speak, she shook her head.

"Surely."

"Nope, never."

He lowered his lips to her ears. "You move beautifully. Such a perfect partner." The words were ten times sexier with his accent. Before she knew what happened, his lips were on hers. They were standing in the middle of the dance floor, mouths locked together. Her arms wound around his neck, her fingers tangling in his hair. His hands slid around her waist, holding her against him. His tongue parted her lips and his hands slid to her bottom.

Adventure was one thing, this was quite another. Megan pulled back and put her hands against his chest, pushing him away. "I'm sorry. That... was amazing, but I can't."

Marco raised an eyebrow and caught her hand in midair. He pressed his lips to the back of her hand and looked up at her through long black lashes. "No worries, *mi corazón*. I will wait for you."

Megan grabbed her camera and fled, sure her pounding heart was audible to everyone on the ship. She didn't stop speed walking until she got back to her own cabin and slammed the door shut. She let out a huge breath and pressed her fingers to her lips. Wow. Thirty-four years on the planet, and she'd never been kissed quite like that.

Pushing away from the door, she set the camera and the bunny down. "Stop judging me," she told the towel.

Chapter Eleven

Seeing Marco The Omelet Man's tongue halfway down Megan's throat annoyed Eric to no end. He knew he had no right to be. They were friends. Besides, forty-eight hours ago, he'd been engaged to her cousin.

Still, annoyed, he most certainly was.

He scowled at the stupid ocean. Stupid Marco. What a ridiculous name. It was probably fake, along with his stupid fake accent, so when he knocked up a new passenger on every cruise, they wouldn't be able find him. There was probably an army of illegitimate Marcos running around all over the world. His real name was probably Bob, and he was probably from New Jersey and just hit the genetic lottery. Jerk. Eric hoped he went prematurely bald. Preferably today.

Everything was perfectly nice. It was a nice trip. He was having a nice time with Megan. Nice. Then the Omelet Douche breezes in with his stupid accent and... and what? What business was it of his if he swept Megan off her feet?

Trudging back to his suite, Eric slammed the door shut and pulled out his suit for dinner. A dinner he'd be eating alone since Megan would be eating a freaking dinner omelet in

Marco's onboard love nest somewhere in the boiler room. Skeevy jerk.

He flipped his tie around, yanking it this way and that, trying to get the stupid knot straight. When he'd wrestled it into submission, he pulled on his jacket and glared at his watch. Was there even any point to knocking on Megan's door?

He shoved his feet into his shoes and straightened the cuffs of his shirt. He ran a hand through his hair and checked the mirror. Okay, he didn't look half bad. Maybe he'd eat his lobster alone and find some lonely woman on an upper deck who'd think his tale was sad and sweet... and sexy. Yep, now he had a Plan B.

Right.

He'd start with Plan A. Pretend he hadn't seen anything, knock on Megan's door, and go from there. Wing it. If she didn't answer, he'd go back to the sad lobster story with the mystery woman above deck. Maybe Richelle, the female equivalent to Marco.

Every step down the carpeted hallway made him more anxious. He hated anticipating the empty room, the unanswered knock. He cleared his throat, raised his hand, and rapped on the door.

It swung open. "You're late." Her voice was teasing. He startled, and looked at his watch.

"Two whole minutes."

He took in her black dress and heels. She'd put a little makeup on and curled her hair, wearing it down around her shoulders. "You look beautiful."

"Fine, you made up for one minute," she laughed.

"I mean it. You look amazing."

She rolled her eyes. "Let's go. I don't want to be trying cold lobster."

"After you." He stepped aside while she pulled her cabin door closed.

"So it's good, right? Lobster?"

"It's not bad. I've had it a few times." Eric forced himself to think about lobster.

"You don't sound impressed."

The elevator stopped to pick up more passengers dressed in their formal attire. "It's good. I like shrimp better, though."

"Okay."

After posing on the grand staircase for their formal picture, they arrived in the dining room. A waiter in a tux led them through the dining hall, up a rounded staircase and out onto a balcony. Cloth dividers were set up, separating several tables into their own "private" seating. Eric pulled out Megan's chair, then sat across from her. A hurricane lamp sheltered a candle and its flame from the ocean breeze.

The waiter poured two glasses of wine and retreated. Megan sipped her wine. "I guess I didn't say it out loud, but you look great, too. You clean up nice." She smiled at him.

"Thanks." He poked at the collar. "I'm not a big fan of starched shirts and neckties."

"Well, it looks good. So there's that."

"I'll take it." He took a long drink from his own wine.

"Not as good as the seafoam green blazer I was expecting, but it'll do." They laughed.

The waiter reappeared with salads for each of them and quickly vanished again.

"The dressing is delicious. I wonder what's in it?" He tasted. "I think raspberry?"

"I think you're right. The tartness must be vinegar. Maybe red wine vinegar."

"So what did you do this afternoon?" The words were out before he could check them.

Her fork paused halfway to her mouth. "I got a lot of pictures. I'm not sure what else is left on board to photograph."

"Good." He swallowed hard, the spinach in his salad more bitter now. Was she going to mention *him* or not?

"Yeah. Then I ran into Marco."

He raised an eyebrow at her disinterested tone. "The Douchey Omelet Guy?" He failed to keep the snark out of his voice.

"Yes. The Omelet Guy."

"I figured he'd be below deck tending to the chickens or something. Gathering eggs for tomorrow's buffet. Maybe laying them himself."

Megan cocked her head. "Are you finished?"

He shrugged and stabbed at the last tiny speck of salad on his plate. "So what did *Marco* have to say?"

"He said some very pretty things with a very pretty accent."

"I bet."

"And then he gave me a salsa lesson."

Eric snorted. "Oh, I bet he's got some smooth moves. *Salsa lesson.*" He made air quotes with his fingers. "I bet he gives *salsa lessons* on every cruise." He couldn't stop himself.

Megan glared at him. "Stop. Why am I even talking to you?"

He held up a hand. "Sorry, but that guy's ridiculous."

"Because he singled me out? On a ship full of beautiful women, he's paying attention to me, so he's ridiculous?" She yanked the cloth napkin from her lap and tossed it on the table. "Or are you trying to say *I'm* ridiculous because I'm too naïve or stupid to realize what's going on?"

"Wait. What? I didn't say anything even remotely like that. The guy's slick. He's got a good game going. Look, do what you want. It's not like we're here together. If you want to go shack up with Egg Man for the rest of the trip – except breakfast time, of course – then knock yourself out." He snatched his glass of wine and drained it.

"Why are you being such a jerk?"

"Me? He's the guy who's trying to get laid."

"Wow."

"You think he's not?"

Megan rolled her eyes and shook her head.

The waiter reappeared and cleared their salad plates. "How is everything?"

Eric barely glanced up. "Great. Fan*tas*tic."

Megan nodded vigorously. "Wonderful."

The waiter looked back and forth between them, then made a hasty exit with the salad plates. Megan grabbed the wine bottle and filled her glass. Before she could set it back down, Eric took it and filled his glass to the brim.

They both stared out over the ocean, the silence as thick as the salty air.

Several long moments passed before Megan said, "I'm not stupid, you know."

Eric lifted a shoulder. "I would never suggest you are."

"It's rather flattering to get attention from someone like Marco."

Eric fiddled with the stem of his glass. "I would imagine so."

"But..." she trailed off.

He looked up at her. "But what?"

The waiter reappeared, pushing a cart. He lifted a covered plate and placed it in from of Mega, then did the same for Eric. With a flourish, he lifted the cloches, revealing the lobster and garlic mashed potatoes.

"*Bon appetit.*"

Megan answered, "*Merci.*"

"You speak French?" The tension seemed to lessen with the

arrival of the food, so Eric decided to let it go. He didn't want to ruin good lobster by talking about the Omelet Douche.

She grinned. "You just heard most of it. Four whole years of high school French, and I only remember about seven words."

"Why French?"

"Well, you see, I had a theory. At the time, I thought it was much more likely I would end up trapped somewhere in French-speaking Canada than anywhere Spanish speaking. So it seemed more prudent to take French." She rearranged the cloth napkin back on her lap.

"In case you were ever taken hostage in Canada."

"I don't think Canadians take hostages, do they? They're too nice."

Eric chuckled. "They do, but only if they have to. And they treat them really, really well."

"No, I was thinking more along the lines of being stuck in the snow or something. I'm not getting stuck in the snow in Mexico."

"Good point."

"Exactly. And since we never traveled anywhere, and since we're much closer to Canada, voilà. My airtight reasoning."

"Can't argue with that logic."

Megan bit into her lobster.

"Well?"

"It's okay, but I think all the flavor is from the sauce. The meat itself is pretty mild."

"I'd have to agree."

"But the potatoes are delicious. And so are the green beans."

"I'd agree again." Garlic mashed potatoes was one of his favorite dishes. Right next to macaroni and cheese.

"Let's disagree on something."

"I thought we already did that."

Megan gave him a flat look. "Food, Eric. Let's talk about the food."

"The wine kind of sucked. It was bitter."

She laughed. "I'd agree. Pick something else."

Eric squinted. "Okay, then the wine was delicious."

"No, it wasn't."

"Yes, it was. It was full bodied and tangy."

Megan laughed again. "It was over-aged and spoiled by, I don't know, too much light in the bottle."

"I completely disagree."

"So do I."

Shaking his head, Eric said, "You can't agree about disagreeing. Then we're agreeing again, and you wanted to disagree."

"Then stop agreeing with me."

"I wasn't." Eric smirked behind his glass.

"Yes, you were."

"Was not."

"Why are you fighting with me?" She asked.

"Because you told me to."

"If you're doing what I told you to, it doesn't count as fighting."

"Good, because I don't want to fight with you."

She set her glass down. "Then don't."

The gentle roar of the ocean was the perfect background music, occasionally punctuated by laughter from the "private" dining spaces on either side of them.

The waiter eventually cleared their dinner plates and returned a few minutes later with cheesecake drizzled with strawberry topping. Eric couldn't read Megan's face in the dimming light. She seemed upset with him, but he wasn't sure why. Unless it had to do with the Omelet Douche. Whatever. He'd cross that bridge when he came to it.

"St. Maarten looks amazing." Megan was the first to break the silence.

"I'm excited about the helmet diving."

Megan raised an eyebrow. "I'm nervous about it. I don't know what to expect, and the brochure isn't very helpful."

"There's all kinds of YouTube videos. Let me see if I can find the one I saw." He pulled out his phone, connected to the wifi and spent a minute searching for the video. "Here it is." He scooted his chair closer to hers and held his phone so they could both see the screen. Eric put his hand on the back of her chair while they watched the video, not touching her, but almost. Her fruity perfume, or maybe it was her shampoo, filled the air and immediately became his new favorite scent.

Goosebumps covered her arms. "Are you cold?"

She nodded. "I should have brought a sweater. I guess I should have realized the 'private dining' would be outside."

"Take this." He slipped his jacket off and hung it over her shoulders.

"Thank you."

"*De nada.* Four years of Spanish." He winked at her.

"Good. Stick close when I get thrown in prison for drug trafficking."

"What?"

Megan laughed. "Sorry, inside joke with myself. My mom told me someone would plant drugs on me so I'd get arrested and then I'd be trapped in a Mexican prison."

"We aren't in Mexico."

"Completely irrelevant."

"I see."

She shook her head. "I doubt you do, and consider yourself lucky you don't."

"Is she still blowing up your phone?" Families could be such a pain, but Eric couldn't imagine life without his. They supported him through thick and thin, but it seemed like Megan's family must be a whole study in dysfunction. Or maybe he was being unfair. He didn't know.

Megan slipped her arms through the sleeves of his jacket. "I asked her last night to only message me through Facebook, because the texts and voicemails are costing me a fortune. This morning, I Skyped with her for a couple of minutes, and before dinner, I checked my phone and I had a dozen texts and two voicemails. It's driving me insane."

"Can't you ignore them?"

She shook her head. "I can't. I know why she is the way she is... and the last thing I'd ever want to do is hurt her feelings. It's hard for her to have me this far away."

"Yeah, but you're entitled to live your own life, right? Set some boundaries."

"It's complicated."

Eric reached across the table and slid his dessert plate so it was in front of him. A wave of gratitude for his own family settled in his chest. "I'm listening, if you want to talk."

Megan picked up her fork. "Some other time."

"Okay."

They finished their cheesecake in a much more comfortable silence, but he couldn't help but wonder what she was thinking about.

Chapter Twelve

Megan scraped the last of the strawberry syrup off her plate. Cheesecake was her favorite, and whatever they did to it on the ship made it a hundred times better. She avoided Eric's eyes. It was too easy to talk to him. There was no pressure with him, mostly because there was no relationship. Just a casual, convenient ten day friendship.

Even so, she couldn't bring herself to talk about her mom's issues, or her brother. It felt like a violation, even though it affected her life, too.

Affected?

More like defined.

She drank the last of her wine and set the glass down, watching the last streaks of a brilliant orange sunset fade from the sky.

"You should have brought your camera."

Megan shrugged. "I thought it would be rude."

"I wouldn't have minded. I like watching you work. You get this intense look on your face, like you're putting a puzzle together in your head."

"Yeah, kind of. I try to visualize the frame in my head

before I take the shot." She considered for a minute. "It's more like taking a puzzle apart. I try to see what a section of what I'm seeing will look like in the frame. So I'm looking at individual pieces that will work on their own."

"Like the trash can in the lobby with the wrought iron."

"Exactly. Who wants to look at a trash can? But when you get down close to it, the design of the frame was quite beautiful."

"You have a gift."

Megan blushed and gave a shrug. "I guess."

"Do you like doing weddings?"

The waiter cleared their dessert plates.

"Shall we walk and talk?" he asked.

"Sure."

Eric stood up and followed her through the dining room. They rode the elevator up to an open deck and walked the perimeter.

"Weddings." She sighed. "They're great, don't get me wrong. I like working with brides... well, I like working with *most* brides. I love the lace and satin and the gowns and the flowers. Especially the flowers. They're my favorite part. And it makes me a good living, so I can't complain."

"That's not what I asked."

"Hmm. Do I like doing weddings. I guess I'd say yes, I like doing weddings. I don't love doing weddings."

"And the family portraits?"

"They're more fun than weddings, but less lucrative. Now, I do love maternity shoots. Those are so much fun. Baby shoots? Not so much. I think they're the hardest for me, even though I've done some amazing work with newborns. But I love love love doing senior portraits and prom sessions. Teenagers are entertaining. They're so creative and have some great ideas. Most people don't believe me, though. Like teenagers are surly and brooding all the time."

He laughed. "I have three nieces and a nephew. They're all teenagers except the youngest, who's six. I think they're wonderful. Smarter than I'll ever hope to be, though. It's kind of scary."

"No kids of your own?"

"No. Maybe someday."

"So you want kids?"

"I'd rather find the right wife. Kids would be great, but honestly, it's not a deal breaker one way or the other for me. I have my brother's kids to spoil."

"Would you have had kids with Brittney?" The question seemed to pop out of nowhere, but now that she'd asked it, she was curious about the answer.

He sighed. "Can I be honest?"

"I'd prefer it, yes."

"I'm sure I would have, and I'm equally sure I would have regretted it."

"Why?"

"I don't think a marriage with Brittney would have been destined for longevity."

She stared at him. "Then why would you have gone through with it? Seems kind of..."

"Pathetic? Stupid? Ridiculous? Weak? Pitiful?"

"I wouldn't have put it so strongly."

"But it's fairly accurate?"

"Honestly? I don't know. I guess I don't get it. Why would you try building a life with someone you don't want a life with, and can't even *see* a life with long term? The whole point of marriage is to be with someone for the rest of your life. It doesn't make sense to me."

Eric stopped walking and leaned his hip against the railing, facing her. "It doesn't make sense if you're looking at it logically. But who lives by logic? Brittney cheated on me. With a close friend of mine. Business partner, in fact. I ended things. Over. Done. Everybody told me I'd done a good thing. When we got back together, everybody thought I was stupid. Crazy. Both. Maybe I was. But I'd made my decision, and I was going to see it through. And to follow through with my commitment. I'm a man of my word. If I could show everyone how wrong they were, then I'd be right."

"You were trying to salvage your pride."

"Basically."

"And prove beyond a shadow of a doubt you're stubborn and obtuse?"

"That, too."

"Do you love her?" Megan looked him hard in the eye.

A long moment passed. "No. I couldn't trust her. And I don't believe love can exist without trust," he added.

"If she wanted to try making it work again, would you?"

"Absolutely not."

Megan shook her head. "I still don't get it."

He gave a half-laugh. "I don't, either. Lucky for me she bailed."

"Are you glad?"

He grew serious. "I am. I knew it was wrong, and I was going through with it anyway. I'm not sure what that says about me as a person. It was like I was taking a rowboat over Niagara Falls. I knew it was a disaster and I'd end up getting killed, but I kept rowing." He shrugged. "I'm learning."

Megan studied his profile. "I guess we all are, huh?"

"Live and learn, right?"

"Okay, so we talked about my job. Now tell me about yours."

"The one I just quit, or the one I just started?"

"Either. Both. Pros and cons of each. What did you love about having your own business?" A strand of hair blew across her face. She brushed it away.

"Sometimes I loved the travel. I got to see parts of the world I never would have otherwise seen. The downside is I mostly saw them from the window of the plane or a board-room. Or worse, a golf course. I hate golf. I hated schmoozing with people I didn't like. But being on the golf course beat being in an office."

"Where were your favorite places to go?"

"Beijing. Sydney. Moscow. Cairo. They were all amazing, and all completely different. Those are the places I'd most want to go back to."

"Cairo? Did you see the Great Pyramid?" She couldn't keep the envy and excitement from her voice.

"I did. From a distance. It was closed to visitors when we were there."

"Oh, what a shame. Why?" She felt a pang of disappoint-ment, almost as though she'd been denied the opportunity to see it herself.

"Terrorist activity in the country at the time."

"I would have been so bummed."

"We were. It's the only time Stewart was able to travel with me, and we didn't get to see the best stuff. Is that where you'd go if you could go anywhere?"

"Absolutely. Egypt is the number one place I want to see someday."

"What's number two?"

"I don't know, I don't think about it too much."

"Why not?"

Megan turned and started walking. "What's the point? I'll depress myself if I try to dream too big about places I'll never get to go. But hey," she joked, "with Google Maps it's *almost* like I've been there, right?" She felt exposed, like she'd admitted some deep, dark secret.

Eric grabbed her hand and held it as they walked. His fingers were warm and strong and comfortable laced with hers.

After a while, he squeezed her fingers and said, "Why are you willing to live a life with small dreams because your mom has anxiety?"

"You don't understand."

"I don't. But maybe it's not so different from my situation?"

"Ugh. Totally different."

"Making critical decisions about our own lives because of what other people will think? Sounds pretty similar to me."

"Maybe we should stop talking."

He chuckled. "Fine."

They strolled around the deck. At the end of the ship, a band was playing. White lights were strung up around the deck, giving it a soft glow. Several couples were slow dancing on the wooden floor.

Megan looked up at him. "Shall we?"

They stayed at the edge of the floor, half in the shadows. Eric pulled Megan into his arms and they swayed with the music.

"I'm not much of a dancer."

"You're fine."

"Not like –" He mumbled, but stopped himself.

Megan narrowed her eyes. "Really? Come on, Eric."

"Sorry. It's none of my business."

"No, it's not." She laid her head on his shoulder, and felt his arm tighten around her waist. She spread the fingers on the hand he held against his chest, lacing them with his.

The warm air swirled around them, fluttering Megan's skirt.

She still wore his jacket.

"This is nice," he said into her hair.

"It's none of your business," she said, "but I'm not seeing Marco again."

"Well. If it *was* my business, I'd be glad to hear it."

"But it's not." She smiled into his chest, knowing he couldn't see her expression.

They danced for a while without speaking.

Megan finally pulled back. "It's getting late. I need to get some sleep before our big adventure tomorrow."

"I'm excited. I think it'll be a lot of fun."

"I think so, too. As long as I don't panic."

"You'll be fine."

He walked her to her cabin door. Megan leaned over and hugged him. "I'm having a nice time."

Smiling, he nodded and gave a little wave before he walked away.

She closed her door and kicked off her heels. Her phone vibrated.

"Crap." She scrolled down through the frantic text messages.

> Emergency!
>
> Call home immediately!
>
> Megan call home!
>
> 911!

With shaking hands, she flipped through the ship's information pamphlets to get the codes for international dialing. She tapped in the numbers and waited for a connection. She heard nothing but a series of beeps and clicks. She hung up and connected to wifi, then to Skype.

"Come on, come on, come on," she murmured to the screen.

Eventually, her mother answered. "Megan, where have you been?"

Relief at making contact nearly made her dizzy. "Mom? What's going on? Where's Dad? Was there an accident? Are you okay?"

Her mother, on a few second lag, looked confused. "Everyone's fine."

"What? I got all your emergency messages. What the heck is going on?"

Alice sniffed. "For all you know, we *could* have been in an accident. Your father could have had a heart attack and it took you –" she held her arm to the camera and pointed at her watch, "three hours to even check in."

Megan's wildly pounding heart was settling. She squeezed her eyes shut against the anger, frustration, and helplessness she felt. "So you were trying to scare me into calling home. You decided to lie to me and pretend something awful happened, for the sole purpose of making me miserable."

Eye rolling. "I'm just showing you where your priorities need to be. You shouldn't have gone on that trip at all. What if something happens back home? You won't even know, and you certainly couldn't get back home if it did."

The heat rose, up across Megan's chest and throat, into her cheeks. "It's late and I have a big day tomorrow." She spoke through clenched teeth. "I will talk to you at some point tomorrow. Until then, I suggest you go back and re-read The Boy Who Cried Wolf."

Alice scowled and opened her mouth to speak, but Megan disconnected. She turned her phone off and shoved it in her underwear drawer.

Then, she sat down and cried.

Chapter Thirteen

Eric didn't mention Megan's red, puffy eyes. "Got everything?"

She smiled and patted her drawstring backpack. "Just the essentials. Need to leave room for all those tacky St. Maarten souvenirs, right?"

They scooted into the shuttle for a fifteen minute ride to the excursion site, where they locked their valuables, changed into their swimsuits, and went through instruction on the dive. When it was their turn, they stepped onto a floating platform, then were sent a few rungs down on a steep ladder, where the guide instructed them to wait. He flipped a long yellow hose around, checking it for kinks, then lifted a white, space-age helmet up and over Megan's head. She gripped the railing with white knuckles.

Eric gave her a thumbs up as her guide led her down the ladder and into the warm water. He waited while the guide checked his hose and set the helmet on his shoulders. The helmet was heavier than he'd expected. It was a relief to get underwater, where the weight was lessened.

Megan was waiting for him, holding onto the guide rope. When he was beside her, she turned and followed the other divers along the long metal platform serving as their path along the ocean floor. A school of yellow fish darted in and out around the group, while guides in scuba gear swam around, encouraging the fish closer to the tourists.

The guide pointed out a coral reef to the group, and another scuba-clad guide snapped pictures of each person in front of each point of interest. A guide brought a sea urchin over and handed it to Megan, whose eyes were wide with wonder. She grinned as she handed it to Eric. He had to admit it was pretty cool.

More colorful fish darted around, shimmering in the streams of sunlight flittering down through the water. The guide motioned for Eric and Megan to stand together while he snapped a picture in front of a statue of King Neptune, then motioned for them to keep making their way around the platform. Megan was taken with the colorful coral. He was watching her when she flapped her arm, reaching out toward him. She pointed excitedly.

Eric followed her finger and saw the turtle swimming toward them. The rest of the group and the guides noticed as well, and started pointing and waving to get each other's attention.

The creature was graceful underwater, its long neck sticking out, its pinched upper lip drawn into what looked like a smile. It swam closer, close enough for Megan to reach out and touch its head. It turned away from her, and Megan trailed her fingers along its shell as it navigated away. Eric glanced and saw the guide with the camera hovering nearby. He hoped he'd gotten a shot of Megan touching the turtle. It would make her day.

After the turtle, the rest of the walk was something of a letdown. The water grew cloudy, making it hard to see beyond a few feet. The guides led them back to the ladder, where the tourists climbed out.

Megan gave Eric a thumbs up, then began to climb out. He followed her, careful on the rungs that felt rather old and less stable than he would have liked. At least the rickety ladder distracted him from her bathing suit, which was modest, but still...

Above water, a guide pulled off his helmet and grabbed his arm to help him back onto the ramp where Megan stood, waiting.

Back inside the cabana, they dried off and retrieved their clothes and valuables from the lockers. Eric touched Megan's elbow. "You got the dolphin pictures, can I get these?"

She nodded. "Sure."

He filled out the order form and handed it to a khaki-clad employee. Now they had an hour to kill. They changed and perused the rows of tacky souvenirs, buying several, before settling onto a bench shaded by palm trees, overlooking the diving platform. Megan collected her sand, and they watched the next group of tourists sink below the surface, one by one.

"I hope the turtle comes back for them. He was awesome."

"Definitely the best part."

Megan's smile was infectious. "I couldn't believe he came right up to me. Did you get to touch him?"

"Just the tips of my fingers."

"It felt like a seashell. Rough and bumpy."

"They make great soup."

She elbowed him in the ribs. "Stop. You're not eating my turtle."

Rubbing where she'd assaulted him, he laughed. A few minutes later, he said, "I thought we'd be under longer."

"Me, too. It lasted what, about twenty minutes?"

"A little longer, but not much."

"It was worth it, though. I hope it's clear for these people. It was getting too cloudy there at the end to see much. I was surprised how heavy the helmet was, but it wasn't bad under the water. It wasn't hard to breathe or see, either, which was great."

Activity in the building drew Eric's attention, so he stood to get a better view. "Looks like they're handing out the pictures."

They retrieved their packet and learned the shuttle back to the ship would be another two hours.

"How about we get a taxi and see if we can find some good coffee."

"Sounds great."

A man in Hawaiian shorts standing nearby spoke. "Excuse me, did you guys say you're getting a cab?"

Eric sized him up. They were about the same age, and this guy obviously worked out. But Eric had way better hair. "Yes? But we're not going straight back to the dock."

The man scratched his close-shaved head and looked a little embarrassed. "Actually, I, um, heard you say something about coffee. My wife has been dying for a good cup of coffee. Do you know a place?"

"Yeah, my brother recommended a coffee shop. We're going to go check it out." Eric glanced for the first time at the petite woman standing next to the man. "I'm Eric, and this is Megan."

The man held out his hand. "Chuck and Emma. We must be on the same ship."

Eric shook his hand. "I remember those shorts from the shuttle ride in."

Emma groaned. "I told you they were ridiculous."

"What?" Chuck looked down at his neon yellow and orange flowered shorts. "I think they're great."

Eric held up a finger. "Excuse us a second." He pulled

Megan aside. "Do you want to share a cab? They seem nice enough."

"Sure, if you don't mind sharing your secret coffee spot." He turned back to the couple. "Let's hit the road."

They shared a cab to a fifties-style bakery/coffee shop along the lagoon. The humidity seemed to have multiplied during their ride. They hurried from the sweltering heat into the cool shop.

Megan reached down and grabbed his hand. "Holy crap, look at all these pastries. I want to taste everything."

Chuck said, "Me, too."

Eric caught an odd tone in the comment and glanced over, but Chuck wasn't looking at the pastries. His eyes were glued to Megan's backside. Before he said something he'd regret, Eric let Megan pull him over to a display case full of the most delectable desserts he'd ever seen. Every color of the rainbow was represented, and quite possibly every pastry known to man.

"Stewart said we need to try the chocolate chip croissants." Megan pointed into the case. "There. They do look incredible. But the coconut macaroons look good, too."

"You get one, I'll get the other. We'll share."

Chuck and Emma exchanged a glance. Chuck said, "Do you want to share, too, baby?"

Emma giggled. "Of course."

Eric couldn't quite figure out what was so funny about sharing dessert, but whatever. This guy was annoying. Lesson learned. No more cab sharing. He and Megan made their selections and went outside on the huge wooden porch overlooking the lagoon and sat at a plastic round table. The shade and overhead fans tempered the heat and humidity.

A blanket of boats covered the surface of the lagoon.

Megan sipped her coffee. "Cinnamon. And something else. Nutmeg, maybe?"

Eric smelled. "I think you're right." Shaking his head, he tasted his and said, "It's good, but nothing special. I don't think I'll bother getting any to take with us."

Chuck and Emma joined them at the table. "This is so nice," Emma said. "Where y'all from?"

Megan set her large mug down. "Pennsylvania. You?"

"Georgia."

"Is this your first cruise?"

Emma laughed. "Oh, heavens, no. We cruise at least once every year. Sometimes twice."

Chuck chimed in. "It's a great way to... get to know other people, away from home. You know, make some new... *friends*."

Eric leaned closer to Megan. Something about the way Chuck looked at Megan was getting on his nerves. She didn't seem to notice, or if she did, she was hiding it well.

"Whereabouts in Georgia?" Eric put his arm around the back of Megan's chair.

Emma answered, "About an hour outside of Savannah."

Eric's eyes shifted toward Chuck again. "Savannah's nice."

Megan put her hand on Eric's knee and leaned closer to him.

So she did notice Chuck's stare.

Chuck drained his coffee. "How long have you guys been married?"

Megan spoke before Eric had a chance. "Less than a week."

Eric kept his face neutral. He had no problem being Megan's pretend husband if this guy got the message. "It's our honeymoon." How could Emma be so totally oblivious to her husband's leering?

Emma sighed. "Oh, how sweet. I remember our honeymoon."

"Where did you go?" Megan asked.

Chuck leaned on his elbows, facing Megan. "We took a cruise through the Caribbean with some open-minded friends."

She frowned. "How open minded do you have to be to go on a cruise?"

Chuck's half-smile set Eric's teeth on edge. "Oh, it wasn't just the cruise. We're rather... non-traditional. So another couple helped us celebrate our marriage." He put his arm across Emma's lap.

Eric squeezed Megan's shoulder, hoping she didn't ask any more questions. She didn't, but Chuck continued.

"It can get boring, committing yourself to one person for the rest of your life. So Emma and I sometimes find another couple to get *friendly* with."

Megan was staring into her mug with one eyebrow raised. "Good for you." She turned to Eric. "We should get some of those croissants to take back to the ship."

He nodded as she got up from her chair. Before he could join her, Emma jumped up. "I'll go with you. I want to get a slice of cake to take back."

Eric leaned back in his chair, but was anything but relaxed. Chuck, on the other hand, didn't seem to have a care in the world. He leaned back and crossed his arms. "So, Eric, man to man, I think you saw where I was headed, right?"

"Pretty sure," he bit out the words.

"Communication is key in these situations. Misunderstandings have ruined a lot of good friendships."

Friendships? No way was there going to be any friendship with his meathead and his wife. Maybe they should go be friends with the Omelet Douche. "Maybe you ought to spell it out for me."

"If you're cool with it, I'd like to have sex with your wife. So would Emma. We'd totally be into some three or four-way action. Whatever works for y'all."

Eric was on his feet, the plastic chair clattering backwards against the deck. His fists and his jaw clenched tight.

"Whoa, simmer down." Chuck held his hands up, something between a smirk and a grin curling his lip. "If it ain't y'all's thing, it's cool. Doesn't have to go any further than this conversation."

Unsure of his next move, Eric simply turned and picked up his chair. He set it back at the table, and without a word, walked into the bakery. Megan was holding a paper bag, waiting for Emma to pay for her purchase.

She smiled at him, but it quickly faded as she studied the expression on his face, her own expression an obvious but silent question.

He gave his head the slightest shake. "We need to get back to the ship," he said, steering her toward the door as Emma went back out to Chuck.

On the sidewalk, she asked, "Are we leaving them here?"

"Yup." He would have rather left them floating out to sea on a dinghy.

"Are you going to tell me what's going on?"

"Not right this second, Megan."

She fell in step beside him. He spotted a taxi and waved it down.

"Are you sure we should –"

"They'll be fine," he snapped.

They slid into the minivan with three other passengers, obvious tourists. Eric was settling himself when Chuck and Emma climbed into the seat behind them. Great. At least they didn't try talking to them, although Emma did give Megan a confused look as she got in.

Megan looked at him questioningly, but he kept his eyes

fixed out the window, anger at the people behind him growing with each passing second. It occurred to him that Megan might think he was angry with her. He reached over and put his hand on her knee, rubbing his thumb against her skin. She put her hand over his and squeezed.

The ride back to the dock felt like it took hours. Eric's jaw ached from clenching his teeth. When they stopped, he practically threw money at the driver so he could get as far away from Chuck and Emma as fast as he could.

He put his hand on Megan's back, urging her to hurry. She kept glancing at him, but didn't slow down.

It wasn't until they were back on the ship and out of sight of Chuck and Emma that he breathed a sigh of relief.

Chapter Fourteen

Megan let him lead her through the crowd returning from shore, then through the ship, but when they got back to her cabin, she pulled him inside before closing the door. She slipped her backpack off and set it on the bed before turning to face him, her fists planted on her hips.

"Spill it."

Eric looked uncomfortable.

"And don't lie to me."

Running a hand through his hair, he said, "Chuck was being kind of inappropriate."

She crossed her arms and raised an eyebrow. "Inappropriate? I'm guessing there's a little more to it than simple inappropriateness."

"Do the details matter?"

"We're on the same ship. We could run into them again, you know."

"We hadn't run into them before, so maybe we won't see them again."

"Eric."

"They're swingers," he blurted out. His face was beet red.

Megan's lip twitched.

"You knew." A horrified expression crossed his face. "You're not... No. Nope, huh-uh." He made an incredulous barfing face.

"Eric! Get a grip." She shook her head. "Emma propositioned me at the bakery counter. Well, she propositioned *us*, if it makes you feel any better." It was hard not to laugh at his reaction.

"It doesn't."

"I told her we weren't interested, she said okay. The conversation ended there."

Eric grumbled, "Well, Chuck was a little less *genteel* about it. I thought I was going to have to punch him."

Megan put a hand over her mouth. "Oh, no, what did he say?"

"I'm not repeating it. You already know the gist of it." He scowled.

"Hey, there's no use in being mad about it. They asked, we said no, it's over and done with." She smirked. "If nothing else, you have to admire their chutzpah."

Eric shook his head. "I don't admire anything about it. Who does that?"

"Ironically enough, I have an ex-fiancé named Charles, although he despised the nickname Chuck. I could almost see him doing that."

"Guess that's why he's an ex?"

"He's an ex because my mother interfered when he was moving to California for his medical residency. I was all set to go along, but she told him otherwise and he left without me. It's all for the best, but I sure didn't think so at the time."

"But-"

"It's not something I really want to talk about."

He stared at her for a long moment, then softened his tone. "What time do you want to get something to eat?"

"About an hour? I'll come up."

After Eric left, Megan got in the shower, trying to scrub the skeevy off. It was one thing to be hit on by a random guy. But a random guy *and* his wife? While she was with a guy they thought was her husband? On their honeymoon? Ew. She'd played it off to Eric as not a big deal, but the whole situation left a bad taste in her mouth, too.

Wrapped in her fuzzy towel, she slid open the dresser drawer. Her phone lay there, taunting her. She tapped it, lighting up a long list of missed calls and messages. Text, voicemail, Facebook, Skype... She yanked out her clothes and tossed the phone back into the drawer, then slammed it shut.

Megan tried to fight the knots in her stomach. She'd thought being this far away from home would help her relax, but her mother's anxiety had actually tightened its stranglehold on her neck. She took a deep breath and focused on soothing things. The sway of the ocean. The sound of the ship cutting through the water. The food. Eric. Their easy rapport on this trip. The dolphins. The sea turtle. The weather. For Pete's sake, St. Maarten was right outside her window.

Reaching back to rub her neck, she decided she was going to have a nice evening, and not going to devote any more time to indulging her mother's insecurities tonight. She'd done it for nearly twenty years, she could take ten days off.

She changed and pulled her hair back, grabbed a sweater, and headed up to Eric's cabin.

"What's wrong?" He asked as soon as he opened the door.

"Wow, no poker face here, huh?"

He stepped into the hallway and pulled the door closed. "Burgers?"

"Sounds perfect."

"So...? More calls from home?"

How was he able to read her so easily? He'd only known her for four days. "Yeah. I had twenty-two different messages. Facebook, text, Skype..." she trailed off.

He simply nodded. "I think I'll try the sweet potato fries. You?"

She looked up at him. "Chicken fingers."

"Did you look at your newsletter today?"

"No, why?"

"Jeffrey David Wallace comedy show tonight. Have you ever seen him?"

"I've heard of him."

"Stewart and I saw him one time in Vegas. He's hilarious."

"Sounds great." She could use a good laugh.

Two hours later, Megan was clutching her stomach, laughing so hard she could barely breathe. Eric was beside her, wiping his eyes, his shoulders shaking.

She gasped for air and clapped, hard, then jumped to her feet for a standing ovation, along with the rest of the crowd. The comedian chuckled at his own closing joke, then thanked the audience. Jeffrey stepped down off the low stage and greeted the people who stayed behind. Megan and Eric walked over and complimented his performance. Jeffrey posed for a few selfies with them before moving on to talk with other fans.

"I've never laughed so hard in my entire life," Megan said.

Eric was still chuckling at random times as they walked down the hallway. "He was even better than when I saw his show in Vegas. I can't wait to tell Stewart about it. He'll be so jealous."

Megan grabbed Eric's hand without thinking about it. "I'm blown away. I've been to a few comedy shows, but no one's ever had me laughing so much for so long. Tomorrow I'm going to feel like I did a million sit ups."

"Yeah. Tomorrow." Eric sobered.

"What?"

"The horses."

Megan grinned. "Aruba! I'm so excited. I haven't ridden a horse in years."

"I've never been on a horse."

"Ever?"

"Not unless you count pony rides at the fair when I was a kid." He paused. "I have been on a camel, though."

"I can't imagine it's much different."

"I hope it's a *lot* different." He grimaced. "I fell off the camel."

"Oh, no." Megan bit her lips together to keep from smiling.

"Thanks a lot."

Her chin quivered.

"I thought you'd be more sympathetic."

"I'm sorry. It's just the image in my head, and all the laughing tonight... and I can see you weren't permanently damaged."

"Pfft, maybe not physically, but the emotional scars are still there."

"What happened?"

"We were in Cairo. We decided it'd be fun to camp in the Sahara. So we had to ride camels out to this touristy campsite. We got all our gear packed onto the camels, and then it was time to get on." He shuddered. "Stewart hops on like he's been riding camels his whole life. His camel jumps up, ready to go. I'm putting my leg over my camel and the stupid thing stands up. I'm hanging off the side of the beast, trying to heave myself up over, meanwhile the guides are laughing their asses off, pointing at the stupid American."

Megan was losing the battle. She snerked and pressed her hand over her mouth.

"So the camel stands the whole way up, I lose my grip and fall face-first into the sand. To add insult to injury, my shoe stayed hooked in the saddle thing, and then the camel spit at me. So there I am, laying on the ground, camel spit covering my pants, sand in my mouth, my shoe stuck on the camel, with everyone pointing and laughing at me, including my jerk brother."

Megan couldn't hold back anymore. She guffawed loudly and grabbed the wall. Spasms rocked through her midsection, doubling her over. She laughed, tears streaming down her face, holding her belly, leaning on the wall so she wouldn't fall over.

"I'm so sorry," she managed between gales of laughter.

Eric mock glared at her. "Yeah, you seem sorry."

"No, I am," she wheezed.

He stood against the wall, laughing at her laughing at him. "If I didn't know better, I'd think you were drunk."

Megan composed herself. She smoothed down her dress and patted her hair back into place. "Okay. I think I'm okay now."

He shook his head and held out his arm. "You sure?"

A giggle escaped. "No."

"Alright, let's get you back to your cabin."

Megan was still trying to get her giggles under control when Eric stopped at her door. She cleared her throat. "Okay, I'm good. I'll see you at breakfast, okay?"

A stern expression was on his face, but she knew he wasn't serious. "I'm not sure I want to have breakfast with you. You're kind of mean."

"Aww, come on. If I can climb the rock wall, you can climb a horse."

"Yeah, yeah."

"I'll see you at breakfast."

"Fine." He planted a quick kiss on her forehead. "Breakfast."

Megan was still chuckling as she climbed into bed, remembering jokes and imagining Eric sliding off his camel. She sobered a bit, hoping he wasn't truly afraid of the horses. She'd ask him in the morning. If he was, they could do something else.

Chapter Fifteen

They stood in the sand, waiting for the guides to match everyone up with their horse. Eric watched Megan sling her tanned leg over her horse and sit up in her saddle like she belonged there. She reached over and patted her horse's mane.

Eric, on the other hand, was not looking forward to climbing onto his beast.

"She knows you're afraid," a guide said at his elbow.

His eyes flicked to Megan. "I'm sure she does."

The guide laughed, deep and hearty. "The horse, mon, not the girl." The man clapped Eric on the back. "Kimba's gentle, you'll have no troubles," he said as he held the stirrup steady. Eric put his foot in and took a deep breath.

"Okay, horsey, I don't want to die today." He swung his leg up and over and settled into the saddle. The ground looked like it was a long way down. He glanced over at Megan.

She gave him a huge smile and a thumbs up. "Good job."

He felt less than confident as Kimba stepped to the side. He held the reins in a death grip.

A guide rode up alongside him. "Relax, mon," he said before riding to the front of the group.

Kimba started walking along with the rest of the horses.

Megan was next to Eric. "How you doing?"

He gulped. "Not dead yet."

"You'll be fine." She snapped a photo of him.

"Oh, great. The main attraction for your 'Abject Terror' gallery opening?" He muttered, not taking his eyes off Kimba's head.

"Eric. Look around."

Daring to trust the horse – just for a second – he looked to his right. The brilliant blue ocean lapped up to the white sand beach. He relaxed a fraction. Until Kimba shifted again.

"Here we go," someone called from the front. The line began to move toward the water.

Eric clung to the reins as Kimba stepped from the sand into the ocean. He gulped, waiting for the horse to get stuck or sink into the sand and kill them both. He looked around briefly, trying to enjoy the scenery, but ended up watching the back of the horse's neck, telepathically willing her not to get him killed. Kimba didn't seem concerned. Neither did any of the other horses. Or their riders.

He spoke too soon. From the rear, a woman shrieked.

"What's going on?" He couldn't turn around to look.

"A lady and her husband are... hanging back," Megan answered. "There's a guide with them."

Okay, at least he was doing better than she was. He swore that even if he fell off, he wouldn't scream. At least not like the lady was. The horses waded deeper and soon, the warm water touched Eric's feet. It was warm and soothing, but weird to be atop a horse and getting wet. Very, very weird.

The water lapped higher, covering his calves. Kimba kept her head up, walking in line with the others.

Megan called over to him, "How are you doing? Isn't this amazing?"

Somehow, she was sitting on her horse, completely relaxed with the reins loose in one hand while she took pictures with her other hand.

"Aren't you afraid your camera will get wet?"

"Nope. I have a waterproof casing on it. I'll show you when we stop."

"How soon?"

"Aren't you having fun?" She sounded concerned.

He was already stuck here, he might as well lie. "I am, this is great."

"Liar."

Okay, so he wasn't very good at it. "You're enjoying it, right?"

"I am."

"Then that's all that matters."

Somehow, Megan slowed her horse until Kimba was alongside them. "Aww, we could have done something else, you know."

Daring to glance over at her, he said. "I know."

"Hey. Try to relax a bit. Sit up straight. There you go."

He resisted the urge to hunker back down, closer to the horse. "Did the screaming lady ever get going?"

Megan turned and looked around. "Doesn't look like it. You're doing great. What's your horse's name?"

He knew she was trying to distract him, and he appreciated it. "Kimba. I think she likes me."

"Of course she does. My horse is Kiki. They said Kimba is her mom."

"Cool."

If he fell off the horse now, he'd just be falling a foot or two into the water. Kimba was steady and surefooted. He leaned forward slightly and let go of the reins with one hand long enough to pat her mane. "You're a nice horse."

Megan chuckled. "Good job."

Half an hour later, the group began climbing out of the water and back onto a pristine white beach. The guides helped the tourists dismount.

Eric was relieved as his feet hit the sand. Megan was right beside him, grinning from ear to ear. She stood up on her tiptoes and kissed him on the cheek. "You did awesome."

Suddenly, he felt like he could take on the whole world. On horseback, if he had to.

The whole group congregated on the beach as a guide explained the snorkeling portion of the excursion. Eric reached for Megan's hand. "Now *you* look nervous."

"I'm not sure about the whole snorkeling thing. Will it feel like the helmet dive we did yesterday?"

"No, there's nothing weighing you down, so you have to swim. And you have to breathe around the mask like they showed us this morning. It can be a little tricky, but you can do it."

"Stay close, okay?"

"Of course. There'll be guides everywhere. Nothing to be afraid of. This'll be a piece of cake after the rock wall."

The guides handed out everyone's equipment, reminding them of the lessons they'd had earlier in the day. They split everyone into small groups and ushered them into the water. Megan adjusted her mask and snorkel and waited for Eric to finish adjusting his.

They waded out into the deeper water. Eric let Megan take his hand and they kicked off. Her grip loosened little by little as they swam slowly along the surface. Eric pointed to the coral reef. Megan gave him a thumbs up, then pointed to a school of fish swimming toward them.

After a while, he pointed down. She shook her head, so they stayed on the surface. A few minutes later, she squeezed his hand. When he looked over, she pointed down. He squeezed her hand back, and they practiced a duck dive the instructors had shown them.

They dove closer to the reef, and from this distance, they could see more marine creatures. Megan pulled on his hand, waving her other excitedly, then pointing as soon as she got his attention. He followed her finger and saw an octopus unfurl its legs and scoot itself into a tiny crevice in the reef.

A moment later, Megan yanked her hand out of his and lurched for the surface, flailing gracelessly through the water. He immediately followed. She broke the surface and yanked her mask and snorkel off, gasping, coughing, and sputtering.

He pulled his mask up. "Easy, easy."

She gasped for air, her face drawn with panic.

"Hey. Look at me."

Her eyes filled with tears. "I got water in the tube thing and I couldn't remember what to do. I couldn't breathe and I panicked."

"It's okay."

"I'm sorry."

"Megan. There's nothing to apologize for. You're okay. Nothing else matters."

She treaded water, looking back and forth, her wet ponytail slapping against her cheek. "Oh, no. The equipment."

"I grabbed them." He held up her mask and snorkel.

A guide swam over. "Everything good?"

Megan nodded. "I couldn't remember how to clear my tube."

"Easy to forget when you are under the water. Do you remember now?"

"Blow."

The guide grinned. "Exactly." He swam off, checking on others in their group.

Megan coughed a few times. When she calmed, she put her mask back on. "Try again?"

"If you're sure."

She nodded. "If you can ride a killer beast, I can blow a little air out of a tube, right?"

"Right." He was impressed with her. How many times had he heard someone saying they were going to live every moment to the fullest? She actually was. This entire trip, she was throwing herself into every new experience, all in, one hundred percent.

They adjusted their equipment and dove again. Different varieties of fish, blue, yellow, orange and rainbow colored, swam around the reef. They were careful not to touch anything, tempting though it was.

Eric pointed down. A massive starfish lay on the ocean floor, much larger than he'd expected. A crab skittered across the sand a few feet away from the starfish.

Eventually, they rose to the surface. Some of the other tourists were back on the shore.

"Ready to head in?"

Megan pulled off her mask and nodded. "Yeah, I think I need to get more sunscreen on."

"Your shoulders are kind of pink."

They swam back to the shore and staked out two lounge chairs in the shade. Megan sprayed sunscreen on. Once it dried, she pulled her t-shirt on. She tossed the can to Eric. "You could use some more, too."

He obeyed, spraying himself.

The ocean breeze was cool and comfortable. Eric watched Megan dozing for a few minutes before the last of the snorkeling group came back to shore. He nudged her. "I think it's time to go."

She made an exaggerated sad face. "But I really like it here. I think this might be my favorite excursion yet."

The tired group remounted their horses for the ride back. Eric was much more relaxed this time. He was able to look around instead of staring at Kimba's head, willing her not to kill him. They returned to the starting point, and, as always, bought an overpriced package of souvenir photos and waited a thousand years for them to be processed.

The shuttle ride back to the ship was mostly silent, except for the kids, who had a seemingly endless supply of energy. Megan leaned heavily against Eric, and if the road had been smoother, he knew she would have fallen asleep.

"There's a coffee shop right near the dock," Megan pointed out when they exited the shuttle.

"Are you sure you're not too tired?"

She grabbed his hand. "I get the excursion, you get the coffee. That was the deal, right?"

"Sure. I'll make it quick."

The quaint little coffee shop was by far the most modern one they'd been in. They ordered a unique almond coffee. After two sips, Eric bought five bags of the coffee beans to take home.

Megan nodded. "I don't even like coffee much, but this is delicious."

They trudged back into the ship. Megan yawned. "I think I'm going to take a nap before dinner."

"Good idea. I think I might, too." He walked her to her cabin, then rode the elevator up to his own. It was only a few minutes after five, but today's excursion was more physically taxing than the others. Especially when he was stressed out about the horse, and Megan was stressed out about the snorkeling. Maybe they should both keep their feet on the ground from here on out.

Chapter Sixteen

Megan fell onto her bed and immediately went to sleep. Half an hour later, she awoke, reasonably refreshed. She showered and changed, then walked up to Eric's room.

"You look great," he said as soon as he opened the door.

"I wasn't sure if we were doing the dining room or not, so I figured this would work either way." She smoothed down the front of her yellow sundress.

"Dining room sounds good."

They got to their table, which was empty. "I wonder if Sheila and Morty aren't dining in tonight?"

No sooner were the words out of her mouth than she felt the hug from the side. "Oh, Megan, Eric, I'm so glad to see you two again. Are you having a nice time? We've been sitting over there with those folks," she waved her hand in the general direction of the entire dining room, "but as soon as we saw you, we knew we'd have to sit with you. So how's your trip? What did you do here in Aruba?"

Megan smiled. "We took a horseback riding tour and went snorkeling. How about you guys?"

"We did some shopping and spent some time on the beach. I love all the white sand, don't you?"

"I do. I even got some to take home. It's so pretty. I think I took a thousand pictures of the beaches today."

Sheila patted her arm. "You just reminded me. I want to get pictures of you two." She fished her camera out of her massive purse and flagged down the waiter.

The four of them leaned together and smiled while the waiter snapped the picture. Megan showed the waiter which button to push on her considerably more complicated camera, and they leaned and smiled again while he took a couple more shots.

"Thank you so much," she said as he handed her camera back. She flipped the display and leaned over to Sheila as she scrolled back through some of the day's photos. "This is us with Kiki and Kimba."

Sheila oohed and aahed over the horses and the photos of the beach. "You take such beautiful pictures, Megan."

"Thank you." The more time they spent with Sheila and Morty, the less abrasive and annoying they seemed.

Dinner passed in pleasant, if constant, conversation. When they left, the hallways seemed more crowded than usual. The reason became apparent when they walked to the upper deck and saw the fat raindrops splattering against the windows.

Megan sighed. "Well, it had to rain at least once, right?"

"And it was nice enough to wait until we got back on board."

"It's so warm, though. I was hoping to sit outside for a while."

"You can come to my balcony if you want. It's pretty big. There's a roof so I don't think we'll get wet unless it starts blowing."

"Sounds great."

In Eric's suite, Megan took in all the luxurious details. "Holy crap, this is huge. My room could fit in here three times over."

He looked a little embarrassed. "Yeah, it's a little excessive."

"I didn't mean to sound insulting. It's a great room. Mine's great, too, just a bit smaller."

He pulled open the sliding glass door and let her step through first.

"Huh. I was a little bit jealous of the inside, but this... I am *insanely* jealous of this."

"I've only been out here once."

"What? If I had this in my room I'd sleep out here." She made a face. "I'm lying. I'd be afraid the railing would break and I'd fall into the ocean and drown. But I *would* spend a lot of time out here."

"You're welcome anytime."

Two plush lounge chairs faced the ocean. Megan leaned back on the cushion and stretched her legs out. "I might not leave."

Eric laughed and stretched out on the chair beside hers. "That's not much of a threat."

Megan reached over and took Eric's hand. He laced his fingers through hers. An hour passed, then another, as they listened to the rain falling onto the decks around them, in comfortable silence. Finally, Megan stretched. "I should go. I'm going to fall asleep out here. It's so quiet and peaceful."

"If it's raining tomorrow, we can hang out here."

"Oh, right, we're sailing all day, aren't we?"

"Yup."

"Sounds good. Meet for breakfast? We can figure out our plan for the day."

He nodded and walked her to the door. "I'll see you in the morning then."

Back in her room, Megan checked her phone. Only a dozen messages today. She initiated a Skype call. Her mom picked up.

"Hey, guess what. I got to ride a horse through a lagoon today."

Alice scowled. "That sounds dangerous."

"No, it was fun. And then we went snorkeling over this coral reef." She wasn't going to mention the mishap with her air tube.

"Who's 'we'?"

Crap. "We. The group. There was a whole tour from the ship. Everything is done in groups, Mom. It's not like I'm alone out here, ever."

"Have you seen Eric at all?" She said his name like she was sniffing dog poop.

Uh oh, where is this going? "Yeah, I've talked to him."

"Well, you stay away from him. He's a snake."

Megan knew better than to ask, but she couldn't help herself. "Why would you say that?"

"You know what he did to your cousin."

"I know she dumped him and called it off."

"Because he cheated on her."

Megan kept her face neutral. "Oh."

"Brittney told us all about it. She was so upset when she found out you were still on the trip. She told me to tell you not to trust him."

"It's a big ship, Mom, it's not like I have to see him very often." Technically true. She didn't *have* to see him at all.

"Good. Have you made any friends?"

Safe topic. Megan told her about Sheila and Morty.

"They sound nice. Are they keeping an eye on you?"

"No, because that would be creepy and weird."

"You haven't met anyone, have you?"

Megan deliberately misunderstood. "I've met lots of people."

"I mean men. Don't do something stupid."

"Like have a wild affair with some hot foreign guy?"

Her mother scowled. "It's still not funny."

"Who's laughing?"

"You aren't having an affair with *Eric*, are you?" She practically spit his name.

"Mother! You can't possibly be serious."

"You're naïve, Megan. It'd be easy for you to get used by some guy like him."

Wow. It was a wonder she could be trusted to tie her own shoes. "I don't know what you've heard, but he's been very nice to me. Um, the few times we've spoken."

"Be careful. You know a man like him wouldn't be interested in a girl like you anyway. He's wild and not trustworthy."

Megan bit her tongue.

"What should I tell Brittney?"

She's an idiot and he's better off. "I don't care what you tell her. I've seen him and talked to him a few times. What am I supposed to do, push him overboard?"

"Don't be dramatic. I suppose you can talk to him if you run into him."

Megan bit back one sarcastic response after another. She settled on, "Well, as long as I have permission."

Alice changed tactics. "When are you coming home?"

"You have my schedule."

"You could fly home from Jamaica if you wanted to."

"I don't want to."

"Why not? Don't you miss us?" Alice whined.

"You haven't really given me the opportunity to miss you."

Megan knew it was a mistake as soon as it was out of her mouth.

Alice's chin quivered. "I'm worried about you. We saw there's a tropical storm right where you are. But you wouldn't be worried about a little storm, would you?"

"We're perfectly safe."

"Maybe you'll get lucky and *we'll* have a horrible storm while you're on your *vacation* and we'll all die. Maybe you'd miss us then."

"Stop it."

"You wouldn't even care."

"I mean it, Mom. Knock it off. You're being ridiculous."

"We'll see who's being ridiculous when you come home and we're all gone. Maybe once you get back, your father and I will pick up and go away for a few weeks and leave you all alone. See how you like it."

Her dad walked past in the background. "That's a great idea. When do we leave?" He kissed Alice on the top of the head and waved to Megan. "Hi, pumpkin."

Alice's eyes widened and her mouth pursed.

"Hi, Dad."

"How's your trip?"

"It's awesome. I gotta go, though. We're sailing all day tomorrow, so I'm seeing a lot of shows and doing activities and stuff. I'll send you a message at some point."

"If I'm alive to get it."

Her dad made a face behind Alice. "Okay, whatever. I have to go."

Megan signed off and blew out a frustrated breath.

She sat on the edge of her bed, holding her phone, staring at the carpet. She set her phone on the nightstand and curled up with her towel bunny. She fell asleep in her clothes. Sometime in the middle of the night, she went to the bathroom and changed into her sweats. The zipper from her dress had squished into her skin, annoying her.

Morning came and she felt like she hadn't slept at all. The ship's movement had her a little off balance as she trudged to breakfast.

Eric was waiting by the entrance when she rounded the corner. They found a table near the window. It was still raining hard, the sky a deep gray, the churning water an angry, deep blue.

Megan frowned. "I'm glad we don't have an excursion today. The weather is awful."

"I think everyone on board is here for breakfast. I'll keep the table, you get your food, then I'll go."

Megan piled fresh pineapple onto her tray. "Good morning, *mi corazón*. How are you?"

Megan half-turned, her back to his omelet station. "Fine, thanks. You?"

"Terrible. I'm missing you." His voice sent a tingle down her spine.

"I'm sure you'll find a way to get over it."

"Ah, but will you?"

Megan laughed. "I think I'll manage, thanks." Yes, he was hot. Yes, he could kiss. Yes, his accent could melt butter. Yes, as far as bad decisions went, he could be an excellent one. But no, she wasn't getting involved.

"Megan, you're breaking my heart."

She made the mistake of looking in his hypnotic eyes. "No, I'm not."

"Meet me today."

"Nope."

"Two o'clock. The room where we danced."

Megan shook her head and put the fruit tongs back on the buffet table and stepped away.

"I will be there, *mi corazón*. Waiting for you."

She ignored him and kept walking. Back at the table, she couldn't meet Eric's eyes as he got up to get his food. Then she sat up straighter. No. She wasn't going to be ashamed or embarrassed about Marco, even if he was a bit much. So what if he flattered her. It was good for her ego. Much better than being propositioned by Chuck and Emma.

A small laugh bubbled up. In six days, she'd been propositioned by three people, which was more interest than she'd attracted back home in the past six years. She dunked her tea bag in her mug, then squeezed the water out of it.

What a trip.

Chapter Seventeen

Eric studied Megan's face and slumped shoulders. "Did you bring any Dramamine?"

Megan looked up from her tea. "Why?"

"You're looking a little green. Are you feeling okay?"

"I don't feel quite right, but it was a long night. I didn't sleep much. I don't think I'm getting seasick."

"Maybe you should take some just in case."

She smiled. "Fine, doctor Eric, I'll go back to the cabin and take some Dramamine."

"Now I know you're not feeling well. You didn't argue with me."

He walked her back to her cabin and waited at the doorway. "You might as well come in. We can look at the newsletter and see what's happening today."

He stepped inside and sat on the corner of the bed, scanning the newsletter while Megan fished around for some motion sickness pills. He said, "Looks like there's a cooking class at eleven o'clock. Fancy party appetizers and then you eat them for lunch. Could be fun?"

"You don't sound very convincing. Besides. Only appetizers

for lunch? They better be some big appetizers." Megan sat beside him, reading the newsletter over his arm. She swallowed her pills and finished her bottle of water.

"There's a painting class at ten. It says no experience needed." There was also a hot yoga class, but hot yoga wasn't going to happen in this lifetime.

"Painting could be fun. My friend Beth went to one of those classes a few months ago. They did it as some kind of fundraiser for her daughter's dance group. She said it was a lot of fun and their painting was cute."

"Then let's do it. Since you don't need experience." Eric had no interest in painting, but if it's what Megan wanted to do, he'd suck it up and tag along.

"I bet yours turns out better than mine."

"You're betting against a sure thing, then. I don't have a creative bone in my body." Eric thought she looked a little pale, and she wasn't quite herself. "You sure you're feeling up to it?"

"Yeah, I think as long as I can sit still, I'll be fine. I don't feel *bad*, exactly, just kind of not *good*, you know?"

"If you're sure, we can head up."

"Yup, let me grab my camera."

They found the painting class and sat near the front. The stations were already set up with a 12 x 12 blank canvas propped on an easel, brushes, a cup of water and paint squeezed out onto Styrofoam plates.

"I thought there'd be a ton of people."

The cheerful instructor, clad in a paint-stained apron, gave them a warm smile. "I think the rough waters have a lot of people staying in their cabins with seasickness today. I'm Julie." She shook their hands, then addressed the six people in the room. "If it's all right with you, I'll wait a few minutes to get started, just in case we have some folks coming in late."

Everyone nodded in assent. A couple more people came in

and sat down a few minutes after the hour. At ten fifteen, Julie started the demonstration. "This is a nice intimate group. If you have any questions as we go, feel free to speak up." She pulled the cover off the display painting. "Here's what we'll be working on today."

The display was a beachy scene with a starfish.

Julie walked them step by step through the painting. Every so often, she'd give them breaks so their paintings could dry between steps, and she'd show them other paintings or engage them in a bit of conversation.

"I thought you said yours wouldn't be good." Megan was looking at his painting. "It's great."

Eric leaned over to see hers. "So's yours."

She made a face. "My starfish is deformed."

"He is not. He looks fine."

Julie walked around the dozen or so students, answering questions and complimenting their paintings. "And now the final touch. Sign your paintings. Be proud of yourselves, you all did an outstanding job. Give each other – and yourselves – a hand."

Everyone clapped, and a man in the back said, "How about a hand for Julie, too."

More enthusiastic clapping this time. Julie thanked them and wished them all a good day.

In the hallway, Eric said, "Do you want to get some lunch?"

Megan shook her head. "I think I'm going to lay down for a bit."

Eric carried their paintings back to Megan's room and set them on her dresser.

Suddenly whirling around, Megan lurched into the bathroom and threw up.

Eric maneuvered around her in the cramped bathroom to wet a washcloth to lay across the back of her neck, and helped her into bed after she insisted on brushing her teeth. "What can I get you?"

"I hate to be a bother."

"I think we're past that."

She gave a weak smile. "Would you please get me some ginger ale or something?"

"Of course. I'll be right back." He grabbed her key card and left, hoping she wouldn't get any worse. He'd only had motion sickness one time, and once was plenty. The waiter in the dining room was sympathetic, giving him a handful of cracker packets to go with the ginger ale.

He returned to Megan's cabin and put her key on the dresser where he'd gotten it from. She nibbled on a few crackers and sipped on the ginger ale, then lay back down. Eric pulled a blanket over her. "I'll check on you in a few hours, okay?"

"Thanks. Hopefully the room's done spinning by then."

He pulled the curtains shut and turned off the lights before letting himself out. In his own room, he sat on his balcony and read for a while, then went out to explore.

After wasting another two hours and a whole bunch of dollars in the casino, he was about to head down to check on Megan when he saw her turning the corner of the deck. In a tight red dress.

With Marco.

Furious, he hurried around the corner, following them, and saw her blonde ponytail disappear into the room where Marco had given her a "salsa lesson" days earlier. If she wanted to see the Omelet Douche, fine, but he wasn't okay with being lied to about it. He stood in the hallway for a minute or two, debating whether to confront her or let it go. Nope, might as well get it over with now. He drew back his shoulders and whipped the door open. There was no one in the room.

Confused, he looked around. Another door stood on the far side of the room. His heart pounding, he went over, his shoes squeaking across the polished wood floor, and grabbed the knob. The unmistakable sounds of enthusiastic sex floated through the door. He let go of the knob and quickly left the room. It was Brittney in his office all over again.

He strode blackly back to his cabin, refusing to exchange greetings or make eye contact with anyone in his path. Slamming the door, he stomped to the mini bar, scowled at his reflection in the mirror, then punched his towel dog, trying to vent his impotent rage. The towel flopped onto the floor.

Eric picked it up and apologized, straightening its ears. He sat on the edge of the bed, holding the towel dog. "This sucks. What's her problem, anyway? *Marco*? Really? The biggest sleaze ball on the planet? Seriously? Why do women want guys like him?"

The dog remained silent.

"Maybe I'll act like a creep and use some generic lines of bullcrap so I can hook up with some random woman, too. What do you think?"

The eyeless towel sat still in his hand, probably afraid of being knocked to the floor again.

Eric sighed. "You're right. I know it's none of my business, but she doesn't need to lie to me, you know?"

A rap on the door startled him. He set the towel dog on the dresser, then answered the door. Immediate annoyance pulsed in his head. "Well that was fast."

Megan's brow furrowed. "What was fast?"

Eric rolled his eyes. "What do you need?"

"Um, nothing? I assumed you would have been back a while ago, so I wanted to make sure you hadn't gotten sick, too." She trailed off. "What's wrong?"

A whole string of accusations sat at the ready on his

tongue, but his brain took notice of her loose hair and the same shirt and shorts she'd been wearing when he left her. Unless she was with Marco, ran back to her cabin, changed clothes *and* took down her hair, all to be back up here at *his* door in a matter of fifteen minutes...

Great. Turned out he *was* just as much of a jerk as Marco. Just in a different way. Mentally, he gave himself a sarcastic pat on the back.

A family passed by, smiling and nodding to them as they made their way down the hall. Eric nodded in return, then stood aside to let Megan in, glad he at least hadn't been running his mouth. For once. "Are you feeling better?"

"I am. I'm not sure I want anything much for dinner, but the nausea seems to be gone, and my head doesn't feel as weird. I took more Dramamine just in case, though."

"Good." He gestured to the balcony and slid the door open.

They went outside and sat in the lounge chairs. "Why are you acting so strange?"

Waiting until she was settled in her chair, trying to buy a little time to answer the million dollar question, he said, "Do you want me to be honest?"

"I generally prefer honesty, yes."

"I was on the upper deck and I saw Marco with... I thought he was with you." He felt like an idiot as he played it over in his mind. The woman was shorter than Megan, with longer hair.

How he mistook her for Megan, and his instant assumptions made him feel like a crappy human being. And an even crappier friend.

Megan kicked off her flip flops and pulled her feet up onto the chair, looking rather unimpressed with him at the moment. "After I told you I wasn't seeing him again. Tell me, genius, was barfing my guts out part of a clever ruse I concocted to throw you off?"

"I thought maybe you changed your mind." He stared out at the ocean. The sky was overcast, but the rain had stopped. The water was still choppy, but much calmer than it had been earlier in the day. Hopefully it would be smooth for the rest of the cruise, for Megan's sake.

"I didn't." Her tone was pure annoyance. "So you don't trust me."

Eric leaned back. "It has nothing to do with trust. You have no obligation to me. We're friends, at least for this trip, and it's none of my business if you do anything with Marco or anybody else."

Megan stared at him. "But it's awkward. I don't want things to be weird, so let's spell it out for the rest of the cruise, okay? I didn't come here to meet anyone. I want to build my travel portfolio and experience some new things. I'm enjoying spending time with you, and I would prefer for the rest of the trip to go the same way it's been up to this point. What do you want?"

"That's exactly what I want, too."

"I mean, we'll go back home and most likely never see each other again, so let's enjoy every moment and have ten days of wonderful memories to look back on. No lying. No sneaking. No romantic involvements. No drama." With a wicked smile, she added, "No swinging."

His heart lurched at the thought of never seeing her again, a reaction he wasn't going to explore, but she was right. "Agreed. Wonderful memories, no drama. And for the love of all that is holy, no swinging."

Megan settled back in her chair, grinning.

Eric watched her for a moment. She was still pale, but didn't look as nauseous as she had earlier. He went back into the cabin and grabbed two bottles of water, then settled back to listen to the ocean. Every now and then, the wind would shift, and music from the upper decks floated down to them.

Capping the bottle after a long sip, she said, "Since we're being honest, you might be interested to know the word back home has Brittney as the innocent victim, and you the heartless cheater."

Eric snorted. "Doesn't surprise me." It didn't. Brittney was undoubtedly spreading lies before his plane even took off.

"How are you going to set them straight?"

"I'm not. Everyone who matters knows better. Besides, she always trips herself up. It's only a matter of time before her lies catch up to her." It surprised him to find he didn't care much what anyone was thinking back home. He'd meant what he said – the people who mattered already knew the truth.

"Doesn't it bother you, having people think the worst of you?"

"Nope." He turned to look at her. "Do you believe me?"

She held his gaze for so long he began to think she doubted him. He wished he could see what was going through her mind. Finally, she answered, "I do."

"Then what do I care what anyone else thinks?" Relieved, he reached over and took her hand. "Speaking of home, have you been homesick at all?"

Megan barked a humorless laugh. "Are you kidding? I haven't had the opportunity to get homesick because it feels like I never left. When I got up from my nap, I had a dozen messages. I talked to Mom last night, but she can't go one freaking day without harassing me. I'm so sick of it."

"I can't imagine. Is she always this needy?"

Megan took a long drink. "It's complicated."

Eric watched a parade of emotions cross her face.

Chapter Eighteen

Megan was glad for Eric's hand holding hers. She stared out over the gray horizon and took a deep breath. "It's hard to deal with, but I get it. Mostly."

Might as well just drop the bomb, since there was no easy way to say it. "When I was sixteen, my brother was abducted."

His startled expression was one she'd seen a million times.

"Oh, no. I had no idea." His fingers tightened around hers.

"It was my fault. My parents were away for the weekend, and I was supposed to be watching Danny, who was twelve. I had some friends over. We were hanging out in the basement, and Danny kept coming down and bugging us. So when he told me he was walking to his friend's house. I told him to go." She drew a shaky breath. "He left, and never made it to his friend's."

"Megan, it was not your fault."

"No, it is. I never should have let him go."

"I bet he walked the same way a million times. There's no way you could have known."

Megan shrugged. "Maybe. But it was ten o'clock at night. I had no business letting him go out by himself. The guy had just gotten out on parole. Pulled Danny into his car two blocks from our house."

"Come here." The words were barely more than a whisper.

Megan let Eric pull her over onto his lounge chair and put his arms around her. She snuggled into his shoulder, grateful for the comfortable contact. "It was a nightmare. Police and search parties and dogs and all this chaos and the *not knowing*... Days stretched into weeks, weeks to months... Danny was just *gone*. My parents told me to my face they didn't blame me, but they did."

"I'm sure they didn't." He stroked her hair.

"No, they did. At least my mother did, and my dad didn't refute it. I overheard more of their conversations than I care to remember. 'I told you we never should have trusted Megan to watch him.' was a recurring theme." She felt the memories pulling her backwards, to all the times hushed voices floated into her bedroom through the vent.

"I'm sorry."

"I stopped being Megan, right then, and I turned into Danny's Sister. My mother watched my every move. She'd knock on the door when I was in the bathroom to make sure I hadn't snuck out the window. She listened to my phone calls on the extension. Interrogated my friends. Followed me if I went somewhere. I didn't go on another date until I was eighteen, because she was so petrified of me leaving the house."

Eric rubbed her arm.

"It was so confusing. On one hand, she couldn't stand to have me out of her sight, but at the same time, she couldn't stand to look at me. I turned into the perfect child. I went to bed when I was told. I got up when I was told. If I so much as rolled my eyes, my mother would tell me I'd caused her enough pain."

The words flowed like water gushing from a broken faucet. "For three years, we didn't know where Danny was. If he was alive or dead. What might be happening to him. I turned down three full rides – one of them was UCLA – because I felt like I couldn't leave home. Instead, I graduated with honors from Hickory Hollow Community College." She snorted and wiped her nose. "They found Danny the summer after my freshman year. Hikers with their dogs found him buried near some old hunting cabin. All that time, and he was less than five miles away. They're pretty sure he was killed the night he was abducted."

She fiddled with a button on Eric's shirt. "After the police left, my mother stood up and slapped me across the face. Asked me if I was glad he was dead. Then she told me it should have been me."

Eric sucked in a breath and held her closer. "What about your dad?"

"He was at work all the time. Oh, he tried, but he never heard the worst of it. When she was out of the house he'd try to tell me it wasn't my fault. He did his best, but he'd lost a son, too. He was grieving and I don't think he had any idea how to tell me what I needed to hear. I'm not sure either of them actually realized I was grieving, too, and so full of guilt. They were both consumed with their own pain. I became invisible."

"I'm so sorry. I can't imagine what you went through."

"It was so weird. There was all this constant chaos of people calling and police and false leads and random reporters showing up for the whole three years. We were 'the family of the missing kid' like some twisted celebrity status, and then after they found him, we were 'the family of the kid they found at Cooper's cabin' and we weren't nearly as mysterious or interesting anymore. It was like someone pulled a plug and there was this sudden silence almost as overwhelming as the noise."

"Weren't you glad to be rid of the attention, though?"

Megan sighed. "I was glad we had closure. Not knowing was... it was an indescribable nightmare. But after all the hoopla was gone, there was nothing to distract my mother, and she had nothing to hope for anymore. So for a while, she was horrible. Hateful and mean... I went to a few therapy sessions on campus, and all they told me was to be empathetic. So I did everything I could to make things easier for her. I went to school and worked full time in the family grocery store, taking over what she normally did in the office because she, understandably, could barely function. I cooked and cleaned the house and tried to stay out of her way."

He ran his fingertips over Megan's arm. "You don't owe her your life. Nothing is going to bring your brother back, not even if you're perfect and live every second of the rest of your life the way she thinks you should."

"I know."

"It sounds like your whole life is paying penance for the sin of being alive."

Megan turned and buried her face in his chest, breathing in the subtle scent of his cologne, mixed with the salty ocean air. It was comfortable, laying against him, listening to the steady rhythm of his heartbeat alongside the calming roar of the ocean. Suddenly embarrassed about sharing so much, things she'd never even shared with Beth, she said, "Now you have to tell me one of your deep, dark secrets."

Eric shifted, winding a lock of her hair around his fingers. "I can't compete with any of that."

"Tell me something nobody else knows. Anything."

He thought about it for a minute, then chuckled. "Hmm. When Stewart and me were kids, we had this next-door neighbor, Mr. Hinkley. He had this evil rat dog he'd walk twice a day, and every single time, he'd let the dog crap in our yard. Every day, my dad would go out and scoop up this dog's crap and get rid of it. For *years*. One day me and Stewart were outside playing football. The ball goes over the fence. Our parents told us to go knock on the door, so we did. Mr. Hinkley told us to get lost, then he went out and ran over our ball with his lawnmower."

"What a jerk."

"He was. And now might be a good time to mention Mr. Hinkley's convertible. Ugly old thing. '75 Cadillac Eldorado. It was this awful sun-faded red with rust all over it. Never drove it, just backed it out of the garage every once in a while to wash and wax it. This is also a good time to mention we lived near a creek and my dad took me and Stewart fishing just about every day. We caught a lot of fish. Which we cleaned in the garage, and the guts went into a specific trash can."

Megan giggled. "You didn't."

"I wasn't going to do anything. Until my birthday. We had a party in the backyard. I think it was the year I turned thirteen. Anyway, it was mostly family and a few of my buddies. I'm sure we were loud, but it was a Saturday afternoon in the middle of summer. Mr. Hinkley calls the cops for a noise complaint. Cops come. They tell Mr. Hinkley to stop making stupid calls. Apparently his main hobby was calling the cops on his neighbors."

"Wow."

"That night, after everybody left, I was looking out my window, no doubt sending death glares across the lawn to Mr. Hinkley and his nasty dog, when I saw him leave. He left the garage door up, so I made my move. I snuck out to the garage, dragged the can of fish guts next door and dumped the whole thing in his Caddy. The next day, the cops are knocking on doors, asking everybody in the neighborhood who did it. Nobody saw a thing."

"And even if they did, he was such a jerk they wouldn't have said anything."

"Exactly. I think my dad always suspected Stewart. I was pretty quiet, not the kind of kid who'd dump fish guts into the neighbor's car."

"But Stewart would have?"

Eric laughed. "Most definitely. He was a loudmouth, always getting himself into trouble. But he was charming and good looking, so he always talked himself right back out of it."

"And you were the good boy?"

"I was the younger brother who went along with whatever Stewart wanted. I looked up to him."

"Aww, that's sweet."

Eric raised an eyebrow. "It wasn't so sweet when he blamed me for stuff I didn't do. Like wrecking the car. He parked it like nothing happened, and when Dad came home, he about had a cow. Stewart told him he was trying to teach me how to drive."

"Oh, no."

"Oh, yes. We both got grounded for a month and I had to help pay for the repairs."

"Why didn't you tell your dad the truth?"

He shrugged. "What, and get Stewart in trouble for lying, too? Nah. I always had his back, and he always had mine."

"Sounds like he got the better end of the deal."

"He did. I didn't get into much trouble on my own."

"Did he ever get into any real trouble?"

"Normal teenage kid stuff. Sneaking out, meeting girls, some underage drinking. I think his closest call was when he got caught making out in the backseat of his car. With the sheriff's daughter."

"Oh, no."

"Overall, he was a good kid, and he turned out to be a great man. If I end up being half the man he is, I'll be doing good."

"Wow, most families I know don't talk about each other like that."

"I know, and it's a shame. At the end of the day, all you really have is your family." He squeezed her arm. "Doesn't necessarily mean the one you were born into. Sometimes people have to create their own families."

Megan sighed. "I do love my family. I just don't know how to set boundaries with them."

"I'd imagine if there never were any, it'd be hard to set them."

"It feels impossible. But normal families don't have this kind of history, either, so I don't even know where to start."

Eric rubbed her arm.

"I'm tired of feeling guilty about wanting to be happy. My brother died, yes, and I miss him, but I'm still here. Sometimes I feel guilty about being alive."

Megan let Eric pull her closer. He rested his chin on the top of her head. "I hate that you feel that way. It's not right, it's not fair, and it's not what Danny would want for you."

"I know." Her fingers traced the stitches on his shirt. "Tell me more about Stewart."

"Stewart was quite the ladies' man. Different date every night of the week. Until his junior year in college, when he met Jody. It was like a switch flipped. All we heard from then on was Jody, Jody, Jody. The funny part was, she wouldn't even give him the time of day. She was in school full time and working two jobs, and she had no interest in any kind of nonsense. Stewart did a complete 180. Stopped dating, started studying hard, stopped hanging out with some of his friends...

It was four months before Jody would even give him her number."

"867-5309?" Megan laughed.

"Wouldn't have surprised us if she'd have used that one. They finally went out and he was gone. Done. Head over heels. It took her a little bit longer, though, since his reputation preceded him. They finally got engaged and got married right after Jody graduated. Now they have four kids and just opened the coffee shop. They're still as in love as they were back then."

"Aww, how sweet."

"It's the first time I was ever honestly jealous of Stewart."

"Because of Jody?"

"Because of what they have."

"Did you think you would get it with Brittney?" She was skeptical that he would have imagined a similar marriage to his brother's with Brittney.

"It was closer than I'd ever been before."

Megan looked up at him, not quite believing what he'd just said. "Really?"

"Okay, no. Brittney seemed like a safe bet. It was pretty clear she wanted to be taken care of. I wanted to be married and have a family. We both get what we want."

"Sounds more like a business transaction."

"Pretty much."

"Why did it seem safe?"

She felt him pull in a deep breath. "There was no danger of getting hurt."

"Because you didn't love her."

"And she definitely didn't love me."

"Why would you be willing to have a marriage like that?"

He scratched his head, but didn't answer.

She filled in the blank with a guess. "Because you were hurt before and you didn't want to go through it again. You knew you wouldn't ever truly love Brittney, and she wouldn't ever love you, so you get what you want with no risk of getting your heart broken."

"Very insightful, Dr. Phil."

"What happened?"

"You already know what happened."

"No. I mean before Brittney."

A long silence stretched out. This time, Megan waited for him to speak first.

"Her name was Lila. We got engaged and moved in together. We were planning a wedding and a life and a family. Little things bugged me, but I brushed them off."

"Like what?"

"She was rude to my mom." He held up a hand. "I'm not a mama's boy, but there was no reason for her to be disrespectful to my mother. My parents were always good about staying out of our business. They didn't approve of us living together without being married, but they kept quiet about it. After a while, Lila and I would fight about the stupidest things, and we'd both say the ugliest things to each other."

A gust of chilly air blew in from the water. Megan shivered and drew her knees up over his lap. Eric put his hand on her knee.

"She finally told me she couldn't take it anymore. I was immature and mean and she couldn't live with me. It was a huge wakeup call because she was right. I'd been a complete jerk. Jealous and insecure, accusing her of things she wasn't doing. She moved out. We kept seeing each other, and eventually she moved back in. We even went to a counselor a few times to help us learn how to communicate better. We got married, and things went well."

"Why didn't it work out?"

"It did. For a while. Lila got pregnant. We were thrilled, and then devastated when we lost the pregnancy. Over the next year, we lost two more pregnancies. I can't even describe what we went through – what *she* went through."

"I'm so sorry."

"I told her I was fine with not having kids as long as we were together." He ran his hand through his hair. "She told me I wasn't enough, and if I couldn't give her a family, it was over. I said we could explore other options, like adoption. I thought she was on board, but I got back from a business trip to Thailand to find an empty house and an envelope with divorce papers on the kitchen counter."

"You hadn't talked about divorce?"

"Not even once. After that, I decided I wasn't going to let myself fall in love again, because I loved Lila and all we did was hurt each other. That isn't who I want to be."

Megan looked up at him. Their faces were inches apart. She watched Eric's gaze trace her face from her eyes to her mouth, then back to her eyes. He pulled back. "I'm getting hungry. You?"

Megan sat up, loathe to leave his warmth. "Yes, but no dining room. I'm not sure I could handle Sheila and Morty."

Chapter Nineteen

After dinner and seeing Megan back to her own cabin, Eric got ready for bed, thinking back over the day's conversations. They'd spent all day at sea, but he was more exhausted than the days they'd had physically demanding excursions. It was so easy, talking to Megan. Talking *with* Megan. Even about Lila.

Morning came quickly. Eric jumped out of bed, excited about their day in Jamaica. After the excursion to some waterfalls, he had a list of three coffee shops he wanted to visit if they had time.

He met Megan on the deck. She was practically bouncing with excitement. The weather was perfect, her seasickness was gone, and today's scenery would be a massive addition to her portfolio. They left the ship, opting to hire private transportation instead of waiting on the shuttle.

The trip to the falls was supposed to take an hour and a half. Eric only stopped fearing for his life when they got out of the car and onto firm land – fifty minutes later. From Megan's expression as she climbed out, she hadn't felt much safer.

They donned their water shoes and began hiking up the

falls. They went slowly so Megan could take photos every step of the way.

At the top of the falls, Megan only shot for a few minutes. "Are you ready to head back down?"

"Already?"

Megan nodded. "Yeah. We can get a jump on those coffee shops."

"Is everything okay?"

She sighed and gestured around them. "It's beautiful. Stunning. It's also packed with tourists. It kind of loses something with so many people everywhere."

"Yeah, it's not quite what I expected, either."

"So let's go get you some Jamaican coffee to take home." They hiked back down over the falls and found their driver.

After they climbed in the car and hastily buckled their seatbelts, Megan asked him, "Are there any coffee places nearby? Places tourists don't usually visit?"

The driver smiled and nodded his head vigorously. He mashed the gas pedal. "I got just the place for you."

Eric wasn't sure whether to be glad or terrified. Maybe both. Ten minutes later, the car veered off onto a dirt road and sped down a long driveway. Stones sprayed in every direction as they skidded to a stop in front of a huge white house with a massive wrap around porch.

"What is this place?" Eric asked.

"Plantation. Best coffee in the world. Guaranteed." The driver grinned again and dashed up the front steps, motioning them to follow.

Eric exchanged a look with Megan. She shrugged and started up the stairs.

Inside, a woman was speaking with the driver. She was somehow ageless. She could have been fifty, or she could have been ninety. It was impossible to tell. She greeted them with a smile. "This way."

"Um, what is this place?" Eric asked.

The woman stopped. "You want the best coffee Jamaica has to offer, yes?"

"Yes?" He glanced to Megan. She seemed to be enjoying this more than the trip to the falls.

"Then come." She strode toward a set of double doors, pushing them open as she passed through. "I am Ini."

They followed her and stepped into a huge open room, practically running to keep up.

"I'm Eric and this is Megan."

Ini didn't slow down. She led them through another set of double doors, out onto a back patio. Large tarps covered the lawn, and were full of red berries.

Megan asked, "What's this?"

"Coffee cherries." Eric bent down. "May I?"

Ini nodded her consent.

Eric ran his hand over a pile of cherries, turning them. "These are how the coffee beans come off the plant."

Megan hunkered down and picked one up. "It doesn't look anything like a coffee bean."

He lifted some of the berries up and smelled them before putting them back onto the tarp. "These are wonderful quality. I'm impressed."

"Sadly, you do not have time for the whole tour, but come." Ini walked back into the house.

Inside the room they had passed through, small groups of women sat, talking, laughing, and sorting beans.

"What are they doing?" Megan asked.

Eric answered, "Quality control."

Ini nodded. "Exactly. Machines are faster, but not better."

She picked up a bean. "The machine would pass this. But not us. Our standards are tough." She handed the bean to Megan.

Megan studied the bean before handing it to Eric. "Maybe I'm dense, but why isn't it a good bean?"

The woman took it from Eric's hand and showed Megan two tiny holes. "Weevils," she said with disgust, then tossed the bean into the discard bin.

Eric checked his watch. "I wish we could stay longer."

"You come back. We will take you out to the mountain. You can harvest with us."

He felt like a kid at Christmas. "That would be amazing. Thank you for the offer, Ini. I'll be glad to take you up on it."

She motioned for them to follow her. They went through another set of doors, into a comfortable room with plush chairs and little side tables. "You have time to enjoy a cup."

They sat, and a few minutes later, she reappeared with two mugs of coffee. The rich aroma was intoxicating. Eric breathed deeply. It was the most delicious scent he'd ever experienced. His mouth watered.

The coffee itself was smooth. He looked over at Megan. He knew she wasn't a coffee drinker, but even she was enjoying it.

He smiled at Ini. "Thank you so much for letting us see the facility, and for this." He held up his cup. "This is the best coffee I've ever had."

"Of course it is." She spoke without a hint of sarcasm.

He hesitated, not wanting to offend her, but he had to ask. "I hope this doesn't offend you, but would I be able to buy some coffee to take back home?"

She gave him a knowing smile. "We do not normally allow tourists to purchase our coffee. But for you, we will make an exception."

Eric handed over his credit card and the woman disappeared.

Megan leaned over and said, "How much are you getting?"

"I have no idea."

"And you don't know how much it's costing you?"

"Nope."

Megan shook her head. Eric shrugged. "It'll be fair."

Megan simply raised an eyebrow.

Ini reappeared and handed Eric's card back with a receipt.

He signed it without looking at it, then shoved his card and copy of the receipt into his wallet. "Your coffee is in the car," she said.

He reached out and shook her hand. "Thank you so much. I'll be in touch."

Megan shook her hand as well, then they followed her back to the front doors.

Ini called after them, "Safe travels, my new friends."

The driver was shutting the trunk lid, then grinned at them. "Back to the ship?"

"Back to the ship," Eric answered.

The ride back was exactly as terrifying as the ride to the falls. The car careened around hairpin turns without slowing down, whipping out around pedestrians and donkeys who didn't seem too concerned about the speeding vehicles whizzing past them.

Back at the dock, Eric practically leapt from the car after handing the driver his fare.

The driver got out and popped the trunk. "Here you are, friend." He pulled out two burlap bags of coffee beans, probably weighing ten pounds each. He handed the bags to Eric, jumped in the car and sped off.

Megan's mouth was agape. "Holy crap, that's a lot of coffee."

"A lot of *expensive* coffee. I'm afraid to check my receipt."

"Oh, now you're concerned. Good grief. If I handed over my credit card without knowing how much, you'd think I lost my mind."

"Yeah, because that would be stupid." He gave her a grin and patted the bags. "Totally worth it."

They got back on the ship and dropped the beans in Eric's cabin. He snuck a peek at his receipt and blew out a relieved breath. "It's not too bad."

"Now we head back out for souvenirs." Megan said, rolling her eyes.

"You got it."

Chapter Twenty

Megan loved the feel of the shopping village near the dock, and was happy to spend their last two hours in Jamaica spending too much money on souvenirs. Little stands dotted both sides of a dirt path. Jamaican women were giving tourists braids in one spot, weaving bracelets in another.

"Oh, look." Megan held up a glass bottle with a cork stopper. "These are perfect."

Eric chuckled. "Now you don't have to take your sand home in plastic baggies."

"Yeah, but how am I going to know which is which?"

"Keep the bottle in the baggie?"

"Duh, I guess I could have figured that one out on my own, huh?" She laughed.

"Did you pick up sand today?"

"Yeah, I got some at the falls." She made a pouty face. "I wish we would have had time to do the bobsled."

"You'll just have to come back."

The thought made her smile. "You're brilliant. As soon as I get home, I'm booking another cruise."

"I hope you do. You should travel more."

She sighed, running her fingers along a row of seashells. "Maybe I'll take a European cruise."

"There you go."

Megan bought six glass bottles, one for each stop on their trip. She picked up a seventh, just in case one broke. She turned to pay, then turned back. No. No "just in case" or "what if " extras. Six stops, six bottles. And enough faith they'd be fine.

"I do think I'll book another cruise. This has been amazing." She grabbed Eric's free hand as they strolled back to the ship.

He squeezed her fingers gently. "I think you should."

"Maybe January or February when it's so cold at home. Then I can be in shorts and a t-shirt soaking up the sun while everyone I know is bundled up."

"Over here, please."

A photo station was set up next to the gangplank leading to the ship. Eric put his arm around Megan while the ship's photographer snapped a cheesy tourist photo.

"You should apply for one of those jobs. Live on a cruise ship, travel all over the place, and take pictures of tourists. I bet you'd have lots of free time to build your travel portfolio."

"I don't think they'd hire me. I'm not exotic."

"Vat you mean, Svetlana?"

Megan laughed at his goofy voice. "Svetlana?"

"No? How about Irina or Tatiana? You'll need to work on your accent, though."

"My exotic central Pennsylvania accent?"

"No, your sexy Ukrainian accent."

"Ah. I'm from Ukraine." They walked up the gangplank and waited in line to have their passcard scanned to get back on board.

"Unless you'd prefer Sweden."

"How about Norway. Or Finland."

Eric's hand was on her back. "Nope, not exotic enough."

"Russia?"

"Too common."

She tilted her head. "How many Russians do you know?"

"My cabin steward, Vladislav."

"Besides him."

"I've been to Russia, remember?"

Megan pointed at his chest. "Yeah, but you said you didn't get out of the office much on those trips."

"Enough to meet Annushka." He wiggled his eyebrows. "She inspired my deep and abiding appreciation of fine vodka and borscht."

She gently shoved him with her elbow. "Seriously? You're such a brat."

Eric laughed. "We better get something to eat before the show."

"Way to change the subject." She stepped up to have her passcard scanned and went through security, then waited for Eric to come through.

He said, "Hey, you're the one who wanted to see *Mamma Mia!*, not me. I won't be responsible for you getting there late because you want to argue about my Russian girlfriend."

Megan laughed. "Let me guess. She was a waitress and you never even got her number."

"Not true."

"Uh-huh."

"I did get her number, but it was in Russian, so I couldn't read it." He pushed the button for the elevator and the doors slid open.

"You're so full of it."

"Okay, maybe it was the bill for dinner, but there were numbers. She was totally into me."

Megan rolled her eyes. "Sure, Casanova."

"Casanova? Ah, yes, I have fond memories of Italy. With Giada."

"Give me a break."

"Hey, I can't help my wild and crazy past."

"I think you mean wild and imaginary past." Megan got off the elevator on her floor. "Give me ten minutes and I'll be up."

"Okay, but you better hope there aren't any hot Russian waitresses between here and there, or you're going to the show alone."

"I'll take my chances." Megan watched the elevator close and chuckled as she unlocked her cabin and went inside. She checked her phone. There was only one voicemail. Strange. She hurried to change clothes and freshen up. She shoved her phone in her pocket and grabbed her sweater before rushing up to meet Eric for dinner.

They got a balcony table and ordered their food. "I didn't expect to eat so many burgers on a cruise."

Eric agreed. "Me, either, but this place is great."

"You're just saying that because there's hardly ever anyone else here."

"Maybe."

"Can I be incredibly rude for a minute and check my phone?

I only got one voicemail today, so I'm a little concerned."

"Twelve hundred messages down to one? I'd be concerned, too. Please. Go ahead."

Megan tapped her phone and listened to the voicemail.

The message said, "Megan. This is your mother. I don't appreciate being lied to. We need to discuss this immediately." Every word was short and angry.

"What's wrong?"

Megan had no idea. She played the message for Eric.

He sat back in his chair. "Strange."

"I have to call. I'll be back."

Megan went to the far side of the empty balcony and leaned against the railing. Everything was so perfect. The sun was dipping low. The sky was turning the most breathtaking shades of every color possible. The breeze was warm and salty. The air was warm, not too hot and not chilly yet. The only imperfect thing was the black cloud swirling over Megan's head as the phone rang.

"Hello." Her mother's voice was clipped.

"What's going on?"

"You tell me."

Megan clenched her teeth. "I'm not playing guessing games. Tell me what you think I lied about."

"Think? I have proof." Alice's voice rose an octave.

"About what?"

"You. You and that... lying, cheating scumbag. You promised me you wouldn't talk to him."

"What are you talking about?"

"Oh, don't you try playing innocent with me, young lady. You think because you're far away from home, you can do what you want and it won't get back to us?"

"Would you just say it?" Megan felt the blood pulsing in her throat, strangling her.

"I know you're having an affair with him. With *Eric Caretti*." She spit his name out. "And after what he did to your cousin. You should be ashamed of yourself. Ashamed!"

"This is ridiculous."

"I saw pictures, Megan. Your friend Sheila put pictures on her Facebook."

"Wait. What? Are you freaking kidding me? You started stalking Sheila? What is wrong with you?"

"With me? What's wrong with you? Never mind, I know what's wrong with you. You're an ungrateful little tramp. I hope you weren't sleeping with him before this convenient little *trip*. It'll break Brittney's heart to know you've betrayed her like this. I'm so ashamed of you. I'm ashamed you're my daughter."

"That's nothing new, now is it?"

"Don't you dare try to turn this around on me. What do you have to say for yourself?"

"All I have to say is this: you can think whatever you want. I won't stand here and explain anything or justify anything or answer any of your accusations, because it won't matter anyway, and quite frankly, it's none of your business."

Megan ended the call. She leaned on the railing and squeezed her eyes shut, taking deep breaths to calm herself. She straightened and smoothed down the front of her shirt, then tucked a stray lock of hair behind her ear.

She sat back at her seat.

Eric pulled her hand to his mouth and kissed her fingers. "I'm sorry."

She managed a smile and tried to make a joke. "You should be. It's all your fault. Well, Sheila's, actually."

His expression was confused.

Megan pulled up her Facebook and searched for Sheila. Sure enough, in Sheila's cruise photo album, she'd posted the picture of Megan and Eric at their dinner table. She showed it to Eric.

"My mother was Facebook stalking Sheila and saw this."

"Oh. I guess it looks kind of bad, doesn't it?"

Megan looked at the picture. Eric's arm was around her, and she was leaning close to him. They were both looking at the camera and smiling. The next photo, however, was of Megan and Sheila, in an identical position. She shrugged.

The waiter brought their burgers and set them on the table. Megan took a bite of her burger, while Eric poked at his fries.

He said, "I'm sorry this is turning into a mess. I never intended to drag you into any kind of drama."

"You didn't drag me anywhere. The only drama is in people's heads. We haven't done anything wrong or inappropriate in any way. If my mother wants to accuse me of sleeping with you, it's on her."

Eric dropped his French fry. "Wait, what?"

Megan sighed. "Yeah, I'm a no-good tramp and I'm sleeping with you, and she hopes it wasn't me you were cheating on Brittney with, although from her tone she's decided that's exactly what happened... it was lovely." She took another bite.

"You're awfully calm."

"Nope, I'm pissed. I'm seeing all kinds of red right now. I did nothing wrong, and let's be real. Even if I *was* sleeping with you, it's still nobody's business. Even if the timing would be a little sketchy, and the fact Brittney's my cousin is a little on the sordid side, even then, we wouldn't be doing anything wrong. You and Brittney were officially over before this trip, so everybody can just piss off." She shoved a fry into her mouth.

Her phone vibrated.

"You've gotta be freaking kidding me." She swiped to answer the call and hit the speaker button. "Yes?"

"I'm giving you one opportunity to apologize."

"For what, exactly?" She looked over to Eric.

He propped his elbows on the table, listening intently.

"You can start by apologizing for speaking to me the way you did. Then you can apologize for lying to me."

"I didn't lie to you about anything. And I'm not going to apologize for the way I reacted to your nasty accusations." Her mouth went dry. Standing up to her mother wasn't any easier at thirty-four than it was as a child.

Alice's angry sigh seemed to hover over the table. "You

need to call your cousin and apologize."

"For what?" This time, her mother had gone way off the deep end.

"Have you no shame? Your poor father is mortified. To know our daughter is behaving like a... a common *prostitute*, and with no regard for Brittney's suffering."

"Let me talk to Dad."

Alice paused. "He doesn't wish to speak to you."

She didn't believe it for a second. "Now who's lying?"

"How dare you?"

Laughter floated up from the deck below.

"You're being ridiculous. I am not sleeping with Eric, not that it's any of your business, and I have nothing to apologize to anyone for." Megan glanced at Eric, whose jaw was clenched as he glared at her phone. It gave her a burst of confirmation that she wasn't the crazy one in this conversation.

"It most certainly is our business. This is your *family* you're tearing apart. How about you apologize for humiliating me? All you've ever done, your whole life, is cause me pain and embarrassment. You never think of anyone but yourself. Megan, you are a disgrace to your brother's memory. Why you're still here and he's—"

Megan was up off her seat and to the far railing before she knew what she was doing. She paused and looked down at her phone. Alice's voice was coming through, but Megan couldn't make out the words through the hurt pounding through her head.

She yanked her arm back and heaved forward, releasing the phone. It flew outward, bursts of cheerful sun glinting off the screen as it arced over the crystal clear blue waters of Jamaica. It connected with the water, giving a satisfying "sploosh" and then drifted lazily downward. Megan watched it until it sank too deep for her to see.

Her knuckles were white as her fingers gripped the railing. Eric came up behind her and put his hands on her shoulders. She spun around and wrapped her arms around his waist, breathing as hard as if she'd been running, and accepting his comfort.

He put his arms around her, holding her tight.

Megan pressed her face into his shirt, breathing him in, clinging to him like a lifeline. "I don't want to go back home," she said, her voice breaking.

"It's garbage, Megan, every bit of it is nothing but garbage." Anger punctuated every one of his words.

She tried holding back the tears, but they refused to be contained. She cried into his chest while he stroked her hair. "Why does it still hurt? I've heard the same crap for so long, and I don't know why I still let it get to me."

"It's your mom. How could you not?"

She sniffled and wiped her eyes, pulling back from him. "Thanks."

Eric took a step back so she could walk past him. She stopped and gasped, grabbing a fistful of his shirt in her hands. "My phone. I just threw my phone in the ocean."

A slow smile spread across his face. "You sure did."

"I wonder if my insurance will cover it." She giggled.

He looked out over the water, where her phone had landed. "I kinda doubt it."

"Me, too." She laughed harder. "I can't believe I threw my phone in the ocean."

"You've got one heck of an arm. Maybe you should play softball."

"Maybe I can find a team with a giant scarlet 'A' on the shirt." She cupped her hands around her mouth. "*Up to bat next for the Homewreckers, it's Megan Prescott.*"

Eric chuckled. "Stop."

"What else am I going to do? I can't sit around and bawl because my mommy was mean to me. So I'll laugh about it instead. And now my burger is cold." She sat down and lifted the top bun and touched the burger. It was indeed, cold.

"And I think we missed the start of the show."

"Eh, it's okay. You didn't want to sit through it anyway."

"I wanted to sit through it with you, Megan."

"I appreciate that more than I could ever tell you." She finished her soda and looked down over the railing their table was against. "What's going on down there?"

Eric turned in his seat. The deck below them was lit up with strings of party lights. Huge speakers were moved to the sides of the pool, and a small platform had been set up opposite the bar.

Megan grabbed his arm. "Karaoke."

"No." He held up his hands and shook his head. "No way."

"Yes." The weight of the world had lifted from her shoulders, a lightness settling in where the tension had been. Suddenly, all she wanted in the world was to have some fun and not worry about a thing.

"I am absolutely not singing." She nodded vigorously. "Yes."

"No." He objected, but let her pull him out of his seat and over to the staircase. "I'm not doing this."

"Okay." Grinning over her shoulder at him, she said, "If you say so."

Megan bounded over to the sign up table and flipped through the binder of song choices. She made her selection and joined the growing crowd dancing around the pool.

Eric joined her. "I'm not a good dancer."

She laughed. "That's okay, I'm not a good singer."

Chapter Twenty-One

If Eric had known chucking her phone overboard would have such a dramatic impact on Megan, he would have done it himself on the first day. They danced in a cheerful crowd of people, fast songs and slow songs, enjoyed some amazing singing, and endured some awful singing. Megan even indulged in a piña colada or two. Or maybe three.

He was interested to see what song she picked out. And interested to see if she could sing.

Nearly two hours passed before Megan's turn came. When they called her name, she threw her hands in the air and danced her way to the stage while the crowd cheered. Eric made his way closer to the stage. He had to laugh when he recognized the first strains of Leslie Gore's "You Don't Own Me". Megan belted out the words with feeling. He might have been slightly biased, but he was pretty sure she got the most enthusiastic cheers of the night so far when she finished her song and bounded off the stage.

"WOOO! That was freaking awesome!" She wiped her hair back off her face.

"I thought you said you couldn't sing?"

"I can't, why, did I sound okay?"

"You were great." He meant it.

"How much have you had to drink?" She laughed. "Must have been a good bit if you thought my singing was great."

He shook his head. "Nope, I've only had two. I can still hear okay."

"Two?" In question, she held up two fingers.

"Yep."

"You're way behind. This is my fifth. I think. Not like we're driving anywhere." She pointed at the piña colada in her hand. "I freaking love the pineapple wedge thingies." She pulled it off the edge of the glass and chewed the fruit off while she danced. "Delicious."

Eric turned to look at something, and when he turned back, Megan was gone. He looked around and spotted her at the bar, holding a fresh piña colada, swaying to the music. Joining her, he ordered another drink of his own, then steered her across the deck, away from the loudest part of the crowd.

The air was damp and clingy, with a light spray coming off the ocean. The music was loud, the crowd was festive, and the drinks flowed freely. Eric cut himself off somewhere around midnight, but it didn't get rid of the slightly-more-than pleasant buzz he had. He suspected his legs were going to be sore from all the dancing, so he took a short break and got a bottle of water from the bar, then rejoined Megan, who hadn't stopped dancing since they'd arrived.

"What'd you get? Water's good. But not as good as this thing. What's this called again? Like pencil something. Peno. Peen-yuh. No, no, no, Kool-aid. Peen-yuh Kool-aid. That's not right, is it?" She broke off into hysterical giggles. "That's *sooooo* stupid. Why would something so yummy have such a stupid name? I think I'll call it Yummy Good Pineapple Drink." She looked down into her empty glass. "Hey. Where'd it go?"

Eric was convinced Megan was completely drunk, and he wasn't feeling so steady on his feet himself. "Maybe we should go to bed."

Megan whipped around to look at him, her eyes wide. "Are you prepositioning me? Wait. Preposi..." She giggled again. "Prepositions. And conjunctions. Conjunction junction, what's your function? And but and or. Button or... buttons or zippers. Ohmygosh zipper's such a funny word. Zipper. Zzzzzziiiiipperrrrrrrrrrr. Like a tiger. Rrrrrrrr. Maybe a zebra crossed with a tiger. Zzzzzziiiiipperrrrrrrr." She made a claw and swiped at the air a few times.

"I'm pretty sure you're drunk." He grabbed her elbow to steady her as she teetered.

"Pffffft, yeah, well, you're pretty sure *I'm* drunk. Soooo... no way, Jose."

"It's like two o'clock. We better get some sleep or the ruins ain't gonna happen."

Megan poked him in the chest. "Whatev. Shows what you know. The ruins *already* happened. Duh. I want another yummy drink."

Eric put his arm around Megan and led her toward the elevator. "No more drinks. You look sleepy."

"Well, yeah, because it's like two o'clock. Wait. No more drinks? Why? Did they run out of pineapples?"

"Yes. Exactly."

Her eyes filled with tears. "But why? Why aren't they anymore pie-apples? That's soooo saaaad." She stopped short and grabbed his shirt. "Oh, no."

"What?" He tried steering her back toward the elevators.

"If we don't get some sleep then we'll miss our thing tomorrow. Today. It's today."

"We're going to sleep now."

"Good idea. You're so smart." He helped her into the

elevator and pushed the blurry button for her floor. They made their way down the swaying corridor.

Megan tried to get her door to unlock, but couldn't. Eric didn't fare a lot better, but on the third attempt, he did manage to get the light to turn green and pushed the door open. Megan was already half asleep, leaning heavily on him.

The room spun with every movement, but he managed to pull back her blanket and get her situated on the bed. He pulled her shoes off and tossed them on the floor.

"Kay, Megan, I'm going to my room."

"Okay. Hey, hang on." She scooted back. "I just wanna tell you thanks. For all the stuff. Earlier. You're so nice and I really like this cruise with you."

"Me too."

"Okay. Gimme a hug."

Eric leaned down and hugged her. She held him tightly. After a few seconds, a most unladylike snore told him she'd fallen asleep. He tried to move his arm, but his coordination wasn't the greatest, so he ended up awkwardly half-kneeling, half-lying beside her.

He decided to straighten out his legs and lay there for just a minute, until she rolled over and he could move his trapped arm. Or until the room stopped spinning.

Whichever came first.

Chapter Twenty-Two

Megan stretched slowly. Her mouth was full of cotton and her bladder was housing at least a thousand gallons of pee. Rubbing her eyes, she froze.

She wasn't alone.

For one terrifying split second, she thought the black hair of the snoring man in her bed might belong to Marco. She took a breath, remembering the walk back to her cabin with Eric. And the piña coladas. Lots and lots of piña coladas.

Whipping the blanket off, she was relieved to see they were both fully clothed. Unable to wait a second longer, she crawled out of bed and went to the bathroom, where she peed for what felt like an hour. Brushing her teeth couldn't wait, either. When she finally finished in the bathroom, she checked the time.

She shook Eric's shoulder. "Rise and shine, Sleeping Beauty."

He grunted and peeled a squinty eye open. Immediately, both eyes popped open and he looked around the room. "Oh, no. Megan, I'm sorry, I didn't plan on this." He grabbed his legs like he was checking to make sure he had pants on.

"Yeah, I know. But we need to get moving or we'll miss the shuttle."

Sitting up and flinging the blanket off, he said, "I'm really sorry."

"Apologize later. We only have an hour, and I'm starving."

"Okay. Meet me up at the buffet in ten. Fifteen. Better make it fifteen." He stopped in the doorway. "Megan..."

"Go. Fifteen minutes." Megan closed the door behind him and hurried to shower. She towel dried her hair and tied it up in a ponytail, pulled on her clothes and checked her watch. Four minutes to go. She grabbed her camera and her backpack and sat down to tie her sneakers, double checked she had everything she needed, then raced up to the buffet.

Eric was already waiting, his hair damp. He'd filled two trays. They ate hastily, without conversation, dumped their trash and made it to the pickup location just as the crowd started moving off the ship.

"How are you feeling?" he asked.

"Surprisingly fine. I'm tired and have half a headache, but I took some Tylenol and brought extra with me. You?"

"Same. We'll have to be sure to stay hydrated, especially in this heat, or all the booze will catch up with us."

They followed the group to a ferry, a 45-minute shuttle ride ending in Playa del Carmen. There, they climbed on an ancient coach bus. A guide stood at the front of the bus, making jokes and giving a brief history of the Mayan ruins they were going to see at Tulum. Then he started talking about the best Mexican beer.

Megan leaned on Eric's shoulder. "I'm so tired."

"Me, too." He paused. "I honestly didn't intend to stay there."

"Of course you didn't. It's not a big deal."

"Isn't it?"

Unable to decipher his tone, she pulled back and looked at him. "Do you think it is? I mean, nothing happened. At all."

Even knowing nothing happened, not even a kiss, her own lack of guilt about the mere appearance of something more surprised her. Usually, she was the one freaking out about what people might think. But not today.

"I feel bad. Paranoid, maybe. What if someone saw me coming out of your room and it gets back home? I don't want you to have to deal with any more nonsense."

She leaned back against his shoulder. "Well, unless someone posted it on Facebook, we're probably okay."

They fell silent as the bus rumbled through some poverty stricken sections of the country, the guide pointing out falling down shacks serving as homes. Megan tried to doze, but couldn't, so she stared out the window, watching the magnificent scenery speed by.

The bus pulled into a parking space near the ruins and let the tourists out, along with what seemed to be a thousand other busses and a million other tourists.

Megan sighed. "All the brochures make it seem like you get a quiet, private tour of these places. I keep getting my hopes up and then come crashing back to reality."

"That's what Photoshop is for."

"Good point."

They made their way past the super-American stands lining the road that led to the entrance of the ruins.

Megan nudged him and laughed. "Dairy Queen? Subway? Nothing like authentic local cuisine, huh?"

"I'm holding out for a McDonald's."

After a ten-minute walk, they passed through the ticket building and Megan stopped. Even with the overwhelming crowd, the view of the ruins was breathtaking. She started snapping pictures. They followed a tour guide, listening to the fascinating Mayan history for a while, then wandered off on their own, inspecting each building.

"Look at the corner of that one," Eric said, pointing. "You can see a face."

Megan shot pictures of the carved stone from several angles. "It's amazing, how this has all lasted for thousands of years."

"I wish we could actually go into the buildings or at least touch them."

Rope barriers surrounded most of the crumbling buildings. "I know. At least I can zoom in. It's a shame we're not allowed to climb the stairs to the top of the temple. I bet the view from up there is amazing."

"I agree." Pointing, he said, "How come he's allowed to touch?"

They laughed at an iguana, sunning himself in one of the building's windows.

"He's such a natural model," Megan said as she shot some photos of him. "These are going to be great."

"What's everyone looking at over there?"

They followed a path and waited until people cleared away from the edge of the embankment. The view stunned her into awed silence, looking down over lush greenery leading to a pure white beach gradually disappearing into the gently undulating waves of the perfect blue ocean.

Eric stood behind Megan, allowing people access on either side of them. She shot a ton of photos. "I know they all look the same, but I want to capture as much as I can."

"Knock yourself out."

She took one last deep breath of the perfect ocean air. "Okay, I guess I should let someone else have a turn."

"We only have half an hour left. Let's go down to the beach and get your sand."

Holding hands, they made their way down the stairs to the beach, where they kicked off their shoes and put their feet in the warm water. Maybe it was just the lack of sleep and abundance of alcohol, but tears stung the backs of her eyes.

"What is it?"

She gave a self-conscious laugh. "Okay, it's silly, but it just dawned on me that I'm standing in the freaking *Caribbean Sea*. In *Mexico*. This is awesome. I wish we could spend a whole day here, at least."

"I agree. There's so much history. I love the part where they put the human hearts on the pillars."

"Maybe I'll Photoshop one in for you."

Eric laughed. "It'll be the focal point of my living room. Totally *avant garde*."

"For all your many guests."

"Hey. I don't think you're in a position to cast aspersions at my lack of houseguests."

"I didn't say it was a bad thing." She yawned as they put their shoes back on.

He reached over and held her hand as they made the trek back out of the ruins and headed back to the bus. Half an hour later, the tour bus stopped at a little plaza and let them off for lunch and more souvenir shopping.

Megan grumbled, "I would have rather spent another hour at the ruins."

"Me, too, but you have to admit, this is pretty good chicken."

"Fine. I'll concede the point." She licked her fingers. It was the best chicken she'd ever had. "We only have one more excursion, right? Key West, so I might as well go nuts with Mexico souvenirs."

"Why not."

Megan found a ceramic replica of El Castillo, along with

several other Mayan-inspired items. "It would have been fun to see the ruins at Chichen Itza, too. Especially the pyramid."

"It would have." He cocked his head. "Do you really need another mug?"

"Nope." Megan grinned. "I do have plans for it, though. See how it's taller than a regular one? I'm going to put my wooden spoons in it so every time I'm in my kitchen I can be reminded of this trip."

"Genius."

They finished their shopping and followed the group back onto the bus. The tour guide had chugged an energy drink or something, because he yammered a hundred miles an hour the whole way back to the ferry. His voice faded into background noise as she rested against Eric's arm and stared out the window.

Back on the ship, they deposited their stuff in their cabins, then went to the upper deck to watch the sun set. Eric dragged two plastic chairs to the railing for them to settle onto. Megan snapped photos of the brilliant orange sky as the dipping sun reflected across the rippling ocean.

Setting her camera down, she simply watched the sky change color. "I rarely pay attention to the sunset at home."

Eric nodded. "Me, either."

"Or the sunrise. I guess I take it for granted."

"So set your alarm and tomorrow we'll watch the sun come up."

She glanced at him. "My alarm is somewhere off the coast of Jamaica, remember?"

"Oh, yeah. Oops. Don't they do wake up calls?"

"I'll have to check. What time do you think we should get up?"

"Sunrise will be around seven or so, I think if we're up at six, we'll be in good shape."

"Ok, then I'll come up around six-fifteen and we can head up. I wonder what time the sun will set tomorrow night. I keep hearing about the amazing Key West sunsets."

Eric smirked. "You can kiss that goodbye."

"Why?"

He held up three fingers. "I've been to Key West three times. Never once got to see a decent sunset. It was always cloudy. I think I'm cursed. Sorry."

"Maybe if you stay below deck you won't ruin it for the rest of us," she joked.

"Fine. At the first sign of cloud cover, I'll head back to my room."

"And stay off the balcony."

"I'll even close my curtains."

"Good."

After a moment, he asked, "Can I order room service?"

She laughed. "No. Take snacks with you, I don't want to take any chances."

"What's on the agenda for this evening?" Eric asked.

"Food. Then sleep. I'm exhausted. Last night was the first time in my life I've been completely drunk."

"I wish I could say the same."

"Big partier, huh?"

"Nah, but I had a few moments in college I pretend I can't remember."

"Pretend?"

"Let me put it this way. You've got mean drunks. You've got mellow drunks. And then you've got stupid drunks. Guess which one I was."

"I'm going with stupid."

"Very stupid. It's a wonder I didn't get myself killed."

"You have to tell me this story."

"Over dinner. I'm starving." He pulled the chairs back to where he'd gotten them from, and they went to eat.

Even though the evening had cooled considerably, they still chose a table outside on the balcony of the burger joint. They ordered their food, and Eric began his story.

"So. One of the kids I hung out with lived close to campus. Parents away for the weekend, big football game win, lots of... school spirit, let's call it. His family was pretty well off, and they had a big pool behind the house."

"This can't be good."

"Nope. There was a construction site a few miles away. A few of us went out and stole some of this huge plastic half-pipe. About this big." He made a circle with his arms. "Looked like it would make the perfect waterslide. We got it around back of the house and set it up against one of the second story windows."

"You didn't."

"Oh, yes, we did." He shuddered. "Drunk kids sliding down the tube all night long, it's a wonder nobody drowned."

"It's horrifying, but I have to admit I'm a little jealous."

"Jealous? You definitely shouldn't be jealous."

"Not necessarily jealous of stealing construction equipment or being inches away from death, but jealous because I was so afraid to step out of line I never did anything. I was boring. I'm still boring. My whole life is one long stretch of boring." She poked a french fry into a little puddle of ketchup.

"Would a boring person throw a perfectly good iPhone into the ocean in Jamaica?"

"Sounds like someone who was provoked beyond her capacity to reason."

"But not boring. It's a great story." He grabbed her hand and planted a kiss on her palm, then let go and picked up his burger.

Megan smiled. "It *is* a great story, isn't it?"

"And a boring person wouldn't climb a rock wall the whole way to the top."

"Or get stuck and cry afterwards? That was pretty lame."

"It was lovely. Lots of people didn't even make it to the top. But you did."

"Hmm."

"A boring person wouldn't hop into a cab in Jamaica and tell the driver to take them to a remote area."

"Also qualifies as stupid. We could have gotten murdered."

"But we didn't, *and* you got me hooked up with the best coffee in the whole world. The coffee shops I wanted to check out would have been second rate next to the plantation. And a boring person wouldn't swim with a dolphin, or ride a horse through the freaking ocean, or any of the things you've done on this trip. Especially singing karaoke after a gallon of piña coladas."

"Okay, so I've been un-boring for a whole week."

"So? You have to start somewhere."

"Why, so I can go home and back to my boring life that'll be even worse now that I know what I've been missing? Maybe I would have been better off staying home." She swirled her straw in her soda, moody.

Eric reached over and tucked a lock of hair behind her ear. "I'm glad you didn't."

"Me, too. I'm tired and grumpy. I think it just hit me that tomorrow is our last day." Swallowing down the sudden emotion, she crumpled up her trash and piled it in the basket her burger came in.

"Hey." He waited until she lifted her eyes. "We have a whole day left. Key West is going to be great."

He was right. Key West was going to be amazing. Megan

took a deep breath and squeezed his hand. "Thanks. You're right. I'll adjust my attitude."

"It'll adjust itself after a good night's sleep."

"Excellent suggestion." Standing, she leaned over to kiss him on the cheek. "I'll see you in the morning."

The elevator ride down to her floor was too fast. This entire trip was going by too fast. Shaking her head, she tried rethinking it. *A whole day. We have a whole day left. Two whole nights.* It wasn't working. It sucked, thinking their trip was almost over. *Their* trip? Crap. Maybe it had been a mistake to spend so much time with Eric. He wasn't any of the things her mother – and undoubtedly Brittney – accused him of.

Her brain decided to argue. How did she know what he was? Just because he'd been a great companion on this cruise didn't mean he was a nice guy back home. It didn't matter. They had one more day together, and she was determined to make the most of it. Then, the following morning, they'd leave the ship and fly home.

The thought of going home filled her with dread. More than the likelihood of not seeing Eric again, she dreaded settling back into her life.

Her lifeless life.

Chapter Twenty-Three

Eric's mood lifted as soon as he saw Megan. She looked rested and happy. He leaned over and kissed her cheek.

A few other early birds were on the top deck watching the sunrise. They picked two chairs a short distance from the other people and settled in to watch the sun come up. Eric watched Megan snap a couple of pictures, but for the most part, they sat still and quiet, watching the blue push the red out of the sky as the sliver of sun rising out of the ocean became a fiery ball.

Checking his watch, Eric stood and held out his hand to help Megan up. "Hungry?"

"Always."

They took their time at the breakfast buffet, but Eric felt like he was stalling. Like maybe if he dragged his feet, their last day wouldn't fly by. Draining his coffee, he lifted his mug and said, "Key West, here we come."

Megan narrowed her eyes. "What's wrong?"

"Nothing, why?" He lied. In spite of his pep talk to her the previous night, he hated that this was their last day together as much as she did.

"If you say so." She reached for his hand. "Let's go, Key West is waiting."

They followed the crowd off the ship, following the signs on the dock to the kayak group they would be touring with. A dozen or so people from the ship were with them on the quick shuttle ride to another dock, where they rode a small boat to the kayak tour location. There, they got a brief safety instruction, and then got in their kayaks.

Eric stayed close to Megan, enjoying watching her juggle her kayak paddle and her camera. Every so often, she would veer toward the shore while taking a picture and have to furiously paddle to right herself.

The two-hour tour took them into the ocean and around the island, through mangroves with lush greenery and through water so clear it looked dangerously deceptively shallow.

The guide pointed out Southern Stingrays, all manner of fish, and even a Sharpnose Shark. In the mangroves, they saw snakes and birds with feathers of every color of the rainbow. The humidity clung to them like a second skin. Deeper in the mangroves, mosquitoes feasted on the bits of flesh they had missed when spraying on repellant.

After the two-hour tour, Eric and Megan opted to walk around the island, into Old Town.

"Let's do the Observation Tower." Eric pointed to the wooden tower they were half a block away from.

Megan checked her brochure. "We have to go through the Shipwreck Historeum."

They paid for their tickets and enjoyed the blast of cool air greeting them in the cramped museum. They held hands as they read the information attached to the shipwreck treasures.

Men in old time clothing barked out facts and stories in pirate voices, both entertaining and educational.

Finally, they pushed through the exit door and climbed the 65-foot tower to the observation deck. Megan took a deep breath. "This is amazing. Let me take your picture."

Eric leaned back against the railing while she shot a photo. "Perfect. I got our ship in the background."

"Your turn." Eric took her camera and snapped a couple of photos. A woman's voice startled him.

Sheila.

"Oh, look, Morty, it's Megan and Eric. Good gracious it's a climb, but boy is this view worth it. Here. Hand me the camera so we can get both of you together." Sheila breathed hard, gripping the railing, hunched over in exhaustion after the climb to the top, but her other hand was reaching for the camera.

Eric obeyed, handing over the camera and taking his place beside Megan. Sheila blew out a tired breath and stood straight, took a bunch of photos, then handed her camera to Megan. "If you don't mind."

"Not at all." Megan took pictures of Sheila and Morty with the ship in the background, then took a photo of the couple with her own camera. "This is incredible."

Eric watched as she took at least a hundred more pictures of the 360° view. The bell on the tower. Their ship. Random things on the ground that caught her interest. He enjoyed watching her work. She was so focused and it was obvious she knew what she was doing.

Sheila fanned herself with a brochure. "Are you joining us in the dining room tonight?"

Eric exchanged a glance with Megan. "I'm not sure where we'll eat."

"We'd love to dine with you again, right, Morty?"

Morty gave a noncommittal grunt, then nodded. "Sure. That'd be nice." An actual sentence.

How could they possibly refuse after Morty spoke? It was like seeing a unicorn. Eric said, "We'll try."

Satisfied, Sheila poked Morty. "We should start back down. 'Til we make it down the steps, the ship will be pulling out. You know how my knee is. I wouldn't have come up here, but it's the one thing I just have to do every time we get to Key West because you can't beat this gorgeous view. Of course, the last time we were here there was a hurricane coming so it was raining and we couldn't come up anyway. It was such a bummer." She waved toward the stairs. "You kids go ahead of us. I'll just slow you down."

Megan started down the stairs. "We'll probably see you this evening. Have fun."

Eric followed her, pausing periodically while she shot photos. "There's a brown bird over there."

Megan shot pictures. "I wonder what it is. It kind of looks like a pelican. Do they have pelicans here?"

"Beats me. Could be a pelican. I don't know much about birds."

"Me, either."

They exited the stairs. He nudged her and pointed. "That one's a chicken."

Megan laughed, snapping pictures of the rooster and several hens wandering down the street. "Good job."

"Hey, I think we have time to do this." Eric held out his brochure and checked his watch. "Trolley tour of the island. We can get on and off."

"Sounds great."

They located the trolley tour and paid their fare. They rode through the streets of Key West while the conductor pointed out points of interest.

"Let's hop off here," Eric suggested when they reached the Southernmost Point buoy. They got off the trolley and took pictures, then went inside the tourist shop to buy the requisite souvenirs.

"I think this is my favorite stop."

"You've said the same thing at every place we've been."

Megan laughed. "I know, but this is so relaxed and laid back. No rushing."

They boarded the next trolley and rode the rest of the circuit through Key West. "We have to find the Cuban Coffee Queen. Stewart and Jody were there last year and said their sandwiches are amazing."

Eric asked directions, and before long, they were seated in a bustling café, eating sandwiches with pork, turkey and ham on Cuban bread, and drinking Cuban iced caramel coffee with milk and coffee ice cubes.

"Your brother has to put this on the menu." Megan sipped her coffee.

"You don't even like coffee."

She raised an eyebrow. "Maybe you've converted me."

"Have I?"

"No. But I'm not anti-coffee anymore, so you can consider it a win."

"A near-conversion. I'll take it." Surprised and pleased, he raised his glass and clinked it with hers.

"Speaking of menu, what else will you guys have besides coffee?"

"We'll have a very limited food menu. Some bakery items and a very few sandwiches, mostly for the quick lunch crowd wanting their caffeine fix and a bite to eat, but they don't want to stop two places."

"Like a brown bag type thing?"

He nodded. "Sort of."

"Sounds interesting. Are they going to be cold sandwiches?"

"Maybe two cold options and two hot options. Those will be more like slow-cooker sandwich things, like pulled pork or barbeque. A different hot option every day."

The crowd bustling around them had faded to a cozy background noise.

"What about soup?"

"Maybe when it's cold, but then we have to order more stuff like bowls and spoons."

"Good point. Although you could put them in coffee cups."

"Interesting." He made a mental note to talk to Stewart and Jody about soups as a possibility. If Megan was asking, other people might, too.

"When are you planning to open?"

He watched her pop the last bite of her sandwich into her mouth and brush her hands together to get the crumbs off. "The renovations are almost done. Once we can get in to get the place furnished and decorated, we'll set a hard date. We're hoping by the end of the year."

"Which is coming up fast."

"I know."

"How often do you think you'll travel to find new coffees?"

Eric hadn't thought a lot about how frequently he'd travel for the shop. "I'd guess once or twice a year. I'm also managing the books, so I need to be around most of the time."

"How'd you go from world travelling tech consultant to coffee shop consultant?"

"My degree is in business management. The consulting job was kind of a fluke. An old college buddy of mine was starting up his company and I got in on the ground floor as part owner. So I pretty much created my own job." He knew better than anyone his success was as much luck as it was hard work.

"Quinn?"

"Actually, a third friend of ours, Harrison, started it. Then he got Quinn on board and then me. We were equal third partners until Harrison sold out his share."

"Why'd he sell?" She swirled the ice cubes in the bottom of her almost empty glass.

"His wife was in an accident. They were skiing in Vermont and she went over a ledge and into a tree. She was in a coma for two weeks. It was bad. Once she recovered – it was a long road, but she did have a full recovery – he was ready to give up the high life and all the travelling to be home with her and their kids."

"Good for him."

"Quinn and I bought him out, making us fifty-fifty partners, about eight years ago."

"Then you got out recently?"

"I'd been thinking about it for a while. I was never comfortable with the schmoozing. Then Brittney and Quinn had their affair and I started getting my ducks in a row to get out. Quinn paid me three times what my shares were worth. He'll make it back over the next year, the way the company's expanding."

"You didn't leverage against those profits?"

Eric shrugged. "Didn't have to. Quinn's guilty conscience worked in my favor."

"Then you used your profits to invest in Stewart's coffee shop."

Nodding, he finished his iced coffee. "I also bought my house. Most of the rest of it went into savings and investments."

"Smart."

He shrugged. "My parents always drilled financial responsibility into us. They worked hard, and we were comfortable because they were careful with their money." Glancing around, he said, "Key lime pie for dessert?"

"Of course."

When they had their pie, Eric prompted, "Your turn."

Megan nodded. "My parents were big on financial responsibility, too. My dad and Uncle Doug – Brittney's dad – co-own the grocery chain now. My great-grandparents opened the first Prescott's in 1947. They had five children, but only one – my grandfather – was interested in the grocery business. Of course all the siblings worked there when they were growing up, but my grandfather was the one who learned the business inside and out. When he took over, he expanded and now there are five locations."

Eric nodded. "I knew Doug was part owner in a grocery chain, but I didn't realize it was a family business. I spent more time with the other side of Brittney's family."

Megan rolled her eyes. "The Rockefellers? I'm being obnoxious, sorry. Aunt Connie is sweet, but her family is snotty. Her parents threatened to disown her if she went through with marrying Uncle Doug. I guess they didn't speak to her for years, until Brittney was born."

"You're kidding."

"Nope. I can't remember what they do. They're all doctors or something, and when Connie dropped out of college to marry a grocery store manager, they blew a gasket. Of course, this is all family legend, they could be lovely people."

"They're nice enough, but they are very fond of their money. And talking about their money. Oh, and it's a plastic surgery practice."

"That's right. I've only met them I think twice in my entire life. One of Brittney's uncles offered to give me a nose job."

"What? Why would you want a nose job? There's nothing wrong with your nose."

"I didn't. I don't. My nose is perfectly fine. He was a creep."
Eric shook his head. "Some people."

They finished their pie and headed back out onto the street.

Eric hated to point out the cell phone store, but he did. "Going in?"

She sighed. "I suppose I should."

They spent the next half-hour getting Megan's new cell phone set up. The employee showed her how to install a backup from her cloud. "You'll want to make sure you're connected to wifi and plugged in, charging."

"Sounds great."

Eric watched her face. She looked conflicted. When they got back outside, he asked, "Are you okay?"

"It's stupid. After I chucked my phone in the ocean, I panicked, but then I felt kind of free."

"It's not stupid at all."

She grunted. "Eh, the only person it hurt was me. I cost myself hundreds of dollars because I was mad."

Eric put his hands on her shoulders and turned her to face him. "Megan. Don't think of it as an act of anger. Think of it as an act of independence. You've been a different person since you threw your phone overboard, more relaxed and calm. Maybe it was an expensive lesson, but now you can put it in its proper perspective."

"I guess."

Eric wanted to shake her and make her understand. It wasn't about the stupid phone.

Megan took his hand. "Let's check out the aquarium."

Chapter Twenty-Four

Megan grinned, holding up a starfish. "I never touched a real one before. It's a lot smaller than the one we saw in Aruba." She was nearly giddy with the excitement of the touch tank, where they were able to reach in the water and touch the creatures. It was geared more towards children, but she didn't care. It was awesome.

"Me, either." He picked up a starfish at the other side of the tank and turned it belly-up. "Its mouth is kind of scary. If it was bigger, I'd be freaked out."

"Ew, scary." Megan gently put her starfish back in the water, then pet a fish lazily swimming past. It unnerved her when he'd said she was a different person after jettisoning her phone off the ship. She'd felt different, but never thought it would be so obvious to someone else.

They moved to the closed tanks along the wall. She put her finger against the glass. "Look, there's an urchin in the back. It's smaller than the one we held in St. Maarten."

"Oh, yeah, on the helmet tour. They look so wicked."

"I know, right. Whoever looked at one of those and thought there might be something delicious under all those spines?"

Shaking his head, Eric said, "Wouldn't have been me. I never would have been the first person to eat a lobster or shrimp, either."

"Or bacon."

"No way. I know where it comes from, but I'm not going to be the guy to get it out."

Megan laughed. "If it was up to me, I probably would have starved to death. I don't imagine I would have looked at a wild head of lettuce and though it would be good food, either."

"Or a tame head of lettuce."

Megan rolled he eyes. "Ha. Very funny. But speaking of lettuce, you could do salads to go in the coffee shop, too."

"Maybe one day a week instead of a cold sandwich. That could work."

"Have you done any surveys or anything? Like to find out what people would like to see?"

A kid shrieked in terror at the tank they'd just been at. He apparently didn't appreciate his dad's attempts to get him to pet a stingray.

Eric waited until the ear-splitting noise stopped. "Jody's the one who does marketing, and I know she's done a ton of research. I'll ask her."

"I assume she's been in touch with Ellery Cameron?"

"Who?"

"He does the food segments on Channel 14, and he also has a food article in the Times."

"If I had to guess, I'd say she has, but I'll ask." He pulled out his phone and made a note.

Megan moved to another open tank with sea turtles. "I shot his daughter's wedding last year. He's been sending people to me ever since, so I'm sure I can put in a good word if Jody hasn't talked to him yet."

"That'd be fantastic. Thanks."

"Don't thank me until you see my consulting fee," she teased.

"Free coffee?"

"Tea. And you have to promise you'll take me along when you go back to the plantation in Jamaica." She regretted the words as soon as they were out. It was ridiculous to even joke about it. Heat flooded her face, so she turned to study the turtle in the tank in front of her to hide the bright red undoubtedly coloring her cheeks.

Eric's hand touched her back. He leaned close to her ear and quietly said, "I promise," then moved away before she could respond.

Megan pretended to be fascinated by the next few tanks she looked at, using the time to try to talk some sense into her pounding heart.

"We should head back to the ship soon."

Megan groaned. "Already? How did it get so late?"

"We still have time to get your souvenirs."

Megan grinned up at him. "The best part of every port."

They walked across the cobblestone road to a shop. Immediately, she pointed up. "I need that."

A piece of driftwood, approximately a foot long, held many strands of transparent string, probably fishing line, from which dangled dozens of beautiful pieces of sea glass in all shapes and sizes, and every shade of blue and green. The pieces of glass made a happy tinkling sound as the moving air from the overhead fan blew them gently into each other.

"It's so perfect. It makes me think of all the different blues in the oceans. Can you reach?"

Eric stretched up and pulled the wind chime from its hook. "Where are you going to put it?"

"I might hang it in the kitchen window."

"It's nice. I might get one for my mom. She likes stuff like this."

"Does she like blue?"

"I think she'd rather have the yellow one." He went to the next aisle and pulled a smaller yellow and orange chime down. "She'll love it."

"I still need to get a magnet."

"Did you get one from everywhere we went?"

"Yup." She moved her hand. "I can see it now. My kitchen windowsill will have my sand bottles all lined up, and my gorgeous new wind chime hanging there, catching the sun, and my fridge will have all my magnets, each one holding a picture from the place the magnet is from."

"Good plan."

"It'll be awesome."

"Mine will probably get shoved in a drawer and never see the light of day again."

Megan laughed. "That's just sad."

"But true."

"No, you have to put them out."

"Fine. I'll put them out. Somewhere."

"Promise."

He sighed dramatically and raised his right hand. "I hereby solemnly swear I will display the souvenirs from this trip somewhere, instead of shoving them in a drawer."

"Good. Not in the bathroom, either."

He laughed. "Not in the bathroom."

Megan selected a few more souvenirs, then made her way to the register.

"Did you get your sand?"

"Yeah," she said. "I got it when we got off the kayaks."

"Good. Now you have them all."

"I should have gotten one for Orlando, too, but I won't be anywhere near the beach."

"You can still get a magnet at the airport," Eric pointed out.

"You're a genius."

"I kind of am."

"And kind of full of yourself."

"You wound me." He clutched his chest in mock agony.

Megan steered him to a bench outside the store and handed him her bags. "I have to fix my shoe. I think there's a little stone in there." She pulled her sneaker off and dumped it out. "Geez, I think there was a whole family in there." Tiny stones fell out of her shoe. "Do we have to head back already?"

"'Fraid so."

They started walking back to the dock. Megan took pictures of everything along the way.

After a few minutes, Eric put his hand on her arm. "Maybe turn it off," he gently suggested.

"I want to remember every detail." Megan felt a bubble of desperation in her stomach. She didn't want to forget anything.

"I want you to see everything with your own eyes, not through the camera lens."

Her heart skipped a beat. He was right. She was so worried about capturing the photos that she wasn't capturing the moment. Her finger flipped the lever to turn the camera off and she snapped the lens cap on. "Thanks."

He slid his hand into hers, lacing their fingers together. They took their time getting back to the ship.

Megan stopped on the dock and looked up at the massive ship that was now home to some of the best moments she'd ever experienced. "How many people do you think have taken their bags off the ship right here and never gone back home?"

"It's probably not the most practical plan." He let go of his hand and put his arm around her shoulders.

"I can fantasize, can't I?"

"Sure."

She sighed. "Fine, let's go."

They boarded the ship and loaded their bags on the security scanner. Megan went through the body scanner and swiped her passcard, then picked up her bags. "Thanks for carrying my stuff. I didn't realize I'd gotten quite so much."

"You're welcome. It's only half an hour or so until sunset." He put his arm around her as they walked to the elevators.

"Did you want to watch the sunset and then go to dinner?"

"Sure."

Megan gestured to her bags. "I'll put my stuff in my room and come get you, then we can head to the top deck."

"Perfect."

The elevator came to a stop on her floor. "I'll be up in about fifteen minutes."

In her cabin, she deposited her bags at the foot of her bed, then plugged her new phone into the charger and tapped the buttons to load a backup from her cloud. Hopefully she wouldn't have to completely recreate her address book. What a pain.

She changed into jeans for the chilly evening and grabbed her sweater before heading back up to get Eric.

After she knocked, he opened the door and said, "You might want to see this. Then you can decide where you want to go."

Confused, she followed him into the room. He pulled back the curtain to his balcony. The sun was starting to dip closer to the water. Strands of faint orange were appearing in the clouds.

Megan pressed her hand to the glass in awe. "This view... Can we just stay here?"

"I was hoping you'd say that. I bet the upper decks will be crowded anyway."

Eric slid open the balcony door, letting the sound of the ocean rush into the room. He sat on one of the lounge chairs and held his hand out to her.

Accepting his unspoken invitation, Megan took his hand and settled on the chair with him, cuddling together to watch the sunset, her arm over his middle, her head on his chest.

"You don't have your camera." His fingertips traced little lines on her shoulder.

Megan nodded. "I got some amazing pictures of the sunsets in Mexico and Aruba and St. Maarten. This time, I decided to take some great advice and watch this one with my own eyes."

"Wow, great advice. Must have come from somebody super smart."

Megan chuckled. "Yeah, he thinks he's a genius."

"He must be."

They quieted as the colors of the sky began to change. The brilliant blue paled. Streaks of pink and orange and lazily spread across the sky. The sun seemed to swell, its fiery light cooling to an orange glow. It slid lower in the sky, inching closer to the calm ocean. The wisps of color blended at the edges of the sky, reflecting in the rippling water.

The sun touched the water. Gulls cried somewhere overhead. The sun sank slowly, the water absorbing its light. Darker blue streaks formed overhead, darkness pushing the light into the water.

The air chilled as the sun dipped lower, a faint breeze kicking up over the water. Megan pulled her sweater tighter. Eric's breath on the top of her head gave her chills, but she wouldn't move for anything in the world.

The last sliver of the sun was pulled underwater. The brilliant oranges and pinks soon slid below the surface, replaced with darkening blues. Tiny twinkling dots of light popped out of the deepest blue, blanketing the sky.

Eric shifted. Megan looked up at him and he lifted his hand to wipe a tear from her cheek. Her fingers tightened on his collar, and she felt him swallow, hard. She looked up, her gaze holding his.

He moved his fingertips, brushing strands of hair from her face, then lifted his chin and took a deep breath. "We should head up to dinner," he said quietly.

Disappointment flooded her. She nodded and stood without a word. In the hallway, she paused. "I'm wearing jeans. They won't let me in the dining room."

"It's the last night. They won't care."

They rode the elevator to the dining deck. Megan glanced at her watch. "What time are we supposed to have our suitcases out in the hallway?"

"By eleven."

"I still have a ton of packing to do. I don't know how I'm going to fit everything in my suitcase, even with all the extra space I left." She rambled, trying to think about anything but the kiss that didn't just happen.

"I know. I have about fifty pounds of coffee beans. I wonder what the overweight bag fee is going to cost me."

Megan laughed. "Don't forget I have your tea, too."

They entered the dining room. Sheila and Morty were already seated.

"Oh, honey, we already ordered. I wasn't sure you were going to make it."

"No problem," Megan answered. "We were running a little late. We had to catch the famous Key West sunset."

Sheila bobbed her head. "We saw most of it, but Morty was too hungry to wait around."

"Were you on the upper deck?"

"Yeah. Along with half the ship." She sounded peeved. "We didn't get much of a view. Where were you?"

"Eric has a balcony, and it was on the right side of the ship to see the whole thing."

Sheila's annoyance vanished. "You're so lucky. One of these days we're going to spring for a balcony room. I tell Morty every cruise, this time we're getting a balcony, then all I hear is complain, complain, complain about the extra cost. Even though this was for our anniversary and we should have splurged, but no, we got another interior cabin with no view at all."

Megan doubted Morty was able to get three words in edgewise.

Sheila patted Megan's arm. "Be sure to get your pictures. I saw lots of you guys when we were getting ours."

"Where?" She couldn't believe she'd forgotten about the pictures the cruise photographer had taken.

"Deck Four. Around the corner by the piano. There's a bunch of boards set up with the pictures."

Megan looked at Eric. "Don't let me forget to stop there."

"We'll go right after we eat."

"Thanks for reminding me, Sheila."

"Oh, I wanted to give you this." Sheila pulled a postcard out of her massive purse. "Here's my Facebook and email so we can stay in touch. We really enjoyed the time we spent with you two."

Morty grunted his agreement.

"You're so sweet. I don't have anything to write on, but I promise I'll be in touch."

They enjoyed their last meal. Sheila once again provided ample dinner conversation, distracting Megan from her increasing disappointment the trip was almost over.

"So do you think you'll cruise again?" Sheila actually paused and waited for Megan to answer.

Megan nodded. "I think so. It's such a great way to travel.

No worries about anything, just show up and let the ship do all the work."

"Exactly. It's why Morty and I cruise all the time. Once you figure up all the costs, it's actually cheaper. Of course a *balcony room* would add a little expense, but it'd be worth it." She sighed in Morty's direction.

"I'm glad we met, Sheila. Maybe we'll run into each other on another ship."

Sheila grinned from ear to ear and put her hands to her chest. "Oh, that would warm my heart. I hope you have safe travels back home."

Megan leaned over to give Sheila a big hug. "Thanks again." She tapped the postcard. "I'll be in touch."

Leaving the dining room, Megan wiped her eye. "Gee whiz, I didn't expect to get all weepy."

"She kinda grows on you, doesn't she?"

"More than I expected." She grabbed his hand. "Let's go see what pictures are hanging down there."

They went to the lower deck, around the grand piano, where a woman in a red sequined cocktail dress was singing a soulful Billie Holiday set. Under the grand staircase, vertical boards were set up with slatted shelves holding all the photos the ship's photographer had taken over the course of the cruise.

"Of course they're not all together." Eric mumbled.

"You start on this end, I'll start over there." Megan walked to the opposite side of the display and immediately found two of their photos. They met in the middle, each with a handful of pictures. Megan grinned. "These are so cheesy and awesome."

Eric's brow scrunched up. "How can something be cheesy and awesome at the same time?"

She held up her pictures. "Like this."

They sorted through their stack of photos. "I don't see the one from Aruba."

Megan shook her head. "I don't see Jamaica, either." They went back to the boards and searched again.

"Found Jamaica," Eric said.

A few minutes later, Megan answered, "Woo hoo, found Aruba."

They sorted the photos, putting them in order. "This should be all of them."

Megan agreed. She leafed through the pictures. "These are so fun." She held up the photo from when the boarded the ship, where they were greeted by a "pirate."

Eric chuckled. "I'm telling you, we could get jobs on a ship. I could be a pirate, and you could take the pictures."

She laughed and handed the stack to the cashier. Eric shoved his ship card at him. "I'm buying these."

"Oh." Crestfallen, she didn't want to admit how much she wanted them. She was at least hoping they'd split them.

Eric gave her a strange look. "You can have them, Megan, but I wanted to pay for them."

"You don't have to."

"I know."

"We can split them."

Eric put his card back in his wallet while the cashier bagged the photos and handed them to Megan.

"Thank you."

"We don't have to split them, Megan. I know you wanted them."

"You don't?" Megan wasn't sure whether to be offended or glad she had them.

He sighed and raised an eyebrow. "I can't win, can I? Yes, I'd like to have them. But what I really want is for you to have them. We can get copies made when we get back home."

Megan stopped in the middle of the floor and grabbed him in a hug. He squeezed her back.

She reluctantly let go. "I guess we need to get packed."

He kept his arm around her as they rode the elevator up to her floor and walked her to her door. "Do you need help with anything?"

"Nah, my many years of Tetris have led me to this very moment. It will all fit in my suitcase. It will." She pushed the door open. "Oh! Everything *will* fit. I forgot I brought Space Bags."

"What?"

"Space Bags. You put your clothes in these bags and squish the air out of them and it makes room."

"Um, okay. If you say so."

"It's like a vacuum sealer for clothes."

"With no vacuum."

"These are the travel ones. You lay them on the floor and squish the air out with your knees. It's like magic."

"Huh."

Megan laughed. "I'd show you if I had anything ready to pack, but I don't. So you need to hit the road so I can get busy."

He hesitated in the doorway. "Breakfast tomorrow?"

"Of course."

"Okay. Good night. I'll see you early in the morning."

Megan closed the door before she could start getting choked up. There was too much work to do to get packed, and moping around wasn't going to make it go any faster.

She laid out her clothes for the next day, then laid out what she was wearing to bed. She decided to shower so she could put most of her bathroom items into her checked bag. When she was done, she changed into a t-shirt and shorts for bed, then laid everything on the bed that needed to go into her suitcase.

"This does not look good," she muttered. "I'm glad I brought the biggest suitcase I could find."

She folded her clothes and got them in the Space Bags, then dropped them on the floor and set to pushing the air out of them. They fit nicely in the bottom of her suitcase. She arranged her souvenirs and photos, filling every inch of available space, then reopened one of the space bags and pulled out some shirts to wrap the breakable souvenirs in. She put her least valuable camera equipment in the suitcase as well, saving room in her carry-on for the clothes she'd be wearing to bed.

She eyed the towel bunny who was sitting on her dresser. "Sorry, buddy, this is going to be uncomfortable." She laid the bunny on top of the pile and flattened him as much as she could before folding the suitcase's flap over him and zipping it shut.

She took a final look through her cabin, making sure there was nothing else she could put in her suitcase, then locked the bag, double checked the color-coded tag, and wheeled it to the hallway. Pulling her hoodie and the next day's jeans on, she grinned, grabbing the two Space Bags she hadn't used, and went up to Eric's room and knocked.

He opened the door and she had to laugh at his frazzled expression. "It looks like a department store exploded in here."

Piles of clothes were everywhere. "I have no idea how I'm getting this all in my suitcase."

She held up the bags. "I have the answer. Here. Fold a pile of clothes and then slip them into the magical bag."

"Magical? Make them disappear, then I don't have to worry about getting them home."

"Less talking, more folding."

Eric folded clothes and put them into the bag.

"Now check this out." Megan set the bag on the floor, then

knelt on it, squishing the air out with her knees. The bag flattened, pushing air out the valve.

"I have to admit, those bags are pretty cool."

Studying the bag, Megan said, "I think we could have gotten more in here. Let's fill the other one and if we still need more space we'll see if we can fit anything else in this one."

Eric filled the other bag as full as he could, then squished the air out of it. "What time do you disembark?"

"Eight. You?"

"Seven fifteen."

"Wow, that's early. When's your flight?"

"I think it's at ten."

"We're not running into each other at the airport, then. My flight isn't until three."

"Yuck, you'll be sitting in the airport forever."

She shrugged and rearranged some of the things he'd already packed. "I can finish setting up my new phone."

"Did it transfer everything?"

"Not everything, but it looks like my whole address book is there, so I'm happy." She handed him a bag of coffee beans. "You'll have the best smelling suitcase on the plane."

"And the most overweight one."

They managed to get all of his coffee beans and clothes into his bag.

"Do you have room in your carryon for the stuff you're wearing now?"

"Ah, crap. No."

"You should be able to fit it all in here."

He sighed. "Next time, I'm bringing a second suitcase."

"Me, too. And don't forget your towel dog."

Eric grabbed him from the nightstand. "I don't want to leave him behind."

"Did you name him yet?"

"No. I'm thinking I'll call him 'Towel Dog' or something crazy."

"Wow, what imagination." She laughed.

Eric looked around the room. "I think I've got everything."

Megan glanced at her watch. She quipped, "One more turn about the deck?"

"Was that accent supposed to be British?"

"Yes."

"It was awful." He grinned.

"You recognized it, so it couldn't have been too bad."

"Touché."

Eric grabbed her hand and pulled the door shut. They went to the top deck where a few guests were milling about. "I thought it'd be more crowded."

"Me, too. I guess everyone's busy getting their stuff packed."

He sucked in a breath. "Not everyone." He steered her in the opposite direction of Chuck and Emma, who were chatting intensely with another couple.

Megan snickered and pulled him to the far end of the deck, where they leaned on the railing, looking out over the black ocean. She leaned into Eric's side. "I'm tired, but I don't want to go to sleep. As soon as I do, it's time to get off the ship."

"I know what you mean. I'm dreading it myself."

"What was your favorite part of the trip?" The breeze was blowing her hair. She pulled it back and stuffed the ends into her hoodie.

"The dolphins were pretty great. What about you?"

"Horses. Or the dolphins. Nah... the horses. It was awesome riding the horses through the water."

"So if we rode the dolphins, they'd be your favorite?"

"Most definitely."

They fell quiet, watching the stars twinkle.

Eric cleared his throat. "I hate to say this, but we should get some sleep."

"Sleep is overrated." She managed a smile, but she hated, hated the thought of this trip ending. "You're cold, aren't you?"

"Did my relentless shivering give it away?"

"I think it was the chattering teeth." Megan reluctantly straightened away from the railing. "Fiiiiiiiine," she sighed.

"We could grab a blanket and chill on my balcony."

"Perfect."

They made their way back to his suite and pulled the blanket off the top of his bed, then settled into the lounge chair on the balcony.

"Better?"

"Much," he answered.

She snuggled into his shoulder and grinned. "I think you were faking being cold. You planned this, didn't you?"

He laughed. "I didn't, but it seems to have worked out pretty well."

"At least your room is on the right side of the ship. This would stink if we were facing the dock."

"I agree."

The stars filled the sky and reflected on the still water, along with the crescent moon.

Megan yawned. The salty air breeze played with the loose strands of hair, tickling her face. She fought the tears threatening to form behind her eyes. She leaned up and kissed Eric on the cheek before pulling away.

"I should –"

"Yeah."

He walked her to the door, grabbing her in a hug before releasing her. Megan went back to her room and closed the door softly. She carefully double checked nothing else needed to go into her luggage, then curled up in bed, trying not to cry.

Chapter Twenty-Five

First thing in the morning, Eric finished packing his carry on, throwing his half-used toiletries in the trash. He brushed his teeth and ran a hand through his still damp hair. He wanted to be excited about all the coffees he had to share with Stewart, but all he could think about was Megan.

He took one last look in the mirror and set his bag on the dresser, then stepped out on the balcony and pulled in a deep breath. The early morning sky was beginning to lighten. Inside, he picked up his carry-on bag and did one last check to make sure he hadn't forgotten anything before stepping into the hallway and pulling the door shut for the last time.

He made his way through the bustling groups of people filling the corridors and open areas, to the breakfast buffet. The room was packed with tourists and their bags. As he was scanning the room for a spot, a couple vacated a small table against the windows. He snagged it before anyone else could claim it.

A smile burst out when he saw Megan come through the door, her eyes searching the room. For him. He lifted a hand just as she saw him and smiled.

Shoving her bag under the table, Megan sighed. "I think this is the most packed I've seen the hallways since we got on board."

"Go grab your breakfast. I'll guard the table."

"You were here first. And you'll have to leave first. So you go."

Eric stood and shook his head. "Fine."

He grabbed two trays and loaded them with food. The pineapple bowl was almost empty, and he knew Megan would be disappointed if she didn't get any, so he scooped it all onto her plate. Back at the table, he set a tray in front of her.

"You're so sweet. I didn't expect you to get mine."

"Eh, some of the stuff was getting low, I thought I better grab the last of the pineapple for you."

"Thanks. You are the absolute best."

He watched her bite into her favorite fruit, unsettled by how much it mattered to him that she had pineapple.

They ate quickly, half-listening for the disembarkation announcements over the dull roar of conversation and clinking silverware. Every fifteen minutes or so, a group would heed the announcements and exit the room. Eric sipped his coffee while Megan finished the last of her breakfast.

"Let me know when you get home."

"I will," she answered. "Give me your number and I'll text you."

They added each other's information to their phones. The loudspeaker announced the next group.

Eric's heart pounded. "That's me."

"Oh."

He stood. "Well. I guess this is it, then."

"I guess so. I'll take care of your tray, don't worry about it."

"Okay, thank you."

While he was trying to decide what to do, Megan jumped to her feet and threw her arms around his neck. He wrapped his arms tightly around her, burying his face in her hair, breathing in her coconut shampoo. He wanted to say something, anything, to prolong this moment, to put off walking away from her. Looking down into her eyes, instead of speaking, and without the full intention of doing so, he pressed his lips against hers. For a split second, he was afraid it was a mistake, but the notion vanished when she kissed him back.

They stood there, locked together, holding each other, kissing each other, for several long moments, but not nearly long enough. He hated to, but he pulled back. She tasted like pineapple and syrup and sunshine. He reached down and picked up his bag while still keeping one hand on Megan's hip.

Words flew through his mind, swirling, itching to come out as he tucked her hair behind her ear, trailing his fingers down her jaw. He kissed her lightly, then took a deep breath.

She gave him a brilliant smile that almost fooled him. "You better get going."

Smiling back, he nodded, knowing she didn't want him to see her fighting the tears welling up behind her eyes. "Okay. Have a safe trip home."

He blurted out, "I miss you already."

"Me, too," she said.

He kissed her again, then walked away quickly, through the doorway and down the hall to the exit deck, where he joined the line of passengers leaving the ship. Every step sucked. He trudged at the rear of the line, through the gates, into a massive warehouse-sized room filled with a sea of carefully organized suitcases, claimed his bag and climbed into the shuttle bound for the airport.

His dark mood was in stark contrast to the bright sunny

skies with fluffy white clouds. He tried to think about – and then not think about – what would happen when he got back home. At the airport, he checked his bag for his flight, paid the overweight fee, found his gate, and sat, staring out the window, across the tarmac.

Chapter Twenty-Six

Megan sipped her tea, watching the room empty, bit by bit. She'd managed to hold back the tears, though she didn't know how. It had taken everything she had to not run after Eric the instant he vanished through the doorway. But she'd managed, because clinging to him wasn't going to postpone the inevitable.

She double checked her paperwork in the side pocket of her carry-on bag, then flipped her camera on for a few last shots through the window, and of the mostly empty dining room with their long, long buffet tables.

As she emptied their breakfast trays into the trash, a voice behind her said, "*Mi corazón*, how was your vacation?"

His brown eyes were hypnotic, to be sure. "Good, thank you."

"I am glad." No tingles ran down her spine when Marco smiled at her this time. "I hope to see you again, Megan."

Her group was announced over the loudspeaker. "Take care, Marco." Suddenly anxious to be off the ship, she rushed to the exit deck and joined the procession out across the ramp and into the area where she claimed her suitcase. The shuttle driver hefted her suitcase into the back while she took a seat, hoping for a quick and quiet ride to the airport.

"Oh, sweetheart, I'll sit back here with you. Where's Eric?" Sheila squeezed herself into the back, beside Megan. Morty followed suit, squishing himself into the third seat.

Megan forced a smile. "He had an earlier flight."

"What happened with you two? You make such a cute couple."

"We're not a couple."

Sheila's disbelief was evident. "Please."

Megan sighed. "We told you the first time we met. We're just friends."

"Uh huh. I think what you said was 'it's a long story' but you never told me the story."

"It *is* a long story." Megan tried to let it drop.

Sheila patted her hand. "Okay, Megan." She changed the subject, talking about their excursions and the souvenirs they'd bought for their kids and grandkids.

Megan willingly went along with the topic, telling Sheila about her bottles of sand and the postcards she'd mailed her best friend and herself from every port.

They arrived at the airport and parted ways, only to meet back up at the gate.

"Are we on the same flight?" Megan asked.

Morty looked over their tickets. "We sure are." Another full sentence. She couldn't wait to tell Eric.

Fate's sense of humor put them not only on the same plane, but seated them in the same row.

Megan was at the window. Sheila switched with Morty to have the middle seat and delivered a running commentary until they had taken off and were in the air. Then, she changed direction and said, "Now you have time to tell me your long story."

"I guess I do." Megan adjusted her seatbelt and leaned her head back on the seat. "Eric was engaged to my cousin."

Sheila's eyebrows rose the tiniest bit.

"It doesn't matter, but we were never close. They were supposed to get married on this cruise. My dad and uncle thought it would be good for me to tag along and take wedding photos for them. Much cheaper than the package photographer, and my dad knew this would be the perfect opportunity for me to build my travel portfolio. Well, right before the flight, she called the whole thing off. I decided to go anyway, since I'd already laid out a ton of money for the trip, and I could use it for my travel work."

"Sure."

"I had no idea Eric was here until we met in the airport in Orlando."

"So no monkey business."

"None." Megan shook her head. "We'd only spoken twice. Ever. Very briefly, and my cousin was there both times because we were talking about the wedding photos. He just kind of nodded and said we should do whatever she wanted."

"So why did she call it off ?"

"I'm not exactly sure. He had quit a high brow consulting job in order to partner with his brother in a coffee shop. I guess she was afraid the constant flow of money would dry up."

"Hmm. Do you think it's true? Is she like that?"

Megan nodded. "Very much so. Her mom comes from a high society family. They nearly disowned her when she married my uncle. Then when Brittney came along, they were back in the picture. I guess she always had a desire for the finer kind of life."

Sheila's brow furrowed. "Do you think they loved each other?"

"I don't know. Maybe at the beginning? Maybe not. She cheated on him, so I don't think he trusted her."

"Seems kind of quick for him to get over her and be head over heels for you, which he obviously is. Maybe he's glad she called it off. I don't see him being the kind of guy who can turn his feelings off and on."

Morty snorted. Sheila elbowed him.

"Ow. Whadja hit me for?"

"Don't be impolite."

"Don't elbow me."

"Did you have something to say?"

Morty sighed and ran a hand over the few remaining wisps of hair at the top of his head. "Listen. I bet she's good looking, right?"

Sheila glared, but Megan nodded. "She's stunning."

Morty shrugged. "There you go."

Sheila rolled her eyes. "It's not that simple."

"Sure it is. It starts out good, it goes south, but she's gorgeous. A man'll forgive a *lot* from a beautiful woman with a decent rack."

Megan was half shocked Morty was talking so much, and half shocked at what he was saying.

Sheila grunted. "Eric's not like that."

"Sure he is. All guys are. You get what you think is the brass ring, and you hang on tight until you can't hang on anymore. It's hard to believe a good looking woman can be truly rotten inside."

"Ridiculous." Sheila crossed her arms in a huff.

Morty winked over at Megan and patted Sheila's arm. "Hey, most guys aren't as lucky as me. I got a woman who's good *and* gorgeous."

Megan chuckled.

Morty continued. "I'm not saying it's right or wrong, but

he's a decent man, and he intended to see his commitment through, good or bad. I say he got lucky she bailed." With a firm nod of his head, a clear signal he was done talking, Morty leaned back in his seat and settled in for a nap.

Sheila shrugged. "Maybe he's right. I don't know. But I *do* know he's crazy about you."

Megan smiled faintly. "It doesn't matter. My mother was livid I even spoke to Eric on this trip, let alone had fun with him."

"So?"

"What do you mean, 'so'?"

"Does your mother pay your bills? Does she tuck you in at night? You need to live your life to make you happy, not your mother." Sheila pointed a long, bright red nail in Megan's direction. "Mind you, I'm only saying this because I believe there was no hanky panky going on. You didn't have anything to do with them breaking up, you didn't steal him away, or anything."

"There was definitely nothing like that."

"Everything works out like it's supposed to... if we let it."

"Easy to say. It's... everything's so complicated."

"Life's complicated. But I bet it seemed a whole lot simpler when you were with Eric, didn't it?"

Megan leaned back in her seat and turned to look out the window. Yes, life seemed simpler with Eric, but life seemed simpler on a ship in the middle of the Caribbean in perfect weather with perfect scenery and no responsibilities and no mundane daily chores.

Back home, being involved with Eric would be anything but simple.

Chapter Twenty-Seven

Eric ordered some of the tiny bottles of liquor. The flight attendant ran his credit card, then handed the bottles over with a smile. Somewhere far behind him, Chuck and Emma occupied two seats. He'd pretended not to see them board, and they'd returned the favor. In his own row, he sat at the window while Brittney's empty seat separated him from the man in the aisle seat.

He emptied the first little bottle in two gulps.

"You all right there, buddy?" The man had a slow, Texas drawl.

"Great."

"I'm Ted."

"Eric." He reached over and shook the man's outstretched hand. Of course he'd end up seated with a talker. At least it was a short flight.

"Woman troubles?"

Eric snorted. "Isn't it always?"

Ted laughed, a deep chuckle. "All the troubles worth having, anyway. What's your story?"

If Ted wanted to talk, he'd talk. Why not. "Short version? I got dumped and then met the woman of my dreams."

"Doesn't sound like trouble to me." Eric half-smiled.

"They're family."

"Ouch. I had a similar problem with a pair of sisters once. Didn't end well."

"Cousins. They're not close, but still... It'd be awkward and I'm not sure she's up for the kind of drama it'd create."

"Tough one. I suppose everyone's pretty tight knit."

"Geographically, yes. Small town. Loose lips. It's too close to make it okay for her and I to end up making anything happen."

"What are you going to do?" Ted drawled.

Eric held up his second bottle. "I'm going to get drunk."

Ted held up his own mini bottle of scotch. "Cheers, my friend." They clinked their little bottles together and swigged.

After a few minutes, Ted narrowed his eyes. "You know, maybe in the hard light of day, when you get back home, you'll realize she's not as great as you're thinking right now. It's easy to think a woman's great when you're coming off the heels of one who's not. Maybe you get home and start to see the warts and whatnot and realize you're better off swimming in a whole other gene pool."

Somehow, he didn't think so. "Maybe you're right, Ted."

Eric turned to the window. When they landed in Atlanta, he shook Ted's hand again and wished him a good trip. After stopping in the restroom, he came out to see Chuck and Emma heading toward baggage claim. Hopefully their backs were the last he'd ever see of them.

His leg bounced with impatience as he sat and waited for his next flight. More than ever, he just wanted to get home and talk to Stewart.

When he got on the plane, he texted Megan.

> Boarded in Atlanta. How's your trip?

A few minutes later, his phone vibrated.

> You'll never believe it. Sheila and Morty were my seat-mates from Orl to Char!

He laughed.

> No nap, huh?

> LOL No one around us, either.

A few seconds later, another message came in.

> You'll never believe it but Morty actually talked for like FIVE MINUTES!!

A shocked-face emoji ended the message.

The flight attendant came around telling everyone to turn off their devices. It was the first time in his life he was annoyed to be sitting on a plane running on schedule.

> No way. Need proof. Gotta run, ready to take off.

The immediate reply:

> Stay away from the little bottles. I won't be there to carry you home. LOL

He replied with a smiley face, then turned his phone off. This time, the man next to Brittney's empty seat wasn't interested in conversation. Just as well. He ordered a bottle of water and spent the time staring out the window, trying to keep his mind on what coffee brews would work best in the café. His wretched brain was associating every flavor from this trip with Megan.

Half an hour into the flight, he annoyed the person in the aisle seat by climbing over and retrieving his notebook and a pen from his bag in the overhead compartment. He apologized as he climbed back to his seat, where he made notes about menu items, daily specials, and any extras they'd need, such as bowls or spoons. He tried to note which ideas had been Megan's. He didn't want to take credit for her thoughts.

Soon, he was doodling coffee beans and palm trees instead of working on his list. It served its purpose, though, and kept him busy for the rest of the flight.

He waited patiently in baggage claim, watching the board for incoming flights. Megan's flight from Charlotte wouldn't be in for almost three hours. He debated waiting, but then what? What was his plan? How would it look if he was standing there when her mother arrived to pick her up? It would only create more unnecessary drama for her.

A lady nearby was struggling to pull her suitcase off the conveyor belt. Eric grabbed it and heaved it to the floor for her, then caught his own suitcase and pulled it off the belt as she thanked him. Thank goodness for wheels on suitcases. He hooked his carryon bag to the handle of the suitcase and walked through the sliding glass doors. A blast of frigid air went straight through him.

The warmth and bright colors he'd woken up to in Florida felt like a world away. Here, the leaves were gone, the landscape brown and cold. Typical November.

He caught a shuttle to the parking lot, thanked the driver, and popped the trunk of his car. After wrestling his suitcase into submission, Eric started the car and rubbed his hands together to warm them before starting the hour-long drive home.

Chapter Twenty-Eight

Megan's seatmate on the way from Charlotte was moody and silent, glaring at the window from time to time.

"Did you want the window?" Megan asked her.

The woman, probably in her fifties, gave her a filthy look. "If I wanted the window, I'd be sitting at the window."

"Um, okay?"

The woman squeezed her eyes shut briefly. "Sorry."

"I'm Megan. Do you want to talk about it?"

"Carly. No. Yes. I don't know." She twisted a ring around on her finger. "My life's a mess, and it's my own fault."

Megan waited patiently for her to continue.

"My husband left me, my kids hate me, I have no friends, and I'm left with nothing."

"What happened?"

"I spent my whole life building my career, and I let it consume me. I worked late, I missed Little League games and dance recitals. I never took more than a month for maternity leave. Dedicated employee." She snorted. "For all the good it did me."

"What do you do?"

Carly gave a humorless laugh. "Nothing now. I was in pharmaceutical sales. Then the company I worked for was bought out. The new company wasn't particularly interested in keeping any of the old sales staff. Numbers aside, we weren't young and cute. So here I am, moving back home to live with my mom. I get to look forward to a minimum of six months of 'I told you so'." A miserable expression turned her mouth downward.

"I'm sorry."

"Me, too. Here's some advice, Megan. Don't let yourself end up at a point in your life where you look back and regret every decision you ever made."

"You can't work it out with your husband?"

Carly smirked without humor. "I doubt his new wife would appreciate it. As much as it sucks for me, he's happy, and unfortunately the kids like her. She's all sweet and adoring. Barf. They've put up with her for six years. I got tired of her after about six minutes." She scowled at the seat in front of her.

Megan first felt bad for Carly's family, assuming Carly had shared quite a bit of bitterness over the past six years. Then she thought about Carly's comment about regret. The spiteful part of her brain argued that she couldn't look back and regret her life's decisions because she'd never really made any. Which was a bad decision in and of itself. No more.

Carly put her headphones in and closed her eyes, signaling the end of the conversation. Megan gladly retreated into her own thoughts, occasionally snapping a photo of the clouds, or a tiny, random town below. She couldn't wait to get home, yet she dreaded it.

Her new phone had been uncharacteristically silent. She'd sent her mother two messages, one letting her know the other phone had been damaged and the other with her flight information, but had heard nothing in return.

210 · CARRIE JACOBS

The plane touched down. As soon as they were stopped and everyone's phones came out, she called her parents' house, but there was no answer. She tried her mother's cell phone, but it went straight to voicemail. She texted to let them know the plane had landed.

"Good luck," she said to Carly. Carly simply said, "You, too."

Megan took her time leaving the plane. She pulled her bag down from the overhead and made her way to the door, where the perky flight attendant wished her a good evening.

Megan paused in the plane's doorway. "Do you like your job?"

Surprised, the flight attendant gave her a genuine smile. "I love it."

"Did you always want to do this?"

"Pretty much."

"I'm glad. Good for you."

"Are you interested in becoming a flight attendant? We have a brochure."

"No, thanks. I was just curious. Safe travels."

The attendant smiled again and went about her business. Megan followed the last of the passengers down the corridor, out into the hallway and through the gates to baggage claim. She checked her phone. Nothing. She tried calling again. No answer. She texted. No response.

She was starting to feel uncomfortable. They knew when she was getting home. She reasoned maybe there was no reception in the parking garage. She pulled up her email and double checked the information she had given her mother. The flight was right on time. She called again. Nothing.

She dialed Beth's number.

"Hey, are you back home?" Her best friend's voice brought a smile to her face.

"Sort of. I have a massive favor to ask."

"Anything."

"My parents aren't here to pick me up, and I can't get a hold of them at the house or on Mom's cell."

"Do you need me to pick you up?"

"I'm not sure. Would you mind terribly driving by their place and seeing if they're home?"

"Let me call you right back." The line went dead.

Megan pulled her suitcase over to a row of rocking chairs in the lobby near the baggage claim. She sat at the end of the empty row.

A couple of minutes later, her phone vibrated. "Sorry to hang up, but Zach was on his way home from the store. I had him do a loop and see if they were home. He saw your dad coming out of the garage. He didn't see your mom, so he didn't know if she was home or not."

Megan's brow furrowed. "She wouldn't come to the airport by herself."

"Is everything okay?"

"I have no idea. Do you think I can get an Uber or something this far from home?"

"Megs, that would cost a fortune. I'll come get you. It's not a problem," she added, no doubt anticipating Megan's reluctance to accept the favor. "You'd do it for me."

"Yes, but I don't have five kids to worry about."

"Zach just pulled in. He can worry about them. I'm leaving right now. I'll text you when I get to the parking garage, okay?"

"Beth, you're the best."

"I know. On my way."

Megan hung up, both grateful and annoyed. She texted her mother's phone again, this time letting her know she had gotten a ride, then backspaced over a comment that would only cause more drama.

Beth had been her best friend off and on since high school. She didn't need to explain anything about her weird family dynamic. Beth simply understood.

Megan spent the hour watching people come and go. She tried not to openly stare as a woman in a military uniform burst into tears and threw herself into the arms of the man who had come to pick her up. They were both too occupied to notice her snapping a picture of them.

She counted the floor tiles and stairs leading to the next level. Finally, her phone vibrated with a text from Beth.

In parking garage.

Sore from travelling all day, Megan struggled out of the chair and pulled her ever-heavier suitcase up the escalator and toward the parking garage. Halfway down the hall, Beth met her with a huge hug and grabbed the handle of her suitcase.

"So? How was the trip? Anything interesting I should know about?"

Megan snorted. "I figured you would have already heard."

Beth's eyebrow raised. "Heard what?"

"One more way I've humiliated and disappointed my mother." They stepped onto the moving sidewalk and rode through the empty corridor.

"What'd you do, pick out your own clothes?"

Megan had to laugh. "Have I told you lately how much I love you?"

"Not for ten whole days."

"I don't know what I'd do without you."

"Walk, apparently. Or end up hacked to pieces by a psycho impersonating an Uber driver." Stepping off the moving sidewalk, they walked through the automatic door that opened into the parking garage.

Megan shivered against the sudden rush of cold air and shoved her hands into the pocket of her hoodie. "Thanks for coming."

"No problem." Beth hit a button on her key, popping open the back of her red minivan. She hefted the suitcase in. Megan carefully placed her carryon bag beside it, and shut the hatch.

Megan opened the passenger door and picked up a pile of papers and a violin case.

"Sorry, I didn't want to take time to move everything. Chuck it all in the back."

She set the items on the back seat and climbed in.

"Okay, as soon as I figure out how to get out of here, I want to hear everything." Beth leaned forward, following the tiny exit signs to the tollbooth.

Megan paid the parking fee and waited until they were out of the garage and onto the road. "The trip was amazing. I mean, it was everything I could have possibly hoped for and then some."

"The last you told me, the wedding was canceled. What happened there?"

"Yeah. Brittney canceled the wedding... but Eric went on the trip anyway."

Beth's eyes got wide and a grin spread across her face. "Well, well, well. Get you out of Hickory Hollow and all sorts of exciting things happen, huh?"

"Stop. It's not like that ."

"Okay, so what's it like?"

Her mind conjured up an endless parade of images of Eric contradicting her insistence that it wasn't *like that*. "Well... I did end up spending most of the trip with Eric. They had all these non-refundable excursions booked, and I hadn't booked any, so we went together. Not *together* together."

"Mmm. Okay. Sounds fun. What kind of excursions?"

"We did a dolphin encounter and rode horses in the ocean and went to see some Mayan ruins, and some other stuff."

"I can't wait to see the pictures. So... nothing romantic went on?"

Butterflies roared to life in Megan's belly, just thinking about Eric's kiss before he left the ship. "Well. I mean, um..."

Beth was grinning. "Did you kiss him?"

"No." Technically, he kissed her. "Okay. Sort of. Once. It was right when he was getting off the ship and we hugged and then he kissed me. I feel horrible."

"Why? Was it bad? All tongue and slobber? Ick."

Megan had to laugh. "No! The kiss was perfect. I feel bad because he was hours away from marrying my *cousin*."

"So? Once she dumped him, he was fair game."

"Tell it to my family," she grumbled.

"Wait. How did they find out anything other than the two of you being on the same boat? I thought you weren't able to text or call from the ship?"

"I was able to, it's just so expensive once you're out of the country. My mother called me – one of a million calls – and told me I wasn't allowed to speak to Eric. When I changed the subject, I was stupid enough to tell her about this lady I met, and I used her name, so Mom did some Facebook stalking and saw a perfectly innocent picture of me and Eric sitting together in the dining hall."

"Uh-oh."

"So she called me and said I was a liar and told me how I was an embarrassment, you know, the usual."

"She's horrible. What did you do?"

"Well, when we were leaving Jamaica, she called and told me I was a disgrace to Danny's memory, and I kinda threw my phone overboard."

"She said what? Wait, you what?" Beth covered her open mouth.

"I couldn't take it anymore, so we were on a balcony and I didn't even think. I couldn't listen to one more word, so I pitched the phone out into the ocean."

Her surprised laughter filled the van. "Oh, my goodness. Did you try to jump in after it?"

Megan laughed. "No, but I did panic a little bit. I got a new phone in Key West two days later."

"How many times did she call you?"

"I had at least five hundred calls, voicemails, text messages, Facebook messages, Skype calls... you name it, I had it."

"You're exaggerating."

"You know I'm not. I'm terrified of what my phone bill is going to be. There were warnings all over the ship about keeping your phone in airplane mode, but I knew she'd freak out even worse if I didn't get her messages and respond."

"Ridiculous. She should pay it."

"And then there's the bit about leaving me stranded at the airport, which is freaking awesome."

"I can't believe they left you there."

"I can believe *she* did, but I can't believe Dad didn't come get me."

"Yeah, that's a little fishy. I'd guess he had no idea when you were getting back."

"He needs his own cell phone."

Beth put on her turn signal and took the exit the GPS instructed. "Did you meet anyone? Other than Eric?"

"The omelet chef was hot. Like smoking, panty dropping *hot*. He tried to hook up with me, but I couldn't go through with it."

"Wait. You mean actually *hook up* as in no-strings vacation sex?"

Megan giggled. "Yes."

"Wow. Who *are* you?" Beth teased. "Details, please."

"His name was Marco, he was from Portugal, tall, brown eyes, sexy accent, broad shoulders, the whole nine yards. And the image you have in your head right now? He's even hotter."

Beth sighed. "Sounds dreamy."

"He took me into this empty room where they do yoga and dance lessons, and he gave me a salsa lesson, which was like a twelve on a hotness scale of one to ten. Then kissed me, which was about a seventeen. I thought my head was going to literally explode." She tapped her fingers to her temples and flung them outward, miming her exploding head.

"I need to take a cruise." She glanced at Megan. "With Zach, of course."

"Of course."

"How on earth did you resist Marco? Even his freaking name is hot. *Mmmarco...*"

"I'm not an idiot. I'm sure he hooks up with new passengers on every cruise. Probably several. Who knows what kind of critters he's picked up."

"That's what condoms are for."

Megan gasped and laughed, shocked at Beth's comment. "Says the woman who's only been with one guy in her whole life. Who, by the way, is Hottie McHottie himself."

"It's called living vicariously. You don't pick up Hottie McHottie's nasty socks, which never seem to hit the hamper," she grumbled good naturedly. "And romance novels only go so far. Now back to you and Eric."

Megan turned to look out the window at the darkening landscape before answering. "I like him. We had a lot of fun together. He and his brother, Stewart, are opening a coffee shop on Market Square. So after the excursions on each island, we'd find little local un-touristy coffee shops and buy beans to have specials for the shop. We went to this out of the way coffee plantation and they gave him twenty pounds of coffee beans."

"I bet those were fun to fit into a suitcase."

"He was so sweet and we had such a good time. We talked about everything under the sun."

"Including your cousin, I assume?"

"Of course."

"And he had some good reason for it to be over?"

"She called it off. I think that's a pretty good reason."

"Was he cheating or something?"

Megan debated how much to tell, then settled on the whole truth. "No... she was. With his former business partner."

"Wow. That would explain why he didn't stay home and try to win her back. Do you think he was being honest? I mean, it would have been easy enough to make something up."

There was no doubt in her mind. "I do. There wouldn't have been much point to lying when I'd have found out the truth as soon as I got home anyway."

"Do you want to see him again?"

The question was a punch to the gut. "It's not going to happen. Everybody would have a cow if I started dating Brittney's ex-fiancé."

"So?" Beth rolled her eyes.

"Maybe he's not even interested. It was a nice vacation, we had a nice time, and now it's over. No big deal."

"No big deal?" Beth glanced away from the road to look at Megan. "Then why are you trying not to cry?"

A tear slipped and ran down her cheek. She brushed it away. "A lot of reasons. I'm exhausted and angry at my mother and just want to go home." With a sigh, she continued. "Yes, I like Eric. A lot. I'm disappointed we won't see each other here at home. I loved traveling and being away. I felt free for the first time in my whole life, especially after I threw my phone in the ocean. I still can't believe I did that."

"I can't, either." Beth changed lanes and reached over to turn the heat up. "What else?"

"He was a perfect gentleman. Nothing happened. I mean, we spent most of our time together, and we did hold hands a lot, which was so nice, but we talked about it and both of us decided there wasn't going to be anything between us after we got back because it's just too much drama. And now I'm glad to be back home, but I have so much dread it's like a black pit in my stomach because I absolutely have to deal with my family issues. I'm not sure what to do with all these emotions."

Taking one hand off the wheel, Beth patted her arm and said, "You don't do anything with them tonight. Get some rest. You've been traveling a lot, and today was exhausting. Go home and go to bed. If you can't sleep, take a hot bath and have a glass of wine."

"Good advice."

"Now tell me more about the dolphins. How awesome were they?"

Megan told Beth the details of the excursions until they pulled into her driveway.

"Thank you so much for coming to get me." Megan gave her a big hug. "I love you."

"Love you, too. I'll wait until you get inside." Beth pulled the suitcase out of the van and set it on the sidewalk.

Megan grabbed the handle and wrestled it up the staircase leading to her second-floor apartment, then pulled it along the upper sidewalk to her door. She unlocked the door and pushed it open, then turned to give Beth a wave.

Beth waved back and pulled out.

Megan locked the door behind her and wheeled the suitcase straight to her bedroom, changed into sweats, tied her hair up and went to the kitchen to grab a bottle of water from the fridge. On her way back to the bedroom, she turned off all the lights, then flopped down on the edge of her bed to plug her phone into the charger. When it lit up, she saw a message.

> Checking to make sure you got home okay.

It was from Eric, half an hour earlier.
She texted him back.

> Just walked in the door. Exhausted.

> Sweet dreams.

With a smiley face.
Megan smiled at the message.

> You, too.

She stretched and climbed under the covers.

Chapter Twenty-Nine

First thing in the morning, Eric unpacked the coffee beans and took them to the kitchen, organizing them from his least to most favorite. He put a scoop of the Jamaican Blue Mountain beans into his grinder and brewed two big mugs. One for him and one for Stewart, who was coming with breakfast.

Stewart arrived with a bag of doughnuts just as the coffee finished dripping into the second mug. "Something smells amazing."

Eric handed him a mug. "Wait 'til you taste it. It's phenomenal."

Stewart sat at the table and sipped. "Wow."

"I shouldn't have started with the best one. It's my favorite."

"I can see why. Can we order it? This should be a permanent fixture on the menu."

"I'm working on it."

Leaning forward, Stewart picked up another bag of coffee and casually said, "So tell me about your trip. Did you spend the whole time holed up in your cabin, avoiding the other passengers at all costs, only slinking out to procure coffee?"

"Not exactly."

Stewart raised an eyebrow. "Don't tell me you actually went out around people." He narrowed his eyes, suspicious. "Or were you coaxed out of your solitary existence by someone in particular?"

Eric cleared his throat. "I want to show you the coffee I brought home. The bags are all marked with where I got them, and any information I had. I think most of them will be great specials for the menu. We can advertise them as exclusives. Or have a rotating 'Islands Special' or something. Some of them we can figure out the blends, some of them we can order online..."

"Your face is redder than my shirt. Who is she?"

"I thought you had to get to the shop to supervise the display case installation."

"Jody's there. She can handle it."

Eric took another sip of coffee, still avoiding his brother's gaze. "This Blue Mountain is the best. I got about twenty pounds of beans. I'm going to see about ordering more."

"You already told me that. Twice."

"Oh."

"Dude, you're going to tell me sooner or later, you might as well kill the suspense now. Did you meet somebody?"

"It sounds bad. I mean, I got dumped two minutes before the cruise."

"So you *did* meet someone. Please tell me she's not another Brittney." Stewart nearly choked over her name.

Eric swirled his mug, organizing his thoughts. "Nothing happened."

"Well, *something* happened. It's all over your face."

"I mean it, Stew. Nothing happened. I spent a lot of time with someone, and we had a good trip."

"Are you going to see her again? I mean, are you up for a long distance thing? How far away does she live?"

"Um, not far." Eric's face flamed hotter under Stewart's intense stare.

A few minutes passed before Stewart's incredulous question that wasn't quite a question. "The photographer cousin? Holy crap."

Eric couldn't meet his eyes. "I told you nothing happened."

"So it is her." Stewart blew out a hard breath and leaned back in his chair. "Man, that's complicated."

"No. It's not. We had a nice time together. The whole point of her being there was for her to do the wedding photos, but she was also going to build her travel portfolio. So since I had all those excursions and they were non-refundable..." He lifted a shoulder.

"You took Morgan."

"Megan."

"No sense letting the tickets go to waste."

"Right. And since neither of us knew anyone else on the ship, we just happened to spend most of our time together. There was no pressure. No drama."

"Did you kiss her?" Leave it to Stewart to go there.

Eric shifted uncomfortably. It wouldn't do any good to lie, and evading the question would be worse than admitting it. "Once. It was only a goodbye kiss when I was leaving the ship."

"Huh."

"That was the only time."

Stewart stared at him for a moment. "I believe you. But why are you just letting it go? It looks like you're really interested in her, at least from where I'm sitting."

Eric sighed. "I almost married her *cousin*. No, they aren't close, but they're still family. And she has enough issues with her family as it is."

"Such as?"

"Do you remember way back, like almost twenty years ago, when that kid was abducted and later they found his body up at Cooper's hunting cabin?"

"Vaguely."

"He was Megan's brother."

Stewart grimaced and blew out a breath. "Oh, wow. I can't imagine."

"It gets worse. I'm not sure I would have believed it, but I heard part of it with my own ears. Her mother told her it should have been her instead of the brother."

Stewart's jaw dropped. "What? What kind of person says something so horrible? To their kid? I can't imagine ever saying anything so hateful to any of the kids, or anybody else, no matter how angry I was."

"It was bad. And..." he took a deep breath and let it out slowly.

"And?"

"This older couple we had dinner with took a picture of us and put it on Facebook. Megan was telling her mother about the couple, so her mother actually started Facebook stalking this woman and saw the picture of us. Oh, I forgot a part. Megan's mother had forbidden her to spend any time with me. She could be polite if we ran into each other, but no talking."

"You've got to be kidding."

"Nope. Then, after she saw the picture, she went ballistic. Calling Megan names, telling her she was a tramp, an embarrassment to the family and all sorts of ugly things I don't want to repeat. Stew, she called Megan at least fifty times a day, leaving messages and texts and trying to make her feel horrible because she took a vacation away from home."

"That's seriously messed up."

"Megan doesn't need any more drama, and if her family thinks she's involved with me, they'll make her life miserable. I wouldn't ask her to put up with any of that just to spend time with me."

"I take it she's not exactly like her cousin."

"Polar opposite."

"Huh."

"Yeah, yeah, yeah, I know. You told me all along, blah blah blah. I don't need to hear it right now." Eric got up, shoving his chair back and striding across the kitchen to the sink. He rinsed his mug and set it in the dish drainer with more force than necessary.

"I'm not saying a word right now."

Eric rolled his eyes. "You'll save your wisdom for another time?"

"When you're in a better mood." Stewart rose and took his cup to the sink and rinsed it out.

"Pfft. You'll be waiting a while."

"Who knows. Maybe it'll all work out somehow."

Eric scowled at him. "Those are your brilliant words of wisdom?"

"Nope, you didn't want to hear my words of wisdom."

"Fine, get it off your chest. Let's hear it."

"You sure?"

"Nope."

Stewart crossed his arms and leaned back against the counter. "None of us really 'got' the whole thing with Brittney, which is no secret. Your entire family was cheering on the inside – and maybe a little on the outside – when we found out she bailed on the wedding. My point is, you can't let your family dictate who you choose as your partner. Good or bad."

"Easy for you to say. Jody fit in from day one."

"All I'm saying is, maybe this girl needs to worry less about her mother and worry more about what she wants out of life. If she can't, she's not a good match for you anyway. Once you get married, the rest of the family comes second. It has to."

Eric smacked his brother on the arm. "Someday I'll be as lucky as you."

"Never. But you can be a close second."

They laughed.

Stewart checked the time. "I better go check out the display case situation. See what you can find out about ordering those beans in bulk."

"Will do."

Eric closed the door behind his brother. Stewart was right, but he was wrong. Neither of them could ever comprehend the tragedy Megan's family had endured, so neither of them could judge her for the way she interacted with her family.

Chapter Thirty

Megan stood at the wedged open door, keeping her foot at the corner so it couldn't be pushed open.

"Are you going to make me stand out here?"

"Mom, it's not a good time. I'm trying to unpack –"

"Move." Alice shoved the door.

Megan finally stepped back and let her walk in. Might as well get it over with.

Alice pressed her lips together. "This place is a pigsty."

"Thanks."

"Well? Where is he? I know you didn't want to let me in because you're hiding him."

Megan's jaw clenched. "You're ridiculous."

Alice looked around, scrutinizing every inch of the living room before stalking into the kitchen. "How long ago did he leave?"

"You know what? I've had enough. Eric wasn't here, he was never here, you're being a complete jerk, and I want you to leave."

Alice continued as if Megan hadn't spoken. "I know how you got home."

"Well, it was certainly no thanks to you."

"I wanted you to see what it felt like, not being able to get a hold of anyone when you needed to be able to."

"You never *need* me. You don't even *like* me, so I'm not sure why you keep wasting your time keeping tabs on me."

"Watch your tone."

The chastised little girl inside Megan warred with the pissed off adult woman. For a change, the adult was winning and refused to hold her tongue. "No. You need to leave. Now. I have a lot of work to do."

"Work." Alice snorted.

"Are you having trouble hearing me?"

Something in Megan's tone must have gotten Alice's attention.

She snapped her head around, staring into Megan's eyes. "Excuse me?"

"Leave."

"What's going on here?" Megan's father asked from the doorway.

Something crossed Alice's face.

"I was telling Mom to get out of my apartment. She thinks she can leave me stranded at the airport and then drop by and interrogate me. I'm done. I'm so done with this."

Grant's brow furrowed. "Stranded? Your mother told me someone else was bringing you home. Alice?"

"Thankfully, Beth was home when I called, so she came to get me."

A muscle in his jaw twitched. "Somebody better tell me what's going on, right now."

Alice stood straight. "She wants me to leave. So we'll leave now. Let's go."

"No."

"Grant."

"Alice, you better start talking."

Alice clamped her lips shut, unaccustomed to her mild mannered husband speaking to her in a tone that meant business. Turning her head to ignore him, she refused to speak.

"Megan?"

"Dad, I can't do it anymore. She's accusing me of screwing around with Eric – Brittney's ex – and then yesterday she wouldn't answer the phone when I needed a ride home. I sat in the airport for almost two hours, between waiting for you guys and then waiting for Beth to get there. I can't take any more. I can't take the hate and the venom. I'm sorry Danny died instead of me, but I can't keep hearing it."

Grant gasped. "What are you talking about?"

Alice grabbed his arm. "We're leaving!"

He yanked it from her grasp. "What is she talking about?"

"Nothing. She's a liar, and she'll say anything to get the focus off the fact she's been sleeping with her cousin's fiancé on this *cruise*. I think they had it planned the whole time."

"Now wait a minute. Megan going on this cruise was my idea. I mentioned it to Doug, and Brittney agreed it'd be a good idea to have her own photographer. Megan didn't know anything about it until I was ready to order the tickets, so how did she plan anything?"

Alice went to stand by the door. "We're leaving."

Grant sighed. "Please sit down. I think we have more things to iron out here."

"No." Alice turned the knob.

"Sit down!" he roared.

Megan automatically dropped into the chair closest to her. In her entire life, she could remember one single time her father had ever raised his voice, at a group of kids spray painting the side of the grocery store.

Alice's eyes went wide, but she obeyed, slowly lowering herself into a chair across the room.

Grant sat on the chair beside Megan's, looking back and forth between the two of them. "Megan?"

"I... I'm not sure what you want me to say."

"Honey, I don't know where you ever got the idea... We would never wish you were... gone instead of Danny." His voice hitched. "We'd love to have him back, but we can't. We can't change anything, and we certainly don't want anything to have happened to you." He reached over and covered her hand with his.

Megan stared hard at her mother. The truth sat on her tongue, desperate to punish this woman for being so miserable to her. But she held back. "Dad, Brittney called off the wedding. I was already committed. It didn't make sense to waste all that money and turn around to come home. I had no idea Eric was still making the trip until I ran into him in the airport in Orlando."

Grant shook his head. "Of course it didn't make sense for you to come back home. It was a great opportunity for you to work on your traveling pictures. I said as much to your mother."

"Nothing happened between me and Eric."

"I believe you. But even if something did happen, you're both adults, and neither of you are married."

"Grant!" Alice snapped. "How could you condone such loose behavior? From your *daughter*?"

Megan watched the color rising in her father's cheeks. She was afraid to breathe. She'd never seen him so angry. "Go wait in the car." His voice was steel.

"What? You can't tell me-"

"Car. Now." The muscle in his jaw twitched.

Her mother rose, shooting filthy looks at both of them. She walked out of the apartment, slamming the door behind her.

Grant sighed, releasing the tension hunching his shoulders. "Be honest with me, Meggy. I want to know everything."

"Dad, I had over three hundred messages while I was on the cruise. She couldn't stand me being so far away from her. I've always tried to be understanding, because I can't imagine what it's like to lose a child, but I can't be perfect enough to suit her. I can't be close enough or good enough or obedient enough. I can't make up for what happened to Danny. I know it's my fault, but I can't pay for it any more, I can't." Tears streamed down her face.

Grant's eyes were filling with tears. "Oh, Megan." He dropped to his knees in front of her chair and wrapped her in a hug. "I'm so sorry. Honey, I'm so sorry. This is my fault. I should have paid more attention to what was going on. I knew – I know – she's said some nasty things, but you always seem to let it roll off, so I hated to bring it up once it was over with. You've always been so strong and I chose to take it at face value. I'm sorry. Megan, I'm so, so sorry."

She clung to his arms and cried into his shoulder. "I'm sorry, Daddy. I don't want to cause more drama but this has to stop. I can't..."

"Shhh. It isn't your burden to carry, Megan. It's not your fault. It was never your fault. You were a kid, Danny was a kid. Your mother and I let him walk over to Joey's house a million times. It... it just happened. It's not your fault, and I never blamed you, not once." He wiped his face. "I'm so sorry I didn't see you were blaming yourself. At first I was so wrapped up in finding him... Ah, honey." He put his hands on the sides of her head and kissed her forehead

"She told me she wished it was me instead."

His eyes drifted shut as he clutched her hands in his. "I don't know what to say. I'm so sorry, but that's so inadequate."

"I can't take it anymore," she whispered.

"Don't. You're a grown woman, Megan. You-" He smoothed her hair back from her face and stopped short, like he was remembering something.

"What?"

He suddenly looked weary, like he'd aged thirty years in a split second. "That's why you stayed. Why you didn't marry Charles and move to California. Because of your mother. Because you were trying to pay for what you thought you were responsible for."

Megan didn't know what to say. She felt guilty to see her father sitting there, looking so sad.

He sighed deeply. "I'm sorry. I'm sorry I didn't see it. I'm sorry I didn't stop it. I would have. If I had known what was going on inside your head, I would have stopped it."

"I know."

"I love you, Megan. All I've ever wanted is the best for you. That's what this whole trip was about. You're fading, and I can't stand to see it."

"What do you mean?"

"It's like you stopped dreaming. I thought you were happy taking pictures at weddings and whatnot. But when I heard you and Beth talking about doing travel pictures and you sounded so excited and I realized I hadn't heard that in your voice in a long, long time. I thought maybe this trip would be the thing to put a spark back in your eyes. I thought you might even meet somebody."

"You did?" She was shocked.

"Why not? A spicy affair wouldn't be the worst thing in the world."

Megan giggled. "I did meet a Portuguese chef who offered to have an affair with me."

"There you go."

"Tempting, but not quite my style."

"Eh, that's probably a good thing. What about this other guy?"

"He was going to marry Brittney, which makes him automatically ineligible for any sort of relationship."

"Why?"

"Because she's my cousin."

"So? She doesn't want him."

"It seems wrong."

"Seems okay to me. It's not like you and Brittney were ever close. It's not like you did anything to sabotage their relationship."

"Dad..."

Grant held up his hands and shrugged. "If it's a girl thing, fine, but it seems like a silly rule to me. Your best friend's ex? Off limits. Your sister's ex? Off limits. Your next door neighbor's ex? Eh, kinda iffy until somebody moves. Your cousin, who you've only spoken to three times in the last decade's ex? Fair game."

"If only it was so simple."

"Maybe it is." Heaving out a sigh, he said, "What's not simple is the conversation I'm going to be having with the woman downstairs."

"Thanks for having my back. I honestly wasn't sure anyone did."

She walked to the door with him. He leaned over and gave her a hug. "I'll do better. I know I don't say it, but Megan, I'm so proud of you."

"Thanks, Dad."

Megan watched through the curtain as he descended the

stairs and got into the car. She could see Alice, scowling out the opposite window, refusing to look at her husband. Megan didn't even want to be a fly on the wall during that exchange.

Needing to move, she took the dirty clothes from her trip and put them in the washing machine, then took the plastic bags full of souvenir photos to the kitchen table. She put them on a pile, then made a second trip to bring all the bags of loose tea leaves to the kitchen.

She was tempted to text Eric, asking him what he wanted to do with the tea, but she didn't. He hadn't texted her all day, so she didn't want to initiate contact he obviously didn't want. Instead, she vacuumed the living room and sat down at the computer to edit the first batch of vacation photos. One photo showed a tiny circular rainbow among the puffy clouds she'd captured out the airplane window. She enlarged it and moved it to a folder to be printed.

Chapter Thirty-One

"Are you sure you want it here?" Eric heaved the shelving into the corner of the café's kitchen.

Jody glared. "Do you have to keep questioning me? If I told you guys to put it there, I probably want it there, don't you think?"

"Whatever. I thought it might be better along the other wall, but you're the boss."

Jody turned and considered. "Huh. Well, now that you mention it, it would make a lot of sense."

Annoyance flaring for the millionth time, he figured he'd better take a little walk. "I'm taking a bathroom break, then you can decide where you want it for sure."

"You're really grumpy today. In fact, you've been a grouch for the last four days since you got home."

"I'm fine."

"If you say so."

Her tone irritated him, but he tried to keep his own light. He knew she was under a lot of pressure to get the café ready for opening. "Hey, I'm sorry if I don't feel too chipper. Don't take it personally."

"I'm not used to seeing you so moody and distant."

"I'll be back." He turned and headed for the tiny bathroom. It was bad enough Stewart had been pestering him about Megan, now Jody was going to start, too.

He yanked a paper towel off the roll, which sent the entire roll spiraling across the room and onto the floor, leaving him holding the end in his hand. Picking up the roll, he scrunched up his face. It landed in a wet spot, so he pulled off the unusable paper towels and threw them in the trash can. He situated the roll between the plastic ends of the plastic holder screwed into the wall, lining up the open ends of the roll and let go. The roll fell onto the floor.

Eric kicked the paper towels. They bounced off the wall and back toward his feet, unrolling along the way. He picked up the entire roll, wadded it up, and shoved it in the trash can.

He stormed out.

Jody raised an eyebrow, but said nothing.

"We need more paper towels," he snapped. "And a new holder. That one's a piece of junk."

"Okay." She picked up a stack of papers and disappeared around the corner into the dining area where Stewart was putting shelves up.

Eric ran his hand through his hair. Maybe Jody was right. He was moody. So what. He was still tired from the trip. He grabbed the broom and started sweeping the kitchen floor with vehemence.

"Eric?" Jody poked her head around the corner. "Can you come out here?"

"Sure." He leaned the broom against the wall and went to the front of the shop. "What's-"

Megan stood in front of the new display case, looking fantastic in her jeans and gray hoodie, with her hair up in a messy knot. "Hey."

Eric's eyebrows rose and his heart did a little flip-flop in his chest. "Hey."

She held up a plastic grocery bag. "I brought the tea."

"Oh, great." He rushed around the counter and took the bag she held out. Clearing this throat, he said, "Megan, this is my sister-in-law, Jody, and my brother, Stewart. Guys, this is Megan."

Jody leaned over the counter to grasp Megan's hand in both of hers. "So you're Megan. It's so nice to meet you."

"You, too, Eric's told me a lot about you guys."

Stewart interjected, "All good, I hope."

Eric snorted. "Good? About you guys?"

Jody laughed and pointed to the grocery bag. "What's this?"

"We picked up some tea in a couple of the coffee shops we went to. I'm not much of a coffee drinker, so I tried these instead."

Eric opened the bag and pulled out the bags of tea, spreading them out on the counter.

Jody picked up each one and sniffed it. "These are amazing."

"It's too bad there's not a lot in each bag, but it shouldn't be too hard to order more. I found a couple of places online. I wrote the websites on the bags."

Eric nodded. "I think a lot of it is the spice blends, too. We should be able to recreate most of them."

He saw Jody watching Megan with interest. When her eyes flicked to his, he gave his head a small shake. She raised an eyebrow and gave the faintest one-shoulder shrug. "So, Megan," Jody began. "it sounds like you guys had a great trip."

Megan glanced at Eric and smiled. "We did."

"Stewart and I have talked about going on a cruise. What was your favorite part?"

Eric looked at Stewart, questioning. Judging from his

expression, the talk about going on a cruise was news to him, too, but he wisely kept his mouth shut.

"Hmm, it's hard to choose one favorite part. I guess I'd say the animals. The dolphin encounter and the horseback riding were both amazing."

Jody's eyebrows shot up. "Eric was on a horse?"

"He was. He did great."

Eric groaned. "I did okay."

Stewart chuckled. "It didn't spit at you, did it?"

"No."

Now fully interested in the conversation, Stewart chimed in, "Did you tell Megan about your camel experience?"

"Yes, I did. So you don't need to repeat it." Her coconut shampoo filled his senses. "Tell him I told you, or he'll go through the whole thing, and nobody wants that."

She laughed and put her hand on his arm. "Yes, he told me all about it. Camel spit, sand in the face, wretched brother laughing his butt off. Everything."

Warmth spread from where she so casually touched him. When she lifted her hand, it was all he could do to not grab it back.

Stewart held his hands up. "Okay, okay. I believe you."

Jody held up one of the bags of tea. "We need to try this one."

"The one with fruit? It's my favorite." Megan said.

"It smells like orange and something else."

"Pineapple and mango. It's dried, but I bet it would be amazing brewed with fresh fruit."

Eric agreed.

"How was the food?" Jody asked. "Everyone talks about how great the food is on a cruise ship."

Megan groaned. "Oh, my. Everything you've heard is true. The food was amazing. They had fresh pineapple on the breakfast buffet every morning, and I have to say, it was the sweetest, most delicious pineapple I've ever had. So much better than anything we get shipped in around here."

"I love pineapple."

"And the seafood. And desserts. And the burgers. So many burgers."

"Burgers? Why did you waste a cruise meal on burgers?" Jody laughed.

"The dining room was always so crowded. And our tablemates were very chatty, to say the least. Wonderful, lovely people, but they were exhausting. So we found this little out of the way burger restaurant at the top of the ship."

Eric added, "We seemed to eat at weird times, so we usually had the place to ourselves."

"Oh. So you guys spent a lot of time together?" Eric shot her a warning look, which she ignored.

Megan nodded. "We did. I think we both had the same idea of what a nice vacation looked like. We were interested in the same sorts of activities, and we got along great. It was the best trip ever."

"Hmmm." Jody picked up another bag and sniffed. "This one would be great for winter. Cinnamon and something else?"

"Plum."

"No kidding, what a great combination. Maybe we could do a cinnamon vanilla pumpkin spice tea for fall and then do the cinnamon plum in the winter. These are all so amazing. Thank you for showing them to us." Jody pushed the bag back across the counter, toward Megan.

Megan said, "Oh, no, those are yours. I already took out for myself."

"Are you sure?"

"I'm sure. It'll take me all winter to go through what I kept."

"What do we owe you?"

"Absolutely nothing. It was fun to be able to pick them out for you."

Never one to accept something for free, Jody persisted. "I can't take them for nothing. How about free tea after we open?"

"Deal."

Eric watched Megan and Jody's easy conversation. He nearly shuddered to think of the times Brittney had interacted with Jody, always acting like she had somewhere better to be. Why had he ever thought Brittney could fit into his family? Or his life? Bullet, dodged.

"Hey, Stew," Jody called.

Stewart poked his head around the corner. "Yeah?"

"We're going on a cruise."

"Okay, babe. Let me know when." He disappeared back into the back.

Jody grinned. "I thought he'd be harder to convince." She cleared her throat. "I have some, uh, stuff to do in the back. It was great meeting you, Megan. I hope to see you again. Soon."

"Me, too, Jody. I hope you enjoy the tea."

Jody vanished into the back of the store, grinning up at Eric like the Cheshire Cat on her way past.

"You didn't have to give up your tea," Eric said.

"Of course I did. We got it for the café, not for me."

He was so glad to have her standing near him, but he wasn't sure what to say. He settled on, "Are you guys having a big family thing for Thanksgiving?"

She looked down at the newly refinished hardwood floor. "No. I decided I'm going to help serve the Thanksgiving meal at the food bank this year."

"Oh. How'd that go over?"

"Like a lead balloon. But after stranding me at the airport, I can't even stand to be in the same room with my mother."

"What?"

"Yeah, they never came to pick me up and she wouldn't answer the phone. I had to call my friend Beth to come get me."

"Megan, I would have gotten you."

"I know, but I figured we needed some distance." She fiddled with her ring, a silver band with a bit of blue-green sea glass for the stone. She'd picked it up in Aruba.

He saw the exact moment clearly in his mind, her holding it up to show him, that confident smile on her beautiful face.

"Beth came to get me and when I saw my parents the next day, I found out my mother had told my dad I had another ride. It was my 'punishment'-" she made air quotes, "for being incommunicado those last days of the cruise."

"That's insane."

"Yup."

"I wish you would have called me."

"I thought about it."

"Did you?"

She was still twirling her ring. "Of course I did." She looked up. "You haven't called me, either."

"Do you want me to?" The words were out before he could think them through. They hung in the air as they simply stared at each other, neither of them sure of what to say next.

Something crashed in the back, snapping them out of whatever held them.

Megan gestured toward the door. "So, um, I should go. I'm meeting Beth for lunch."

"Okay. I'll walk you out."

Eric pushed open the door and let Megan walk through. "I'm glad you came. It's good to see you. Really good."

"You, too."

He wanted to grab her face and kiss her, but he stopped

himself, guessing she wouldn't appreciate the gesture. He settled for a quick hug, breathing in her coconut shampoo for a brief second, then turned and walked back into the coffee shop.

"You jerks can come out," he said.

Jody practically flew around the corner. "Eric. Seriously? You're going to just let her go?"

"I can't hold her hostage."

"No, you idiot. She's crazy about you. I can't believe you're not spending every waking moment figuring out how to make it work with her."

"I don't want to hear it."

"Come on. You two were looking at each other the way I look at cheesecake."

"Gee, thanks," Stewart said.

"Babe. *Cheese*cake."

Eric shook his head. "We've been over this."

"Yeah," Jody said, "but that was before I saw you two together. She's wonderful, and she *likes* you."

Stewart nodded. "She does."

"Don't you start, too."

Stewart held up a hand. "I'm only going to say one thing, and then my lips are sealed. I think there's something there. Don't give up too easily."

"You're done now, right?"

"Done." Stewart mimed turning a key over his lips and tossing it over his shoulder.

"Good."

"Well, I'm not." Jody insisted and crossed her arms.

Stewart put his hands on her shoulders, quieting whatever she was going to say next.

Chapter Thirty-Two

Megan pulled into a parking space at the diner and squeezed her trembling hands together. She hadn't expected to be so affected by seeing him in person after not seeing or talking to him for four days. Four days. In some ways it seemed so much longer, and in other ways it seemed like only hours.

A tap on her window nearly sent her through the roof of the car.

Beth stepped back. "Sorry," she said.

Megan stepped out of the car. "Sorry. I was in my own little world, I guess."

They walked into Sonny's Diner and got a booth. Corinne, the waitress, quickly took their orders and brought their drinks.

Megan fiddled with the straw wrapper.

Beth shook a sugar packet, ripped it open and sprinkled it into her tea. "Are you going to join me here on Earth?"

Jolting back to the present, Megan nodded. "I'm here. Sorry. I dropped off the tea at the coffee shop."

She stopped stirring her tea. "I take it Mister Perfect was in attendance?"

Megan rolled her eyes. "Seriously?"

"Well?"

"Yes, he was there. Yes, I talked to him."

"And?"

"And nothing. I gave them the tea and I left. Period."

"Please. If nothing else happened, you wouldn't be sitting here with your head in the clouds."

Her head wasn't in the clouds. It was cuddled up on a balcony in the middle the ocean. "He asked me if I wanted him to call me."

"And you said?"

"I didn't say anything. Something fell in the back and I took the opportunity to escape."

"Do you want him to call?"

"I don't know." So it wasn't exactly the truth. If he called, she'd be more than happy to talk to him. Or go out. But it wasn't going to happen.

"You want him to call, but you don't think you should want him to call."

"Maybe. Probably. I don't know."

"So he wants to call you."

"He didn't say that."

"Megan, come on. If a guy doesn't want to call you, he's not going to ask you if he can." Beth resumed stirring her tea. "Fine. Anyway, I wanted to tell you you're welcome to come for Thanksgiving, unless you decided you're serving at the food bank dinner."

"I am. I've wanted to for a while now, but never had the guts to bail on an actual holiday with the family." Her dad had been mildly disappointed, while Alice had made a dramatic comment about Megan abandoning them.

"Good for you. I'll keep some leftovers for you. Maybe even a piece of my famous Boston cream pie."

"Mmm. Those are the best. *You're* the best."

"I know. You're lucky to have me," she teased. They ate their sandwiches. Beth wiped her mouth with her napkin and said, "You should text him."

"No."

"You totally should."

"Why? I don't have anything to say."

"You have plenty to say. Start with something simple, like 'It was great to see you today.' Or 'I never answered you, so if you want to call me, I'd like to talk.' Maybe even, 'I miss you. I want to lick your abs.' Whatever."

Laughing, Megan said, "No way."

"Right, because we don't want to do something silly like tell him the truth."

Everyone seemed to think it was so simple. It wasn't. "You know I love you."

Holding her hands up, Beth said, "Fine, fine, I'm shutting up."

"Besides, you always tell me everything works out the way it should."

"Not when you actively avoid it."

Megan rolled her eyes.

Leaning forward, Beth grew serious. "I hope someday soon, you realize you're worthy of having good things in your life. You deserve to be happy."

"I'm perfectly happy."

"Okay."

Megan finished the last of her fries.

Beth checked her watch. "I better get going. I promised the kids I'd bring them pizza."

Outside the restaurant, Megan gave her a big hug. "Thank you. And we need to have lunch more often."

"Without the spawn? Absolutely. I love having conversations that don't involve Nickelodeon or the word 'Mommom-mommommommom.'"

Megan was still chuckling when she pulled into the parking lot of the commercial building she shared with four other businesses. Her studio was in the front corner, taking advantage of the natural light from the huge windows. An artist used the other front corner as his studio/gallery, and the back was taken up by three offices. Megan wasn't sure what they did, but they were quiet and kept to themselves.

She fished in her purse for the keys to the front door.

Tires crunched on the gravel behind her.

A car door opened.

Then a voice.

"How'd you enjoy *my* trip with *my* man?"

Megan turned slowly, keeping her face neutral. Brittney strode toward her, a vision of poofy blonde curls and style and expensive clothes. Her stiletto heels teetered on the loose gravel. A slight twinge of guilt chased the amusing fantasy of Brittney tripping and falling flat on her face.

"Brittney."

"Hey, *Cuz*."

"What do you want?"

"First of all, I want the money back for my excursions. My parents bought them as a gift for *me*." She held her hand out, wiggling fingers tipped with perfectly manicured talons.

"I already gave it to your dad." Technically, Grant had given it to her dad, but there was no point getting into detail.

"I want proof. You're not going to steal our money like you stole my husband."

Megan pulled her jacket tighter against the chill. "Call your dad. He got the money yesterday. And I didn't steal anything."

A flawlessly waxed eyebrow arched. "No? Well you sure enjoyed yourself on *my* honeymoon."

"I enjoyed my vacation."

Brittney glared. "You should be on your knees thanking me. I was gracious enough to agree to let you go on this trip. Not that I thought your pictures would be any good. I felt bad for you. And thanks to me, you got the trip of a lifetime. With my man. And now you're acting like an ungrateful bitch."

What did he ever see in her? Morty's words rushed back and she found herself aware of her cousin's figure – some of it natural, some store-bought. Eww. If that's what Eric was looking for, it's a good thing they'd agreed to go their separate ways, because she most certainly didn't fit the same mold. "I didn't realize he was still your man after you dumped him."

"You don't sleep with your cousin's leftovers."

"You don't? When did that change?" Megan was shocked to hear the words come out of her mouth, then she was kind of impressed she'd delivered the perfect snarky comment for the occasion.

Brittney's perfectly lined eyes narrowed. "If you're referring to Ross, he's ancient history." Ross had been another cousin's husband. Emphasis on *had been*.

"What do you want?"

"I want an apology."

Megan let out a surprised laugh. "For what, exactly?"

"You turned Eric against me. He won't talk to me or return my calls."

"Maybe because you dumped him?"

"He should still be mature enough to talk to me."

"Whatever. It has nothing to do with me." She shifted the straps of her purse higher on her shoulder. "Was there something else? I have work to do."

"Are you seeing each other?"

"No."

"You expect me to believe you?" Condescension dripped from her words.

Megan sighed heavily. "Brittney, I don't care what you believe."

Brittney paused, clearly not expecting that reaction, not from Megan. "So... you're really not seeing each other?" She seemed uncertain.

"I already said we're not."

Her face brightened considerably. "Great."

"Why? Are you trying to get back together again?" What was Brittney's scheme? Maybe things weren't quite so rosy with Quinn. She mentally kicked herself. Why did she ask a question she might not want the answer to? Why did she ask a question at all and prolong this conversation?

"Not if he insists on sticking with this little coffee shop scheme of his. That'll never get us out of here." Brittney scrunched up her nose.

Little coffee shop scheme? Dismissive, condescending *and* belittling all at once. The trifecta. "You want a ticket out of Hickory Hollow. Not a husband who's a partner and best friend, but someone who can buy you expensive things and live in a big house somewhere far away from here? Do you even care who he is?"

An eyeroll. "Don't act all high and mighty just because you missed your chance to get out of this stupid town when what's-his-face went out west."

Standing in the cold was annoying enough, but this was becoming intolerable. "You know, they invented these nifty things called *jobs*. You could get one and go wherever you want." Without taking time to savor the surprise on her cousin's face, she continued, "I have some work to do. Goodbye."

"I'll see you around then."

Megan turned to unlock the main door. "Just one more thing, Megs."

"What?"

"I believe you when you say you're not seeing Eric."

"Okay." Whether Brittney believed her or not was of zero concern.

Brittney gave her a winning smile. "Now I'm going to need you to promise me you never will."

"Excuse me?" Slowly, Megan turned back around, sure she couldn't possibly have heard correctly, even though she knew she had. Unbelievable.

"I mean, it shouldn't be a big deal, right? If there's nothing going on? Promise me you won't ever get involved with him, and we can put this behind us and get the family back together. You do owe me, after all, without me you wouldn't have had a great trip."

Megan stared at her cousin. Her beautiful, narcissistic, manipulative cousin. She turned and pulled the key from the lock, then turned back, debating which words she would allow to come out, from the tidal wave springing to her tongue.

Brittney gave her a bright, unnaturally white smile. "Promise? Megs?"

Megan slipped her keys into the pocket of her jeans and enunciated every word. "I don't owe you anything, I won't promise you anything, and don't call me Megs."

The smile twisted. "Have it your way. Just remember you're the one who's ripping the family apart. Your poor mother." Brittney clucked her tongue and shook her head, setting those perfect curls in motion. "After all she's been through, this is how you end up. It's a good thing she has me to talk to. You know, she says I'm the daughter she always wanted."

The words, intended to cut her, had no effect. Either Brittney was lying, which was likely, or she was telling the truth, and Alice had done too many things that were far, far worse for this to hurt her. "You can have her." Megan pulled open the door and stepped through, locking it behind her.

Inside her studio, she waited for the jittery nervous feeling that always happened after any sort of confrontation. It didn't come. She waited a few minutes, and nothing. *Huh. Maybe I picked up a backbone in the Caribbean.*

Pleased she hadn't let the encounter with Brittney upset her, she spent the afternoon editing photos from the cruise. She created a folder for the photos she wanted in her portfolio, then created a folder for the ones she wanted to have printed.

Chapter Thirty-Three

It was five minutes before kickoff on Thursday Night Football when Eric's doorbell rang. What was football without pizza delivery? He grabbed his wallet and pulled open the door, then his head snapped up. "What are you doing here?"

"Can we talk?" Brittney's hand rested on her hip, her head tilted so her blonde curls danced across her shoulder.

Eric slipped his wallet into his back pocket. "We don't have anything to talk about."

"Some of my things are still here. I'd like to get them."

He frowned. "I'm pretty sure you got everything."

Brittney edged past him, deliberately brushing against him with her chest. She stood in the middle of the living room, avoiding looking at the comfortably worn black leather sofa she'd always hated. She inclined her head toward the television. "Are the Mets playing tonight?"

"Sure." What was she doing? She hadn't come here to talk about football. Or baseball.

"What inning are they in?"

"They're getting ready to kick off."

"Did anybody get a point yet?"

"No, Brittney, nobody's gotten a point, including me. I have no idea what your point is in being here."

"You don't have to be rude," she pouted.

Instead of answering, he simply stared, stone-faced, and waited.

"I ran into your girlfriend today."

"I don't have a girlfriend." Eric had already been on guard, but his hackles raised further.

"Oh, I'll be more specific. I ran into *my cousin* today."

"And you think that should interest me why?"

"It's tacky, Eric. I mean, she was there to photograph our wedding, for crying out loud. It's almost as cliché as screwing the wedding planner."

"I think you mean it's as cliché as screwing your fiancé's business partner."

Her eyes hardened. "I thought we were past all that."

"We are. We're past everything." He wished she'd leave so he could watch football in peace. "What did you leave here?"

"Some... stuff."

"What. Did. You. Leave. Here?" Eric's jaw was beginning to ache from clenching his teeth.

"I think some clothes." She reached out and ran her finger along his forearm. "Shall we go look?" she practically purred.

Eric blinked. He wasn't the best at reading signals, but even he couldn't mistake her meaning. He took a step back.

"I've missed you."

He found his voice. "Get out."

"What?" Her eyes widened with shock.

"Leave. Now." He reached over and yanked the door open. "Get out."

The pizza delivery kid was standing with his arm raised, ready to knock. "Um, large pepperoni and mushroom?"

"Yes." He shoved a few bills at the kid and took the box. "I don't need change."

The kid grinned. "Wow, thanks!"

Eric managed not to groan as he realized he'd handed over two twenties for a fourteen dollar pizza, not two tens like he'd intended. "Happy Thanksgiving a week early," he grumbled.

The kid jogged back to his car and waved as he got in.

Eric didn't close the door, letting the cold air swirl in. "Go."

Brittney went to the doorway. "It's too bad for you, though, what with Charles Carter being back in town."

"Whoever."

"Her fiancé. Well, ex-fiancé, I guess, but not for long." Brittney made a show of checking her designer watch. "I'd say they probably finished dinner and are well on their way to rekindling their romance right about now."

"I'm done with this. You're trespassing, and I will forcibly remove you in five seconds."

Something in his voice must have convinced her he was serious, because she stepped onto the porch and turned. "Don't shoot the messenger. If you need someone to... *talk to*... later, call me."

"Say hi to Quinn for me."

"He's out of town until Saturday." She arched an eyebrow. "*Late* Saturday. FYI."

Eric slammed the door in her face. The announcers were excitedly talking about a jaw-dropping 99 yard return for a touchdown on the opening kickoff. All he wanted was a quiet night with football and pizza. Now he missed what would certainly be the most exciting play of the game, had drama on his mind, and undoubtedly he'd end up with indigestion. What had he ever seen in her?

He considered texting Quinn to let him know Brittney was up to her old tricks, but he decided not to. Quinn had made his bed, let him lie in it.

Chapter Thirty-Four

Megan let out a deep breath before answering the phone. A call first thing Friday morning was never a good thing. "Hello."

"Hey, Megs."

"Dad. I thought it was Mom calling." She immediately relaxed.

He chuckled. "Guess that's why you sounded so thrilled, huh?"

"What's up?"

"Just reminding you about dinner on Sunday."

"What dinner?" she asked, even though she knew very well it was their family's big annual Thanksgiving dinner, held every year on the Sunday before Thanksgiving.

"It's at Doug and Connie's this year."

"Great. So Brittney will definitely be there."

"I'm sure she will."

"I don't want to deal with her." Understatement of the year.

"So don't. I'll put you at opposite ends of the table. I want you to come."

"I don't know..."

"Megs. Please. You're not coming for dinner on Thanksgiving, so it's important to me to have you come to this one."

She sighed. "There better be pie."

"Pumpkin. With crumbles. And homemade whipped topping. I'll tell you what. I'll make an extra one you can take home."

"My own *whole* super-secret pie?" She smiled into the phone.

"Yup."

"Fine. I'm in. I'll bring macaroni and cheese." She'd already bought the ingredients, knowing she couldn't get out of two family dinners.

"Good. Maybe this will be the first step to you and your mother patching things up."

"We'll see," was her noncommittal response. Her mother had a lot of patching to do.

Megan ended the call with a smile. It quickly faded. She hadn't asked how his conversation with her mother had gone, and he hadn't offered any details. As for dinner, dealing with her mother and Brittney both, for at least three hours, was not going to be fun. She'd try to figure out a way to avoid them, even if it meant hiding in the bathroom. For her dad's sake.

Megan fixed herself a bowl of cereal and planned out her day. She didn't have any photo sessions scheduled until the weekend, so she would have plenty of time to finish editing her cruise photos at her office, where there were fewer distractions.

On the way to the studio, her cell phone rang. She didn't recognize the number, so she let it go to voicemail. After unlocking the studio, she listened to the message. Jody. Megan called her right back.

"Hey, I'm so glad you called me back. I was wondering if

you could stop by the café sometime today? If you have some time, I mean?"

Megan was suspicious. If this was a setup to get her together with Eric without his knowledge, she wasn't interested. "Um..."

As if she'd read her mind, Jody said, "It's not a trap, I promise. I wanted to see if you were interested in doing some art for the café walls."

"Oh. Sure, I can stop by around eleven?"

"Perfect."

The morning flew by as Megan worked on editing a batch of photos from a newborn shoot. She checked her watch, then decided she had time to check her email. There was a message from the cruise line. Assuming it was a survey, Megan shrugged. They might offer a coupon or discount on another cruise. Which she was definitely going to be taking.

She clicked the email open and took a long swing from her water bottle. As she began to read, she choked on the water. Coughing and sputtering, she read the message a second time, then a third. There was no way this could be a legitimate message.

Dear Ms. Prescott,

We hope you enjoyed your recent Caribbean cruise with us. We came across your Instagram account and are very interested in discussing the possibility of purchasing a few of your photographs.

Please call me at the number below at your earliest convenience.

Sincerely, Amy Abbott

Internet Specialist Majestic Cruise Lines

Megan read the message at least a dozen times before convincing herself it had to be a scam. With a sigh, she shut her laptop, grabbed her camera bag, and headed to the café to meet Jody.

In minutes, Megan had put the email to the back of her

mind. Jody showed her the wall she wanted to cover with giant photos, then gestured for her to sit at a table where she'd put a box.

They sat down and Jody pulled the lid off the box and pulled out a stack of pictures. "I had an idea. We have a bunch of photos from way back when the building was first constructed. I think one of these," she laid out four photos, "would be perfect for the first panel. We could do a sort of timeline from when it was built on up through the current renovations."

Megan looked through the stack Jody handed her. "These are fantastic. But I'm not sure a lot of them can be blown up as big as you're talking. We'll need to get them scanned at as high of a resolution as we can, then cross our fingers."

"Can you do it, or do I have to take them somewhere?"

"I can do it. I'll see if I can get a sharp scan."

"While you're here, do you want to take some photos while we're still in progress? Even if we don't use them, we'll have them for posterity, right?"

Megan smiled. "Sure." She walked around the café and shot a bunch of photos, then measured the wall and wrote down the numbers. "I think this is a great idea. Have you thought about doing black and white?"

"I had the idea last night, so no, I haven't given it a ton of thought. What are you thinking?"

"We could start with the oldest photo here," Megan walked over and tapped the wall, "in black and white. Then photos here, here, here, and here, also black and white, in chronological order. Then this one," she touched the last space, "would be of your new coffee shop, in color."

"I love it. Yes. I can see it, and it's exactly what I had in mind." Jody sat back down and motioned for Megan to do the same. "Now let's talk about your fee."

She pulled one of her brochures out of her bag. "Here's my standard fee schedule, but I don't want to quote you until I see how well the scans turn out and I know for sure what size canvas we're dealing with."

Jody glanced over the pamphlet. "Great."

They both looked up as someone came in the door.

"Oh, am I interrupting?" Eric stopped abruptly.

"Not at all," Jody said, getting to her feet.

Megan stood, hoping her face wasn't as red as it felt. "We were almost done." How could simply seeing him make her heart feel like it was going to leap out of her chest?

Eric shifted.

"So I'll let you know how the scans turn out," Megan said to Jody.

"Wonderful, I can't wait to hear from you."

Jody pushed the box of photos toward Megan and hurried to the back of the building, not even trying to disguise her attempt to leave them alone.

"Hi."

"Hello." Did he have to look so good in a pair of jeans? "I wasn't expecting to see you here."

"Jody wants me to see if I can blow up some of these old photos of the building."

He nodded. "She said something about doing pictures along the back wall."

"Do... do you have some time? Can we maybe get some lunch? I got a message today I want you to look at. I'm not sure if it's a scam."

Chapter Thirty-Five

"Sure." The word was out of Eric's mouth before he could stop it. He added, "It'll have to be quick, though. I have a lot of work to do here." The peevish part of his brain wondered why she wasn't having *Charles* take a look at it.

"No problem. We can just grab a sandwich. This won't take long."

He watched Megan struggle with the box and her camera bag for a second before reaching over and taking the box from her. "Here, let me help."

"Thanks. I don't want to drop it."

They walked outside, where Eric put the box in the back seat of Megan's car. "Sonny's is quick, meet you there?"

"Perfect."

Eric got in his car and drove the few blocks to Sonny's, checking his rear view mirror a few times to see Megan behind him. They parked side by side and went into the busy pizza joint.

"Corner booth." Eric made a beeline for the table. He had no idea what to say to her. He wondered if she'd bring up the fact her ex was in town. Then again, why would she?

Their waitress took their orders and brought their drinks.

Megan pulled out her phone and began tapping and scrolling.

Eric drummed his fingers on the table until she looked up. "Sorry, I'm trying to get this message up so you can see it."

"Oh. Right." He immediately felt stupid for acting impatient. They were here so he could look at this message, so it made perfect sense she'd be on her phone. Getting the message. He ran a hand through his hair.

"Here it is." She slid her phone across the table.

Eric's eyes widened as he read the email. "Megan, this is great."

"I'm not sure if it's legit."

He pulled out his own phone. "Did you google this person?"

"No, I haven't had time to do anything. I got the message right before I left to go see Jody."

Doing a quick search, he immediately found Amy Abbott on the cruise line's "About Us" page. "Looks like she's legit. If it makes you feel better, call the number on their website instead of the one in her email. Have them transfer you."

"Good idea."

After running another search, he handed Megan his phone and said, "Check this out." He watched her face as she read the article he'd found about a cruise line purchasing photos.

She handed the phone back with a stunned expression. "You don't think they'll pay me that much, do you?"

"I wouldn't expect it, but you'll never know unless you call." He studied her face. "What's wrong?"

"Nothing's wrong at all, but I'm a little overwhelmed. First Jody wants to hire me to do the café artwork, and now this."

"This is what you wanted, isn't it? To get away from weddings and babies?"

She nodded. "It is. It's wonderful."

"So enjoy it. You've worked hard. You deserve it. And you can share this whole new life with some other guy and everything will be great. Good for you."

Megan sat back abruptly, her eyes wide and shimmering. Eric felt like he'd just slapped her, and her expression couldn't have been more hurt or shocked if he had.

Her mouth opened as if she was about to speak, then snapped shut.

Corinne set their plates in front of them, smiled and left to wait on another table.

Megan fumbled around in her purse, threw some money on the table, grabbed her phone and stood up.

"Megan, I-"

She hurried away, weaving around the crowded tables and out the door.

Eric put his head in his hands. A few minutes later, Corinne reappeared and boxed the untouched food.

"Thanks." He handed her money, took the boxes, and went back to the café.

Jody was wiping down the wall behind the counter. "Wow, quick lunch."

"Yeah."

"Megan seemed excited about doing the photos for the walls. She had a great idea to do them all in black and white, except for the newest one, which will be in color. I think that'll be perfect."

Eric grunted in reply. He was in no mood to talk.

Jody stepped off the stool she'd been standing on and turned to face him. "What happened?"

"I don't want to talk about it," he grumbled, even though he knew it was useless. She'd needle him into talking eventually anyway. He gave a recap of the conversation. Even trying to put himself in the most favorable light possible, he sounded like a jerk. Because he was.

"You're an idiot."

"Her ex is back in the picture," he defended himself.

Jody planted her hands on her hips. "So?"

"What do you mean, 'so'?"

"I mean, so what. Your ex is *still* in the picture, and I bet you wouldn't be too impressed with someone who wrote you off because of her."

"That's completely different."

Jody rolled her eyes. "Whatever. Are they together? Did she tell you her ex is back? What did she say?"

He shifted uncomfortably. "She didn't say anything about it."

Silence stretched until it was nearly unbearable being caught in Jody's laser beam glare. "Oooooooooooooh, so someone else told you. Someone with no ulterior motive, I bet. Idiot." Sarcasm dripped off her words.

Eric wanted nothing more than to walk into the back office and check invoices. "Okay."

"You *are* an idiot. I spent all morning with her, and I'm telling you, she's awesome and she's crazy about you. And you're going to fool around and screw this up because you're an idiot." She shook her head in disgust. "I don't even know what else to say to you. Idiot."

"You can stop calling me an idiot."

"Stop acting like one!" Jody's shout amplified in the empty room.

Eric took a step back. He couldn't remember a time Jody had ever yelled at him.

Stewart came around the corner, paint splotches in his hair and all over his clothes. "What the heck's going on out here?"

Jody whipped her rag into the bucket. "Nothing." She stormed out of the room.

Stewart's eyebrows rose. "Glad it wasn't something, or else she'd *really* be mad."

"It doesn't concern her anyway. She's mad because I said something stupid to Megan."

"Ah, geez. Are you *trying* to screw this up?"

"You, too? Thanks, brother." Eric snatched his jacket and shoved his arms back into the sleeves. He grabbed his boxes of food and stomped out the front door.

He got into his car and tossed the boxes on the passenger seat. The lid popped open on the top Styrofoam container, sending French fries raining down over the seat and onto the floor. Eric swore and shoved the key into the ignition.

Chapter Thirty-Six

Megan sat back in her studio, hurt and humiliated. She hadn't realized how much she'd been holding out hope for a possibility something could work out between her and Eric until he'd laid it out so clearly.

Wiping her face, she straightened her shoulders, tied her hair back and got to work scanning Jody's pictures. No use in being upset over someone she wasn't involved with anyway.

Hours later, a tapping at the office door startled her straight up out of her chair. The sky had turned dark, and the streetlights were glowing. Megan had been so involved in her work she hadn't noticed the day slipping away.

She pushed the glass door open, letting a blast of cold air into the hallway. "Jody? Come in. I haven't gotten much done yet, I'll call you when-"

Jody held up a hand. "No, no, of course I'm not here about the photos. I'm not the world's most patient person, but I promise I'm not nearly that bad."

"Then why are you here? I don't mind, but..." she trailed off.

Jody fidgeted with her keys. "In spite of evidence to the

contrary, I *am* aware none of this is my business. But. Eric was upset after your lunch and while he didn't tell me anything in particular, he did say he'd been a jerk, so I wanted to stop and make sure you were okay. I mean, not that I thought you'd be curled up in a fetal position, sobbing uncontrollably because my brother-in-law is an idiot, but still. I was going past on my way home and saw the lights on, so I decided to stop and check on you."

Megan wasn't sure what to make of this visit. "I'm fine. We had some miscommunication, but he cleared it all up today and we are definitely on the same page now."

"Uh-huh."

"What?"

"It didn't seem to me like anything was cleared up at all. He was pretty upset."

Megan crossed her arms. "I appreciate your concern." Eric was upset? He was the one drawing the line in the sand.

"I know, I know. I'm butting in, and I'm sorry. I just... even aside from Eric, I think we're going to be great friends, and I want you to know I'm here if you want to talk."

"Thanks, but definitely not about this."

"Gotcha. I hope you're not too mad at me. I know I'm way overstepping."

"I'm not mad at all. I really do appreciate you checking on me."

Jody leaned in and gave her a hug, then left. Megan sighed. Jody had been right about one thing. She needed to talk to a friend. She picked up the phone and called Beth.

"Are you at the studio?" Beth's voice was desperate. The background was loud and chaotic.

"Yes, but I'm leaving right now to go home." She held the phone out to protect her hearing from an ear-shattering scream.

"Perfect, I'm on my way to your place. If I don't escape, I'm going to lose my mind." The line went dead.

Megan chuckled. Zach was going to have his hands full with the kids. Fifteen minutes later, Megan pulled into her parking space at home.

Beth parked behind her and jumped out of her minivan. "I swear, one of these days someone's going to find me rocking in the corner."

"What happened?" Megan found her key and unlocked the door.

"What didn't happen? The toilet backed up first thing this morning, Elsie barfed all over me while I was plunging the toilet, Sophie and Benton decided to 'help me out' by making koolaid for lunch, which they spilled all over the kitchen floor. Grape. Bright purple. Did I mention I had just mopped? Nickie was having a screaming hissy fit because her pink sweater was in the laundry, and Trevor was crying hysterically because Mister Giraffe was missing. Only he wasn't missing. Mister Giraffe mysteriously ended up in the toilet drain, along with a matchbox car and half a dozen checkers. It all went downhill from there."

"Oh, no. How about a glass of wine?"

"How about you give me the bottle?" Beth joked.

Megan handed her a glass of wine and settled onto the couch with her own glass.

Beth took a sip. "So what's up? Eric troubles?"

"Sort of." Megan told her about the email from the cruise line, Jody's ideas for the café, and ended with the conversation with Eric.

"Are you sure that's what he meant?"

"There aren't too many ways to interpret 'go share your life with some other guy,' now are there?"

"I guess not, but from everything you've told me, it seems pretty out of character for him."

Megan shrugged. "I don't know. I mean, we had agreed we weren't going to pursue anything once we got home. I guess he was making sure I knew we weren't going anywhere."

Beth frowned. "It almost sounds like he's jealous."

"Jealous of what?"

"Maybe he *thinks* there's something?"

Megan thought back over their conversations since the cruise. "No. Nothing I've said could possibly suggest there was anybody else."

"Maybe it's not something you said. Maybe somebody else put a bug in his ear."

"Why? Who would do something like that?"

Beth cocked her head and raised an eyebrow. "You can't think of one single person who might want to keep the two of you away from each other?"

"Brittney? But we already talked and I told her we weren't seeing each other."

"Maybe she took out a little extra insurance policy."

"It's ridiculous, though. It wouldn't take long for him to figure out I'm not seeing anyone else, so it doesn't make sense."

"Hmm, maybe not. It just seems like a weird thing for him to say out of the blue."

Her heart seized. "Unless *he's* getting involved with someone else."

Beth took another sip of wine. "I hate to say it, but it could be a possibility."

Megan shrugged. "Well, why would I care? It's none of my business. I don't care."

"You sure about that?" Beth motioned to Megan's computer. The screensaver was showing a slideshow of cruise photos, most of them featuring Megan and Eric's smiling faces.

Megan rolled her eyes. "Pssht. So what? I had a nice trip with the guy, nothing more. I have some nice memories and there's nothing else to it."

"I think you miss him."

"No."

"Not even a little bit?"

Megan swallowed more wine. "Nope. Why would I?"

"Your scowl and crossed arms are totally convincing."

"There's no point, Beth. He was pretty clear."

"No, he wasn't. Before you get your panties all in a bunch, maybe you should have a conversation with him and find out what he actually meant. Crazy, I know."

"Maybe I'll give it a few days. Get through Thanksgiving and go from there."

"No. Thanksgiving is six days away. Give yourself a day or two and go from there."

"More wine?"

Beth sighed. "No. Half a glass is my limit. I need to get back home and help Zach get the monsters in bed. Can I take it with me?"

"Nope. I'm going to change into my jammies and finish it myself."

"Call me if you need me." Beth gave her a hug. "But don't let it go on forever. I'm serious. A day or two, at most."

"Aye, aye, captain." Megan saluted and closed the door behind her friend.

With a sigh, she put the wine in the fridge and edited some more cruise photos until the clock struck midnight and she crawled into bed.

Chapter Thirty-Seven

On Saturday, Eric found himself wrangling four kids through Target, trying to find supplies for Stewart and Jody.

"Okay, guys, in and out." Eric pressed the button on the key fob to lock the van. At first, he'd resisted driving it, but once he'd seen the amount of French fries lodged between the seats, he was glad they weren't in his car.

"Yeah, right." Samantha, his oldest niece, rolled her eyes.

"Do you have your lists?"

Mindy, his youngest niece, grabbed his hand. "I don't have a list."

"Your list is in my pocket." Eric patted his coat.

Darren, Samantha's twin, darted away from their small group.

Tess rolled her eyes. "He spotted Charlotte." She inclined her head toward a pretty blonde.

Eric sighed. How did Stewart and Jody wrangled these four kids on a daily basis?

"Does everybody have their list?" he repeated. "I don't."

"Min, I have your list."

"I want to carry the money."

"Nope."

"You're supposed to be fun."

He squeezed her hand and chuckled. "So are you."

She pondered that while he talked to Darren. The boy pushed his glasses up the bridge of his nose and tried to look cool. "Whatever."

"Hey. I was your age once, remember? So the faster you answer me, the faster you can go off on your own."

"Yeah, I got my list."

Eric glanced at the blonde. Her back was turned, so he grabbed Darren's arm. "Listen up. You're getting stuff for your mom and dad. Not stuff to try and look cool."

"Whatever." Darren yanked his arm away and hurried away. A chipper brunette bounced up alongside Samantha.

"Heeeey, Uncle Eric."

"Phoebe." Samantha's boy-crazy friend had been crushing on him forever, much to his chagrin.

"You look great today. Do you work out a lot?" She giggled and batted her false lashes. Why a kid that young needed fake eyelashes and a pound of makeup, he'd never know.

"Um, Sam, back here in forty-five minutes so we can check out."

Samantha locked arms with her friend and they walked away, giggling, their heads together.

Eric shook his head. "Ladies, shall we?"

Tess and Mindy flanked him as they walked down the hallway.

"Where should we start?"

Two hours and two carts full of items later, Eric sat exhausted in the food court with Mindy while Tess used the restroom. He had a new appreciation for Stewart and Jody. How did they manage this chaos every day and remain upright?

Mindy sipped happily on her slushy, her pink sneakers swinging beneath her chair. "Did you have fun today, Uncle Eric?"

"Sure thing, Buttercup."

Mindy giggled. "My friend has a pony named Buttercup."

"Huh. Great name for a horse."

"A pony."

He surrendered. "Great name for a pony."

"Will you get me a pony?"

"Nope."

"I could keep her in my bedroom."

"Ponies live in barns."

"My pony doesn't have to. She can live in the house."

"I don't think your parents would want a pony in the house."

"Why not? They like ponies." A reasonable argument.

"Everybody likes ponies. But ponies live outside."

"Not Peaches," Mindy insisted.

"Who's Peaches?"

"My pony."

"Oh."

"Peaches has a long tail. She's pink."

Eric chuckled. "Is your friend's pony pink, too?"

Mindy heaved an impatient sigh. "Of course not. Buttercup is *brown*." She shook her head. "Don't you know *anything*?"

"Apparently not."

"Grown-ups," she muttered.

"Indeed." Eric finished his soda and glanced at his watch. "Do any of your siblings know how to tell time?"

Mindy shrugged. "I don't know how. Maybe I'll know how when I'm seven. Peaches can show me."

"Can ponies tell time?"

"Not all of them. But Peaches is special."

Eric reached over and gently flicked one of Mindy's braids. "So are you, kiddo."

The rest of the kids finally emerged with their items. He paid and loaded everything – and everyone – in the van. Pushing the empty cart into the corral, he looked around to make sure there were no cars coming before he walked back to the van.

Waiting to let a lady walk past, he gave a I'm-not-a-creep half-smile that didn't require eye contact. Her pointed glare surprised him. She looked vaguely familiar, but he couldn't quite place her. Until she was past him and he realized he'd just encountered the infamous Alice. She shared Megan's eyes and mouth, except hers was set in a permanent scowl. Without a word, she'd made him uncomfortable. It was a wonder Megan had been able to stand up to her at all.

Chapter Thirty-Eight

Megan pulled the macaroni and cheese out of the oven and placed it in the insulated travel bag. It smelled delicious, but if the churning in her stomach didn't stop, she wouldn't be enjoying much of anything from dinner.

She zipped the bag shut and texted Beth.

> Wish me luck!

The phone vibrated as she was pulling into her uncle's driveway.

> If you need to come over when you're done, I restocked the wine!

A line of smiley faces completed the message.

Megan smiled and slipped her phone into her back pocket. Beth's invitation would give her something to look forward to. The front door flew open as she stepped onto the porch. Aunt Connie pulled her inside, simultaneously hugging her and taking the food from her hands.

"Megan, I'm so glad you came. I want to hear all about your trip. Your dad told us the cruise line wants to buy some of your pictures. I'm so excited for you."

Connie's bubbly conversation was contagious.

"I couldn't believe it when they contacted me. At first, they were only interested in one picture, but after I talked to them, they're going to get six to start with, and they want to see more."

Connie squeezed her again. "How wonderful. Remember us little people when you're jet setting all over the world taking pictures."

Megan's smile froze when Brittney flounced into the kitchen, giving air kisses to everyone. She stopped in front of Megan and grabbed her shoulders. "I'm so glad you came. We're going to have *such* a good time tonight. I can just feel it."

"Okay." Megan didn't suspect Brittney of being sincere for a second. What in the world was she up to?

Megan turned and busied herself by helping set the food out. "You don't have to help with the food," Connie said.

"It's no trouble at all."

A few minutes later, she heard Brittney's sickly-sweet screech. "Oooh, Auntie Alice, it's so wonderful to see you."

"Auntie?" Megan muttered under her breath.

Connie was beside her, shaking her head. "Yeah, I'm not sure when that started."

Megan couldn't quite read her aunt's comment. Maybe she was tired of Brittney's nonsense, too. Of course she'd ever take Megan's side against her own daughter, but it felt good to know she wasn't oblivious to Brittney's fakeness.

Uncle Doug's voice boomed from the dining room. "I'm starving, people. Let's go."

Megan's dad appeared in the doorway. "Hey, pumpkin, I

didn't hear you come in. Doug was showing me the new additions to his train set."

"Sounds fun." She wrapped her arms around him in a tight hug and spoke low into his ear. "Where's my pie?"

Grant chuckled. "It's in the car."

"It better be."

They carried the rest of the food to the dining room. Megan picked the seat next to her dad.

Alice leaned in and gave Megan an air kiss. Megan gave her a confused expression. *When did we start air kissing?*

"It's so nice to see you, sweetie." Alice never called her sweetie. Ever.

"Sweetie? Okay." Megan looked at her father, who simply gave her a shrug. For his sake, she'd let it drop.

Doug pulled his cap off, revealing the beginnings of a receding hairline. "Let's say grace."

Brittney put a hand on his arm. "Daddy, we can't. Not everyone is here."

"When is Quinn getting here?"

She glanced at her phone. "Any minute."

Doug sighed as the doorbell chimed. Brittney grinned and practically skipped from the room while everyone settled into their seats. Megan heard Brittney and Quinn enter the room behind her. She could only imagine the obnoxious way Brittney was hanging all over him.

"And *you* can sit *here*." Brittney tapped the back of the empty chair next to Megan.

"Why would Quinn sit –" Megan's mouth hung open as she turned her head. "Charles."

Brittney giggled, pulling Quinn to the other side of the table. Charles sat beside her. "Hey, Megan. It's been a long time."

Megan turned to her father.

"I had no idea," he whispered.

The smug smile on Alice's face revealed she had definitely known.

Megan bowed her head as Doug said grace. She twisted the napkin in her lap, at a complete loss for words.

The food made its way around the table. Charles handed her the bowl of mashed potatoes. "I'm sorry, I thought you knew I was coming."

Megan spooned potatoes onto her plate. "No clue. I didn't even know you were in town."

She passed the potatoes to her father. For the briefest second, she seriously considered hurling the bowl into her mother's face. Anything to wipe the smug look away.

When her plate was filled, Megan studied the food she had no desire to eat. Turkey. Potatoes. Gravy. Stuffing. All of it delicious and picture perfect, none of it the least bit appealing. A drop of gravy slowly stretched itself from the edge of her plate and dripped onto the beautiful rust-colored tablecloth.

Charles was eating beside her, methodical and precise. One food at a time, none of them touching on his plate. From the corner of her eye, she could see him glance her way, but he said nothing. She heard his silence louder than the inane chatter her mother and Brittney were lobbing back and forth on the other side of the table.

Eventually, the forks stopped clinking against the plates as everyone finished eating. Charles leaned over. "Can we go somewhere and talk?"

Megan finally looked directly at him. "Sure. But not here. Too many prying eyes."

"So I see."

Connie brought in pie and coffee and served everyone. Megan wanted to refuse, but offending Connie was something she just couldn't do. Instead, she forced down a tiny sliver of pie. Each bite settled like rocks in her belly. Her parents complimented the aroma of the coffee, but to Megan, it was a pale imitation of the exotic fragrances she'd grown to appreciate. She waited until Connie stood to clear the plates, and jumped up to help.

She loaded the plates into the dishwasher.

"Doesn't Charles look more handsome than ever?" Alice came up behind her.

Megan didn't answer.

"I see. You're still giving me the silent treatment."

"No, I just had no response. I'm not sure why you'd ambush me with Charles."

Alice looked at her like she was stupid. "He's a *doctor*, Megan. Try not to screw it up this time."

Megan bit her tongue. *She* wasn't the one who screwed it up the first time.

Connie came in with a stack of cups and silverware. "Aw, Megs, you're so sweet, but I didn't invite you here to work."

Alice snorted. "Let her do something for someone else for a change."

"Excuse me?" Connie's expression was puzzled. Alice rolled her eyes and left the room.

"I see some things never change." Her aunt watched Alice leave the room. "Are you okay?"

Megan nodded, but kept her focus on the dishes, not wanting Connie to see the tears threatening to spill. She felt Connie's hand rubbing her shoulder. She both craved the comfort and wanted to run from it.

"Everyone come back to the table!" Brittney's shrill voice rang throughout the house.

Connie hurried back to the dining room, while Megan lagged behind. When everyone was back at the table, Brittney and Quinn stood.

"We have some super exciting news." Brittney clutched Quinn's arm and grinned. "Actually... we have two exciting things to tell you all."

"Well? Are you going to keep us in suspense?" Doug asked. He didn't sound like he was anxious for the news, more like he was anxious to get away from the table.

"First, I'm having a baby!" Brittney placed a hand over her perfectly flat stomach. "It's super early, but we couldn't wait to share the news."

Megan glanced around the table. Doug and Connie were exchanging a glance, while Alice was clasping her hands together in rapt adoration.

"Aren't you going to congratulate me – us?"

Doug cleared his throat. "Congratulations, Brittney."

"And Quinn."

He continued. "This seems fast. You were engaged to Eric, what, three weeks ago?"

Brittney's expression darkened.

Quinn put his arm around Brittney. "Sir, I know you must think-"

Doug stood and held up a hand. "I'll thank you not to make any assumptions about what I think. What's your other news, Brittney? The game's about to start."

She poked out her bottom lip. "You're ruining it. I wanted this moment to be special."

No one spoke. Megan glanced over at her father, who was keeping an eye on his brother.

Finally, Brittney shook her head, as if to shake off the bad vibes, and flashed her bright, white smile. "I'm getting married!" She held out her left hand. A large diamond caught the lights from the candles on the table. "Isn't it pretty?" She cast a sly glance to Megan. Under her breath, she said, "Eric could never have afforded a ring like this." Alice leapt to her feet, rushing to hug Brittney.

Doug and Connie were looking at each other, some silent conversation passing between them. Doug gave his head a slight shake, then left the room.

Beside her, Grant sighed and put a hand on Megan's shoulder. "I better go talk to him."

On her other side, Charles sat, checking his phone.

Megan watched her mother fussing over Brittney, touching her belly and wiping away ridiculous fake tears. She went to the back bedroom where the coats had been stashed. Before escaping, she remembered her dad's pie. Avoiding the dining room, she slipped through the kitchen and down the basement stairs.

"Just what we need. Another imaginary grandbaby. I think this is the fourth one." Uncle Doug snorted. "We've been setting up imaginary college funds."

Megan pretended not to hear. "Dad? You down here?"

"Yep. Over here at the train station."

Megan crossed through the main room, into Doug's sanctuary, where a miniature town took up the entire space. "Wow, the last time I saw this, it wasn't even half this size. Sorry to interrupt. I'm leaving, so I wanted to get my pie."

Doug was holding a can of beer. He lifted it and pointed to Megan. "You're a good kid. You turned out great. So much happened to you, but you still ended up being a wonderful young woman."

"Thanks?"

He chuckled. "No, I'm not drunk. Yet."

Grant nodded. "He's right. You've turned out to be an amazing person. In spite of your mother and me."

"There's the problem," Doug said. "Megan's had to fight for everything, so she knows the value of hard work and being a decent person. Brittney had everything handed to her on a silver platter and here we are." He trailed off, shrugging.

Megan couldn't think of anything to say.

"Let's get your pie," Grant finally said. He led Megan out the basement door and unlocked his car. He walked to her car and set the pie on the back seat, then wrapped her in a tight hug. Without a word, he went back into the house.

Megan got into the car, but before she closed the door, Charles jogged over.

"Hey. Can I escape with you?"

"Charles. Sorry." She'd forgotten he was there, let alone that he wanted to talk to her.

"No, please. I'm sorry. I thought you knew I was coming tonight."

"I had no clue. I didn't even know you were in town."

He glanced back at the house. "Can we go somewhere else and talk? Away from here? Quinn picked me up, so I don't have my car." He still had the same boyish grin that had charmed her nearly a decade earlier.

"Sure. Get in."

Megan backed out of the driveway. With every turn away from the house, her anxiety eased. "When did you get back to Hickory Hollow? And how did they find you?"

"I got here about six months ago."

"You're back living here?"

"Yeah. My wife and I separated, so I came back home."

"Sorry to hear that."

"Yeah, it's hard on the kids."

"Kids?"

"Two boys and a girl."

Megan couldn't imagine leaving children behind. She felt a pang of sympathy for him. "It must be hard to be so far away from them."

"The hardest part is seeing how much of my check disappears." He gave a little laugh.

She let the comment pass, but couldn't ignore the bad taste it left. "Where do you live?"

Charles gave her an address. "But you don't have to take me home." His tone suggested something she had no intention of exploring.

"It's no bother. So what are you doing since you're back?"

"I'm working at Mercy General. Eventually I'd like to get into private practice, but for now, the ER pays better, so that's where I'm at."

"Good for you." She turned onto a secondary road.

"Are you still taking pictures of babies and stuff, or did you end up getting a real job?"

"A real job?"

"Relax, I'm kidding." There was no hint of humor in his voice.

"I own my own photography business."

"Make lots of money?"

Megan wondered how awful it would be if she stopped along the edge of the road and told him to walk home. "It pays the bills."

"You want to do more than pay the bills. You should find something more practical. Build up a nice nest egg and retirement accounts. Have you thought about nursing?"

"No."

"How much do you have in your retirement fund?"

"Charles, my finances are none of your business."

"I see."

Megan clenched her teeth and let out a slow breath. "Where do I turn?"

"Up here on the right."

Megan could feel the annoyance radiating from him. She turned. "Now where?"

He directed her until they pulled in front of a nondescript townhouse. She pulled into the driveway. "Nice place."

"Yeah, they're all new construction. You want to come in?"

"No, thanks. I need to get home. It's been a long day."

Charles reached over and put his hand high on her thigh. "Why don't you stay here tonight?"

"What?"

He leaned toward her, his gaze intense. "Spend the night with me."

"Charles, I'm not-"

"Shhh. You don't have to say anything. I know we both feel it." He put his other hand on her face and leaned over to kiss her.

Megan shoved him back. "The only thing I'm feeling is the need for you to get out of my car."

Charles looked genuinely surprised. "I don't understand."

"What don't you understand?"

"Look, I don't want to be insulting. I assumed you..."

"I what?"

"You like having a good time."

"A good time. By 'good time,' I assume you mean sex. And I can only also assume you got the idea from Brittney."

He shrugged. "Come on. It's not like we've never done it before."

"Excuse me? Do you think that means you have lifetime access? I assure you, it does not." When had Charles become a total idiot? He hadn't been like this eight years ago when she'd last seen him.

"Of course not. But after your crazy family dinner, I know you could use a little... stress relief. And we both know I can get the job done." He tried another winning smile.

"Get out of my car, please." Why had she bothered to say "please"?

Charles pulled the handle and opened the door. "I'm disappointed. I wasn't expecting tonight to end up like this."

"I get exactly what you were expecting."

He blinked, confused. "Sorry. I was totally wrong, and I apologize."

"Apology accepted. Brittney's on a mission to make me miserable, and you were one more unlucky pawn in her game."

"Wow. I'm guessing you didn't wreck her wedding then, either?"

"No, I didn't."

"Oh. Wow, I look like an absolute jackass." He blew out a long breath. "I'm really sorry. I've been a complete jerk. Megan, can we please pretend this whole evening never happened?"

"It's fine. For what it's worth, I'm glad you're doing well. Good luck."

He pulled a card and a pen out of his jacket, scribbled on the back of the card and set it in the console. "Give me a call. I'll take you to dinner and we can catch up. See if it goes anywhere?"

"Good night, Charles." The card was going in the trash, but he didn't need to know that.

Megan pulled out of Charles's driveway and shook her head. This whole evening was ridiculous. She wasn't sure whether to be relieved or offended her ex-fiancé had been living less than two miles from her, and he hadn't tried to contact her once. Until he'd gotten word she slept around. Not a ringing endorsement of his character. Eric wasn't the only one who'd dodged a bullet.

It wasn't seven yet, and she was starving. She'd left so quickly she didn't grab the leftover macaroni and cheese. And she needed gas. The knot in her stomach was gone. It growled, demanding more than the few bites she'd taken at dinner.

Pulling into Sheetz, she swiped her card at the gas pump, filled her tank, then went inside, filled a large soda cup and ordered a sub, then absently thumbed through her phone while she waited.

She texted Beth.

> Hang onto the wine. I'll fill you in later.

"I'm surprised to see you here."

Megan startled. "Why, exactly?"

Eric was plainly not happy to see her. "I thought you were having a nice cozy dinner with your new old boyfriend."

"You're mistaken."

"You're saying you weren't having dinner with your ex?" His tone was accusatory and more than a little annoying. Who did he think he was?

"I'm saying it's none of your business." Megan's order number was called. She pushed away from the counter and grabbed her food, stalking past Eric without another word.

Chapter Thirty-Nine

Eric followed Megan out to her car. "Wait." He grabbed her elbow.

She whirled around, smacking her sub on the side mirror. The flimsy plastic bag split open. A few pieces of shredded lettuce flew out of the opening. "Great. My freaking sub is squished. Are you happy now?"

"I'm sorry. Wait. Please." Megan glared at him.

"I'm going about this all wrong. Which is nothing new. I'm not sure what I said to upset you the other day, and here I am putting my foot in my mouth again." He waited for her to respond, but she said nothing. "Can we go somewhere and talk? I think there are some things I'm missing."

"No."

"Megan, it's too cold to stand out here."

"Too bad then." She turned abruptly, sending the bag with her sub into the mirror again. This time, the rest of the side ripped out of the bag and her sub fell to the pavement. The paper wrapped around the sub fell open. Tomatoes and pickles flew, and the bread didn't stop rolling until it was under her car. "Are you freaking kidding me? Nice." She glared at Eric. "Would you like to dump out my drink, too?"

"I'm sorry. I shouldn't have said anything about your ex. I assumed –"

"Know what, Eric? You assume an awful lot. You assumed I was screwing Marco. Now you assume I'm romantically involved with my ex. Neither of which should bother you, since we're just friends, which you've made abundantly clear. But obviously we're not even very good friends, because you think I'm lying about things that shouldn't even matter to you."

"Okay, so they matter." He bent down and picked up the ruined sub and paper, and shoved them in the trash can at the edge of the sidewalk.

"Wow. It matters to you who I'm seeing, but you're too thick to maybe trust me and give me the benefit of the doubt when I say I'm not? Especially when we both know exactly where your insider information is coming from."

"I didn't know where this was from. I blocked Brittney's number. This came from someone else." He held out his phone.

She stared at the screen. "Are you freaking kidding me?"

Eric couldn't place the change in her voice. Disgust? Disbelief? Resignation? "What? Do you recognize the number?"

"I sure do. It's my mom's."

"Why would your mother send me this?"

"You're awfully dense, Eric. She sent it for the same reason she invited Charles at all. It's part of some scheme she and Brittney cooked up. Brittney is miserable and hateful and wants to make sure I stay far away from you. My mother thinks the sun rises and sets out of Brittney's backside, and I'm the stupidest person on the planet, so she's perfectly fine with making me miserable. Penance for yet another misdeed on my part. Today was the big family Thanksgiving. I show up, then Charles shows up. He thought I knew he was coming. It was embarrassing for both of us. More so for me, because not only did that miserable little bitch invite him, she also insinuated – no, flat out told him – I'd be more than happy to have sex with him after dinner." Megan was talking fast.

"What?"

"Oh, yeah. So it's been a fantastic day, and of course I barely ate, and then I forgot my macaroni and freaking cheese, so I come here to get some food and my sub gets smashed." She held the empty plastic bag up. "Then you stand here in the middle of the parking lot, accusing me of who knows what, being too much of an idiot to see a stupid picture is an obvious setup. I can't imagine this day getting any worse."

Eric grimaced. "You might not want to turn around."

Megan slowly turned her head, then turned back toward him. "No freaking way."

"Megan! Come over here!" Alice's shrill voice split the air between the sidewalk and the gas pump. She was standing behind her open car door, as if she needed to protect herself from something.

Megan looked panicked. "I don't want to."

"Don't. Pretend you didn't hear her and get in your car."

"It won't work."

"Where are you parked?" He wracked his brain for some way to help her out of this situation.

"The pump beside them."

"Oh, no."

Alice called Megan's name again. Eric wanted to grab Megan and wipe the trapped expression from her face. He also wanted to strangle her mother. Neither option was likely to happen.

"Do you want me to walk with you?"

"Okay."

Eric didn't bother pointing out Megan was still carrying the empty plastic bag. She walked in front of him, her steps halting, like someone being led to their execution.

When they reached the car, Alice glared at him, then dismissed him with a flick of her head. "Where's Charles?"

"Home."

"Why aren't you with him?"

"Because I'm not interested in having sex with him, in spite of what you and Brittney told him, and quite frankly it's disgusting."

"I beg your pardon?"

"Oh, stop it. Charles told me all about it."

"He wouldn't."

Eric could feel the anxiety rolling off Megan like waves.

"What's *he* doing here?" Alice didn't look his direction.

"Getting gas, I would assume."

"How convenient."

"Well, they are called 'convenience' stores."

"Hey, pumpkin, I thought you were heading home." Grant came around the front of the car and clapped Eric on the shoulder. "Nice to see you. I hear you found some new coffee for your brother's café while you were on your trip."

"Yes. We did, thanks." Eric wasn't sure what to make of the situation. Megan's dad apparently didn't share his wife's hostility for him.

Alice glared daggers at her husband. "Don't talk to him."

Grant raised his eyebrows.

"I'm serious. He's nothing but trouble and I won't have my family associating with him."

Megan moved closer to him. He wondered if it was a reflex or an act of defiance. Probably the former.

"Megan, you're coming with us."

"Stop being ridiculous. My car is right here."

"I don't want you anywhere near him."

Eric wanted to pull Megan into his car and leave, but he was rooted to the spot. Megan moved closer, until she was practically leaning against him. She was clutching her drink. And the empty plastic bag. Eric could see her hands were shaking. He put his hand on her back.

"You can't tell me who I can spend time with." He was impressed with how steady her voice was.

"Then you're making a decision. Let me make this clear. If you choose to continue to associate with this... *person*..." She sneered and looked over him like he was dog crap. It was better when she was ignoring him. "Then your father and I will not speak to you until you come to your senses."

"WHOA." Grant's voice boomed. "Enough."

Customers at the other gas pumps looked.

Alice opened her mouth to speak, but Grant cut her off, pointing a finger at her. "I've had enough. You will *never* keep my daughter from me. I don't care if she leaves here and blows up a busload of orphans and nuns, she is still my daughter and she is *always* welcome in my home. I've already lost a son. No one, and I do mean no one, will ever stand between me and Megan. Ever. Including you. Am I making myself clear?"

The fury on Alice's face was frightening. Eric half expected her to start swinging. Or shooting. Or stabbing. Instead, she sat back down in her seat and slammed the door shut. Her face crumpled and she began to cry. Eric almost felt bad for her. But not quite.

"Let's get out of here," Eric said quietly.

Grant grabbed Megan in a bear hug. "I'm so sorry. This is not going to happen again." He kissed her forehead and looked over at Eric. "Make sure she gets home safe."

"I will." Eric opened the door of Megan's car and stood there while she got in. "Are you okay to drive?"

"Yeah, I'm fine. It's not like this was unusual."

"I'll meet you back at your place, okay?"

She didn't answer, but she didn't argue. He supposed he should be grateful to Alice for overshadowing his own offenses just enough for him to convince Megan to speak to him. He watched as she drove out of the parking lot, then went back inside and ordered a sub and got a fresh soda from the fountain. Extra ice, the way she liked it. He paid, then tapped his foot impatiently until his number was called.

On the way to Megan's, her words stuck in his head. She was right about him making an awful lot of assumptions about her, and none of them gave her the benefit of the doubt. He defended himself in his mind. Yeah, but he saw a woman who looked exactly like Megan with Marco. Yeah, but he was texted a picture of Megan beside her ex. Yeah, but. Yeah, but. Yeah, but.

He caught himself. What was actually in the picture, anyway? She didn't look happy. She didn't look captivated by his conversation. She wasn't looking at Charles like she looked at him. In all of their cruise pictures, except maybe the first one, Megan was smiling and leaning towards him. Or touching him. Happy.

The picture he'd been sent? She wasn't looking at Charles with any more affection than she would a stranger. Which the man was now. Charles might know most of her past. He didn't know how much Megan loved pineapple, or how she enjoyed binge-watching Little House on the Prairie, or how hilarious she was after half a dozen piña coladas. He didn't know she kept little bottles of sand, that she dreamed of seeing the Great Pyramid, or how she was terrified she'd spend the rest of her life trapped in Hickory Hollow.

He turned down the road leading to her apartment building and sighed. Jody was right. He was an idiot. And he had a lot to apologize for. No wonder she couldn't trust him, he'd done nothing to earn it.

Chapter Forty

Megan ignored her growling stomach. She'd thought Eric was right behind her, but she'd been home for fifteen minutes. She changed into her sweatpants and yanked her hair up into a messy bun. A quick glance in the freezer revealed a quart of ice cream. With a start, she remembered the pie in the back seat of her car. Jackpot.

In her socks, she ran downstairs and grabbed the pie from the back seat of her car. She'd stepped back into the apartment when headlights turned into the space behind her car. So he'd come after all.

Megan held the door open. "I thought you decided not to come."

"Sorry. It took me a few minutes to get you this." He held up a sub and followed her into the kitchen.

"Thanks. You didn't have to."

He nodded at the pie. "I see you made other arrangements for dinner."

"My dad's specialty. He only makes pies once a year, and this year he made me my own super-secret pumpkin pie."

"Sounds great."

"You have no idea. It has an amazing crumble topping. And a homemade whip on top."

"I already had dinner, but you're making me hungry again."

"Let's see how you behave while I eat the sub, and maybe I'll share a slice."

"I'll be on my best behavior."

Megan got two glasses of water and sat at the table with Eric. "So. Enough drama for you?" She began eating her sub. He'd remembered to get pickles on it. Point in Eric's favor.

"It's mind blowing that a grown woman would behave like a toddler because you spend time with someone she doesn't like. Or send a picture to try and stir up trouble."

"Welcome to my entire life. Wanting to control every single aspect of my life. It was there before Danny died, but afterwards, it kept getting worse. I figured as I grew up and *proved*," she made air quotes, "I was responsible and trustworthy, she'd loosen her hold a bit. Never happened."

"I'm sorry. I can't imagine."

"I think what bothers me most is that it feels normal. I mean, when I think about it, I know in my head it's the exact opposite of normal, but in the moment, it's just how my life is. No offense, but it's kind of the same thing with you. You tell me to get lost, then you act like a jealous boyfriend when you think something's going on. I'm not a switch you can just throw off and on."

He had the decency to look contrite. "I know. When we got interrupted, I was trying to say I'm sorry. I know it seems like I don't trust you or I jump to all the wrong conclusions, but I think maybe it's because I don't know what we are, so I'm not sure how I'm supposed to feel or react to anything. Am I making any sense?"

"Kind of."

Picking at the lace on her tablecloth, he said, "If we're just friends, it wouldn't bother me if you decide to see someone else. But it does bother me. A lot. I don't know what that means."

Megan studied his face. "Are you sure it means anything?"

"I think it does."

"You think. Not exactly a ringing endorsement, Eric."

Megan got up, partly to throw away the sub wrapper, and partly to put some distance between them. She slowly and deliberately sliced the pie. She set a plate in front of Eric and sat down, her eyes fixed on her own slice.

"If it tastes anything like it looks and smells, this is going to be amazing."

"It is."

They ate their pie in silence, except for the clinking of their forks against the plate.

"Would it be a horrible breach of etiquette if I licked the plate?"

Megan grinned and lifted her own plate to her mouth. "Who cares?"

Eric followed her lead and licked his plate clean. "Can I wash the dishes?"

Megan snorted. "Like there's a chance I'll stop you."

He grabbed the plates and took them to the sink. Megan studied his back while he washed the plates, forks, and the cups she'd left in the sink.

She ran a hand through her hair. "So, what do you think we are?"

He kept washing and for a minute she thought maybe he hadn't heard her. He put the last cup in the drainer and turned and leaned back against the sink, wiping his hands with a towel. "Maybe it matters more to know what we want to be."

"And what do we want it to be?"

He captured her gaze and held it until she could hardly

breathe. Her heart was pounding in her throat, not knowing what his answer was, hoping for what his answer was. She couldn't stand the pressure anymore and looked away.

He cleared his throat. "I would like for us to be together."

Megan raised an eyebrow and lifted her chin, challenging him. "With all the drama? Really? You've told me a million times you're not into drama, and you just got away from drama. So you want to jump into all this?" She held her arms out. "You want to sign up for showdowns in the Sheetz parking lot? The very definition of drama?"

"Big difference. There's drama, and there's *drama*. You know that. It's one thing to be the creator of all kinds of ridiculous drama, and quite another to be collateral damage in other people's."

"So I'm collateral damage? You think you can fix me? Make yourself feel good about helping someone up out of the sludge of a horrible life?"

"It's a pretty big leap from what I said to what you just threw out there."

"No, I'm pretty sure you said I was collateral damage. I'm a fixer upper."

"You're deliberately misunderstanding me. I said your drama was collateral damage."

Megan wanted to fight with him. She wanted to push back against the notion that someone that *he* – could experience even a moment of her family dynamic and still want to be with her. *She* didn't even want to be around it.

"Charles dumped me because my mother told him I 'wasn't allowed' to move to California with him during his residency. Instead of talking to me, he called me after he'd already landed across the country, and told me he couldn't be with me because my mother was crazy, and I would be, too."

"Sounds like a real peach."

"What's your breaking point going to be, Eric? When are you going to wake up and realize I bring so much misery and you can't stand it anymore?"

"When are you going to wake up and realize you are an amazing woman and you have so much to offer? When are you going to stop believing you're responsible for someone else's crazy?"

"You don't even know me."

"Bull. Other than Beth, I bet I know you better than anyone else."

Megan snorted. "Yeah, right."

"Who else has seen you calm and relaxed, not carrying the weight of the world on your shoulders?"

"That was an illusion. It was Vacation Megan. Baggage included."

"No, it was you. You, Megan, without all the responsibility. Without all the looking over your shoulder, afraid of making a single wrong step."

"I left Vacation Megan at the airport in Orlando and brought Old Megan along home."

Eric sat down and took her hands in his. "No, you didn't. You're sitting right here. Old Megan would never have stood up to her mother. She would never have sold pictures to a cruise line, where millions of people will see them. She wouldn't have answered the email."

Megan studied their hands. His tan, strong fingers entwined in her slender, pale ones. "I'd like to believe that."

"Hey. The old Megan wouldn't have gone on the cruise. So I think Old Megan started fading longer ago than you think." She shook her head and pulled her hand away. "And what are you going to do when Old Megan comes back to stay?"

Eric reached over and brushed her hair behind her ear. "This conversation is weird. There's no old or new Megan. It's all you, growing and learning and creating your own life. And I'd really like it if that new life had a place in it for me."

"I do kinda like you."

"Your mother hates me." She laughed.

"I think that's why I like you." She laughed.

Eric grinned. "Gee, thanks. I thought you liked me before you knew your mother hated me."

She pretended to think about it. "You might be right. But you became infinitely more appealing afterwards."

"Well, my family adores you."

The teasing mood slipped from her. "Your family's awesome."

"You'll love my parents."

"I'm meeting your parents?" Wow. He wasn't wasting any time.

"I'd like you to. Come over for Thanksgiving."

"No pressure, huh? Let's not simply meet the family, let's meet the family *and* share a major holiday?"

"It's Thanksgiving. It's not like it's Christmas. Thanksgiving is all about food. There's no pressure with food."

"Thanks, but I can't anyway. I'm volunteering."

"When are you done? We can spend some time together afterwards."

"Not until three. After the meal, we have to clean up."

"Which means you'll be exhausted. So I can pick you up and make sure you get fed. We can sit on the couch and talk."

Megan shook her head. "No talking. Football. If you talk while I'm watching football, it won't be pretty."

Eric laughed loud. "Understood."

Chapter Forty-One

Eric woke up on Thanksgiving morning with a huge grin he couldn't get rid of, even if he wanted to. He jumped out of bed and pulled his clothes on. He sent Megan a good morning text, wishing her a good day. She was either going to thank him... or kill him. Whistling, he backed out of his garage and drove to the café, where the rest of the family was waiting for him.

Twenty minutes later, they were being shepherded through a fellowship hall by a short, bossy woman named Lorraine.

"Megan," she called out.

Eric grinned and acted innocent when Megan looked up from the mashed potatoes she was scooping into dishes. She wiped her hands on her apron and quickly came out from behind the island. "Oh, my gosh, what are you – Jody? Stewart? What are you doing here?"

Jody reached over and gave her a big hug. "You didn't think we'd let you have Thanksgiving by yourself, did you?"

Stewart shrugged. "We figured you might be able to use some extra hands."

"What have we here?" Lorraine asked with a warm smile. "How about I take the youngsters out front and they can help serve food." She leaned down to the youngest and tapped her lightly on the nose. "*You* can be on roll duty. What's your name?"

"Mindy," the girl answered confidently. "I'm six."

Lorraine chuckled and stood upright. Jody pointed to each child in turn. "Samantha, Darren, Tess. They'll do whatever job you give them." She gave the kids a Mom Look.

"Wonderful!" Lorraine grabbed some hair nets and plastic gloves and ushered the kids through the double doors leading to the dining room.

Megan pushed her hair back from her sweaty forehead. "I can't believe you guys are here."

Stewart pushed his sleeves up. "What can we do?"

Megan pointed them to a group huddled around a food station. "I think they can use more hands. And you," she said to Eric, "are on dish duty."

"How about us?"

Eric watched as Megan tried to cover her confusion. He proudly put his arm around her waist. "Megan, these are my parents. Patty and Nick."

Megan wiped her hands on her apron again, then reached up and touched her hair net. "Oh. Hi. I'm Megan."

Eric knew she wanted to strangle him.

Patty shoved past Eric and grabbed Megan in a hug. "It's great to meet you. We've heard so many wonderful things about you."

Megan gave a laugh. "I'm sure they've been exaggerated."

Nick gave her a nod and a smile. "Good to finally meet you."

"You, too."

Eric heard the shake in her voice.

Lorraine reappeared. "Do you folks have jobs?"

Patty and Nick shook their heads.

"No time to stand around and chat. We need two hundred to-go meals packaged and boxed up. You can help there."

They followed Lorraine to their assignment.

"What are you doing?" Megan asked him quietly.

"When I told my mom you weren't coming for dinner because you were volunteering, she insisted we all come and help. What were we going to do, tell her no?"

"What about Thanksgiving dinner?"

"We're eating at six. And yes, you're coming. And yes, we'll have football on. But I can't guarantee no one will talk."

Megan's eyes were rimmed with tears, but she was smiling. "Thank you," she whispered before wiping her face. She cleared her throat. "We have to get to work."

Eric spent the next several hours washing dishes. By the time the last plate was rinsed and handed off to the person drying, his back and feet hurt, his fingers were pruned and aching, but it was the good hurt of a job well done.

He'd caught glimpses of Megan from time to time, smiling and laughing with the other volunteers. He'd been worried about surprising her with the whole crew, but now that they were almost done, he was deeply happy his family had immediately jumped on board with him. Everyone should have a family so amazing.

Chapter Forty-Two

Megan stood in the shower and let the hot water soothe her aching shoulders. Her cheeks ached, too. She couldn't stop smiling about Eric and his family and the incredible gift they'd given her.

She carefully picked out her clothes and took extra care with her hair and makeup. She wanted to impress Eric's parents at dinner. Dinner.

Crap.

By the time Eric knocked on her door, she was in full-blown panic mode.

"What's wrong?"

"Dinner. Eric, dinner! I don't have anything to take for dinner. Your mom's going to think I'm some greedy, grubbing moocher!" She flung her hands up in frustration. He was clearly not grasping the problem. "When you go to dinner, you take something. You *contribute*. You don't show up empty-handed. You just don't. There's nothing open, I can't even stop and buy something." She shuddered at the thought, but it would be better than showing up with nothing. Drumming her fingers on the kitchen counter, she fretted, wracking her brain for some sort of dinner-worthy offering she might pull off with something she had on hand. Nothing.

She turned back around. Eric was right there, up in her face. He put his hands on both sides of her head and kissed her until she had no idea what she'd been worrying about. She sank against him, into his kiss.

Eric pulled back and softly said, "No one's expecting anything except you."

"But-"

Whatever she was going to say was lost as he kissed her again.

And again.

In spite of his assurances, her nerves were jittery when they pulled in the driveway of his parents' house.

"Deep breath. It's going to be fine, I promise."

Megan nodded and squeezed his hand. "Okay."

Two hours later, she felt silly for being so nervous. Patty and Nick were as gracious and funny and welcoming to her as Stewart and Jody. They even thanked her for letting them help with the food bank meal, like she'd had anything to do with it. The kids laughed and disappeared when it was time to wash dishes, only to be dragged back to the kitchen by Jody.

When the dishwasher was loaded and the pans were soaking, everyone congregated in the living room. Nick flipped the television on. "I hope you like football, Megan."

"Love it." She settled onto the loveseat beside Eric. The family was divided between the two teams, cheering and trash talking. Even when the twins got into an argument, Megan couldn't pinpoint a single uncomfortable moment.

After the game, she shuffled to his car. "I can't thank you enough."

"You already have." Eric waited until she her feet were inside and shut the door, then went to the driver's side.

The combination of the turkey and the drive home made her pleasantly drowsy. "Glad I'm not driving," she mumbled.

"Me, too."

At the apartment, Megan unlocked the door and leaned into him. "Thank you for an amazing day. I'm so glad you all came to help."

"I'm glad, too. I write plenty of checks for donations, but it meant a lot to actually be doing the work myself. Gave me a whole different perspective. And a whole new thing to be grateful for today."

Megan felt herself tearing up again. "I'm so glad. And I'm so glad I got to share it with you." She leaned her face upward, letting Eric kiss her good night.

Epilogue

Six Months Later

Eric sat in first class, drinking little bottles of airplane liquor, getting pleasantly tipsy. He couldn't wipe the smile from his face. Megan sat beside him, shooting pictures out the window.

Twenty-four hours earlier, they'd exchanged vows in front of their family and friends, laughing and crammed under a tiny pavilion during a sudden spring downpour. His whole family had instantly bonded with Grant, who quickly became the number one customer at the coffee shop. It took a little while for Alice, but she'd come a long way. Spending Thanksgiving without either of her children was the dramatic wakeup call that inspired her to start grief counseling and begin mending her relationship with her daughter.

Megan's fingers clutched his thigh and dug in. "Eric! There it is, there it is, there it is! I see it!"

The "fasten seatbelts" light came on and the captain came over the intercom, welcoming them to Egypt. A few minutes later, the plane began its descent. Soon, they were on their way to baggage claim, from there to their taxi, and then to their hotel room with a view of the Pyramids.

Megan stared out the window, awestruck. Eric held her hand and ran his finger over her ring. He wondered if he'd ever get used to the fact that she was his wife. It seemed too good to be true.

"I can't wait to see inside the Pyramid. I hope I don't have to crop a lot of tourists out of the pictures. The Sphinx looked so small from the air. I can't wait to see it up close." She chattered excitedly. "There's no way I'm going to be able to sleep tonight. I can't wait for tomorrow's tour. I can't wait--"

Cutting her off with a kiss, Eric smiled against her mouth and said, "I can't wait to spend the rest of my life with you."

Enjoyed this trip to Hickory Hollow? Keep those warm fuzzy feelings going and dive straight into Book 2 in the Hickory Hollow series, Caller Number Nine.

When overworked veterinarian Margo Lewis wins a ten-day glamping vacation, she doesn't expect the man responsible for her first - and worst - heartbreak to be in the tent next to hers.

Hickory Hollow. Get comfy, stay a while!

You don't want to miss news of upcoming books, events, and behind-the-scenes sneak peeks! Sign up for my newsletter today at carriejacobs.com!

Author's Note

Shout out to country music superstar Dierks Bentley, without whom I might never have had the idea for this book. His song "Drunk on a Plane" came out in 2014 and one day while singing along (loudly and poorly), the idea for this book grabbed my attention and wouldn't let go. You can check him out at dierks.com.

Writing is a solitary endeavor. For some people, that's a plus. For extraverts like me, not so much. I don't know what I'd do without my writer friends and colleagues. I have too many people to thank individually, but the one person I will single out is Michelle Haring, who owns the most amazing indie bookstore in the whole wide world (located in central Pennsylvania). Cupboard Maker Books is one of my most favorite happy places (books and cats!!!), and Michelle is one of my most favorite people. Her support, encouragement, and knowledge is second to none. Visit cupboardmaker.com.

I have several writers' groups that bring me immense joy. My CPRW group – you guys are amazing professionals and I've learned so much. I've learned so much about the industry from this group, and I'm proud to be a part of it.

My Tuesday Girls – you guys listen to me whine and kvetch and cry. You share snacks with me. You celebrate with me. You take my pivoting in stride SQUIRREL!!

My clever Velociposse – RAAAAAAWWRRRR!

My Fourth Wednesday critique group – Wow. I don't think I could possibly express how much this group means to me. I am a much, much better writer for being a part of this group. I always look forward to the feedback, criticism, and suggestions. You're an amazing group of critters, always delivering even the worst news with tact and professionalism.

Special thanks to my parents. Mom, for instilling a deep and abiding love of reading and being surrounded by books, for transcribing "A Frog Named Tog," and for always nurturing my love of writing. And for Dad, who doesn't read fiction, but he darn sure read my first published story.

For Austin, who thinks it's cool his mom is a writer, and considers it the highest of compliments to have his words compared to mine. I love you to pieces.

And perhaps most of all, thanks to my husband Scott, who proudly supports my dream. I love you.

About the Author

Carrie's love of storytelling began in early childhood and never wavered as time marched onward. She reads in pretty much every genre imaginable, but found her writing happy place in small town contemporary romance and romantic comedy. From that love came Hickory Hollow, a mashup of her hometown and places she's either visited or would like to. Her favorite part of Hickory Hollow? The residents don't have to drive an hour to get to Target, like she does in real life.

Carrie lives in beautiful central Pennsylvania with her family and very spoiled furry editorial assistants.

Connect with Carrie through her newsletter or social media!

Website: carriejacobs.com

f   facebook.com/writercarriejacobs
⊙   instagram.com/carriejacobsauthor
g   goodreads.com/carriejacobs

Made in the USA
Columbia, SC
12 April 2024

34267481R00188